TINSEL ROSE
By Stephen Alix
Published Independently
www.stephenalix.com

Stephen Alix

# TINSEL ROSE

For mom.

Stephen Alix

"The tin soldier melted down into a lump, and the next morning, when the maidservant took the ashes out of the stove, she found him in the shape of a little tin heart. But of the little dancer, nothing remained, but the tinsel rose, which was burnt black as a cinder."

-The Steadfast Tin Soldier
By Hans Christian Andersen

Love has no boundaries

3/15/18.

Stephen Alix

# *1*

Vincent Kojima entered the Alton, a New York City skyscraper located on 38th street and Madison. Sixty stories high, fashioned in glass and metal. Every surface reflected light. Whoever designed this, he thought, wanted to blind everyone who walked in.

He squeezed into a crowded elevator and held his breath. Stuck between Sophie from accounting who sprayed on what he swore must be litter box scented perfume and Paul, a bulbous corporate lawyer who wheezed into his left ear.

"Good morning," he said, surrounded by groans and grimaces. "Twenty please." He smiled; others looked away or returned his gesture with a slight nod.

The elevator emptied by the time Vincent reached his floor. Variations of Edvard Munch's *The Scream* hung on the walls. They shared the level with several other companies. On the far left was his company, the largest on the floor: Mechanimus Inc., a multinational semiconductor chip maker.

He swiped his key card and rounded the corner. "Good morning, Jessie." He leaned onto the cherry wood reception desk. "Benheim in yet?"

"Yep." Her eyes, fixed on her cell phone. She smacked her gum, pursed her lips, and scowled at the screen.

"What's wrong?"

"I guess you haven't heard the news yet." She lifted her cell and showed him an orange screen. "Dead after only two days."

"Oh, shit."

"Yup."

"I can fix this."

"You better see the boss man, he's pissed."

Vincent adjusted his black square frame glasses, fixed his tie, checked the part on his jet black hair, and buttoned his suit jacket before entering Benheim's office located down the hall.

Gregory Benheim was forty years old, medium build, dressed in a white button-down shirt, blue tie, and brown slacks with thick blonde hair littered with gray strands. He squeezed a stress ball that wheezed like a rubber duck. Damn things sounds like my asthmatic mother. Stress reducer my ass, he thought.

His secretary called him. "Vincent Kojima here to see you."

"Let him in."

His desk, littered with photographs of his wife and kids on various trips. Camping, kayaking, and skydiving. They all faced away from him. "Take a seat."

Vincent pressed his thumbs together. "Your pictures are facing the wrong way."

"Before you came in I moved them around. Do you know why?"

"Why?"

"This is why I come in every day. I bust my ass for them. Who do you bust your ass for?"

"I—"

"Labels are important. But even more important is control over what gets labeled. Do you know what they're calling your little fiasco?"

"No, I—"

"The orange screen of death. We're looking at a recall. Twenty maybe thirty thousand replacements and we haven't gotten any final numbers yet."

"I can fix the Lexicon."

"But who will fix our PR? I thought you said you tested this thing."

"We did."

"You're the brainchild behind this whole thing. If our stock goes down, you go down. Get Frank and don't leave the office this weekend until you find a solution."

"I promise—"

"Don't promise me, Vincent, fix the problem."

Vincent stepped into his office down the hall. He flicked on his computer monitors, one by one, and enjoyed the buzz as they vibrated against his fingertips. He lifted the newspaper off his desk and noticed a large brown box on the floor. It's here, he thought. Vincent cut open the box and rummaged through the contents. Broken metal scraps, wires, random screws, and microchips were all scattered at the bottom.

What a mess, he thought and sifted through the packing peanuts. The package contained the core, two synthetic arms, two legs, and a chest plate. He picked up the central core: a titanium hexagon about the size of two human hearts placed side by side— wires protruded in every direction. The model number on the front read 071909. He attached a plug from the core into the monitor on his desk. Images flashed across the screen in a jumbled mess.

A woman appeared; she flickered in and out. The light shimmered against her smooth white skin and wavy, strawberry blonde hair. Her blue eyes turned upward, she spread her lips and formed a sensuous, alluring smile. She sat on her side in a four-post bed, satin sheets atop her body, hugging her curvaceous form, legs and thighs formed subtle shapes underneath. Two slender fingertips swept across her brow, a dimple formed on her cheek.

The images pixilated into a blur then zoomed into a close-up. She appeared luminous, skewed; hair tossed, makeup smeared; a single tear lingered in her eye. Her mouth parted— caught between pleasure and pain.

A knock broke Vincent's concentration. He unplugged the unit and opened the door.

"Frank, you frightened me!"

Frank's robust size ate up the room; the tiny office now seemed even more cramped. "I've never seen you scared. I'm guessing you've heard."

9

"Yeah, what happened? We tested and tested."

"I warned you, but you wouldn't listen. Naming that thing after your ex-was bad luck."

"What's wrong with Lexi?"

"You mean besides that she ran up your credit cards and almost got you evicted from your apartment?"

"I..."

"Once she became part of your routine you couldn't get over her. You don't know when to let things go. Like that tie."

"What's wrong with my tie?"

"I hate that tie. You've worn it every other day for the last month. I bet you even know how many dots are on the damn thing."

Vincent turned his chair around.

"Oh my god, you do don't you."

"One hundred and forty-seven."

Frank palmed his face. Through his fingers he noticed the box and all the parts spilling out over the side. He spotted the core connected to the monitor.

"What's this?"

"This will make the Lexicon obsolete."

"How?"

"This is a Synthetic."

"Are you kidding me? Here? Do you realize what they'll do if they find you with this?"

"They won't know if no one tells them. I set him up, and the thing went off all on its own."

Frank hitched up his pants, placed his hands on his gut, and looked into the blank display. He smirked. "What did you see?"

Vincent jumped from his seat. "Check it out. He reset the monitor. The screen remained blank. "This woman appeared. It seems our buddy here was quite the voyeur."

"They only made, what, ten before the government outlawed them? I heard people did the craziest things with these models. That's what happens when you get this close to the real thing."

"Not close enough." Vincent picked up an arm cut off at the elbow. He inspected the open socket and pressed down on the fingertips. "Still warm, even after being dismantled the heat sensors in his parts remain functional. It's almost like hot blood is coursing through his veins."

"This guy took quite a bit of damage before finally being sent to his maker."

Vincent paused. "Do you think it's true?"

Frank pulled up a seat beside him. Vincent lowered the arm onto his desk, littered with copper wires and scraps of metal. A dozen action figures stood atop his monitors. Frank recognized a few from various Japanese Mangas. "Is what true?"

"The rumors about the first two models: they disobeyed their core program, became sentient."

"Impossible. Let's stick to what we know. We know we built in pain sensors. Lab results proved pain a suitable punishment and kept them on their best behavior."

"What about other things?"

Frank twisted his lips; the thought filled him with disgust. "What's your point?"

"I don't know— if the visual feed is down maybe we can get the audio working. Find out what happened to him."

"Who cares about him I'm more concerned about our asses getting fired. Where did you get him? Who sent you this? His existence is illegal, Vin, serious jail time."

Vincent smiled. "I'm doing someone a favor."

"Is there enough left of him? We'd be lucky if he even turns on."

"The important stuff seems intact. He might hear us and answer our questions."

"Shouldn't we work on the Lexicon?"

"Yes, later. These parts will make something better, and Benheim will forget all about the Lexicon and the orange screen of death."

"I doubt he'll forget. Company stock is plummeting as we speak."

"We've got the whole weekend to work on that. Are you in or not?"

Frank sighed. "Where do we start?"

The monitor buzzed, and a static image emerged on the computer screen. They couldn't make out the picture.

"Let's see if we can clean up the image." Vincent inspected the central core. A microchip stuck out halfway from the slot. He dusted the chip, removed all dirt specs, and nudged it back in with his index finger.

Frank squinted at the monitor. "None of this makes sense. It's visual gibberish." He changed the color and contrast on the monitor. The colors washed over each other.

"Slow down. Now we can't see anything."

Random images flew across the screen. Vincent noticed a string of numbers at the bottom.

"Let's trace his serial number shall we?" He typed the numbers into Google. "He's your typical 'help around the house' model. His report says he was a home attendant for one David Vitas; registered with the name Aeneas."

Frank took the synthetic hand and placed it on his own and formed a handshake. "These models are expensive. Only the super elite owned them. Who was that guy again? The Wall Street hedge fund big shot."

"Gregory Stevens?"

"Yeah, he swore his Synthetic attacked him. Cops found him half dead."

Vincent nodded. "I remember." He studied the images on the monitor. They saw through the Synthetic's eyes, fixed on a windowsill. A leaf blew in and sailed into the house and past his line of sight.

Vincent leaned in closer. "I'm not sure why he's not moving. These models don't stand around and do nothing. My best guess is something went wrong with his motor functions."

Frank searched the box. "Aha!" He held up a small black box. "This should access his speech components."

Another woman appeared on the screen. They fell silent as it played. She walked back and forth from the kitchen sink to the counter, slicing vegetables, and then washed them.

Vincent broke the silence. "I've never seen a machine this fixated on anybody before. He's aware—" Something strange stirred inside him and stopped him mid-thought. "How are we doing on the audio?"

Frank raised his finger. "One second." He then looked up. "Try again. He should hear us from the microphone on his unit, and we'll hear him on those speakers over there. Pretty simple as long as its parts are still in working condition."

Vincent secured the connection and raised the volume. He looked into the box and felt foolish talking to a bunch of scattered metal. "Aeneas?"

No response.

Frank leaned into the speaker and spoke loudly, "Anything in there still functioning? Don't make us throw you in the scrapper."

Vincent covered the speaker. "You're threatening him?" He raised his eyebrow "Really?"

Frank leaned back into his seat and raised his feet onto the desk. "If you got any bright ideas let's hear 'em."

Vincent picked up the central core, turned it upside down and checked for any loose connections. "Hello? If you're still in there, say something." The woman reappeared on the monitor.

"He had a thing for the ladies." Frank read the information sheet on this particular model. "Is there anything else on this guy's channel? I'm getting bored."

The woman's face transfixed Vincent. She looked to be in her mid-twenties He noticed the intense focus on her face. The image, recorded with care. Since when do these models keep records like this? He thought.

The woman's eyes were wide, her lip curled a bit, and her ears lost in her long wavy hair. Vincent wished he could see more. "What would cause a glitch like this?"

A voice boomed through the speaker and sent a deafening ring through their ears. "There was no glitch!"

13

Frank stumbled from his chair."Aeneas?"

Vincent trembled and wondered why he would be afraid of a box of broken parts.

Aeneas spoke again, this time more solemn, almost apologetically. "There was no glitch."

Frank set a toothpick between his dry, chapped lips. He chewed on it like it helped him to think. "Someone's on the rag."

"Don't talk about him like he's not here. I must apologize Frank can sometimes be an asshole." Frank coughed. "Okay, he's always an asshole."

Frank nodded his head in agreement. "Better."

Aeneas lowered his voice. "I must apologize for my tone. Where am I? Once again I am locked away in darkness."

"You're in New York City."

Aeneas hummed. "And who are you?"

Vincent stood and ran his hand over his tie. "I'm Vincent, and this is Frank."

Frank rolled his eyes at the unnecessary formalities. "He can't even see you!"

Vincent took his seat and inched toward the edge; excitement filled his eyes. He ran his hand through his hair and moved to speak. Then paused and tried again followed by another pause. "I have many questions. I'm glad you're still somewhat intact. I worried we'd have nothing left of you to analyze. You have no idea how unique and special you are. I mean, if it's true, what they said about you."

Vincent waited but received no reply. His fingers twitched amidst the uncomfortable silence. He looked over, Frank shrugged.

At last Aeneas spoke. "This is not the first time I've been locked away in the darkness. I feel dead."

Frank tapped his toothpick against the desk. "Well, you are dead, if they find out you're still running, they'll be pissed. You see, Aeneas, your kind doesn't exist anymore, and technically you're not here, and neither are we."

Vincent interrupted. "No one knows what happened. There's so much we can learn from you, I mean, after all, it's not every day one of you glitch and—"

"I already told you there was no malfunction. My program ran properly. I was functioning as designed."

"Not exactly." Frank ran his tongue over his teeth. "Didn't you attack someone?" Vincent felt his finger twitch again.

Aeneas fell silent.

"Weren't you programmed never to harm a human being?"

"I was."

Frank took a deep breath. His large stomach was like a whale washed up on a beach. "The woman in the monitor: why did you hurt her?"

"I never laid a hand on her."

"That's not what this report about your model says. What about the other guy then, the neighbor?" Frank's body now hovered over Aeneas's parts, casting a giant shadow over what little remained.

Vincent stopped mid-thought and looked toward the monitor. The woman's face stood frozen in time. He couldn't shake the feeling he'd seen her before. "Then tell us what happened. So we can understand."

"You're kidding me, right?" Frank sighed. "This is such a waste of time. You're not going to learn anything from his spare parts. If anyone finds out you got this thing we're both in trouble. There's no proof."

"Would you shut up and let him talk?"

"Proof? Proof of what exactly?" Aeneas asked.

"Proof you broke the most sacred rule. Not a single Synthetic is allowed to break it."

The computer monitor went blank and removed the mysterious woman. A ghost-like reflection lingered before it sank into the black screen.

"I was told many times it was impossible. They said I simply could not and would not find what I was searching for, that I was delusional and malfunctioning. They called it a glitch in my programming as if the suggestion of a synthetic who could act on his own free will would spread like wildfire to the others. I don't know what you're afraid of." He paused. "But you see I am afraid your focus is misplaced. All this time you're asking about me, trying to find out what went wrong with me. When in fact it is and always has been about her. What you seek you will not find within me but in her. It was she who brought out this light in me. She made me whole. She gave my life true purpose."

"She's hot." Frank blurted out. "Sorry." He sank into his seat.

"Tell us everything, Aeneas."

Frank rose from his seat. "Hold on if this is going to be one of those long stories let me get a cup of coffee first." He waddled out of the room and murmured. "You're going to get our asses fired."

Aeneas waited until he heard the office door close. "Vincent?"

"Yeah?"

"There is more than you're telling me isn't there?"

Vincent rubbed his temples. "Sort of."

Frank came back in with a cup in hand. "OK, let's get to it ya talking toaster."

Vincent nudged his shoulder. "Ignore his rudeness, please begin."

"I once considered my initial boot up the greatest moment in my existence. Surpassed, the day I met David, his daughter Janie, and…"

"Yeah?"

"And the day I met God."

# *2*

I was shipped in darkness, locked inside a sphere shaped containment chamber. This is where I am first booted up. They don't let me out until I arrive at my destination. Surrounded by birthing gel, I float and ponder my directives.

Assignment: David Vitas, retired mechanical engineer.

Age: Sixty-five years old.

Ailments: recently suffered a stroke.

Location: Hector, Nebraska.

Population: two thousand.

The sphere shifts and I am sent spinning counter clockwise. I bob left and right until the unit is lowered onto the ground. The egg opened and fluid drained out onto the street. I experienced daylight, the wind, and sunshine. All at once they surrounded me, and I was overwhelmed by their essential details. The information contained within each element, minute in scope, and yet limitless.

My new home stood before me. A two-story country house painted a rustic yellow, accented in red and orange along the roof, a forever sunset. The front porch was skeletal—frail and empty, surrounded by a broken fence, riddled with holes.

Several neighbors stepped outside and watched. The delivery men rang the door bell. David answered the door. He stood slightly hunched over, five foot and seven inches. His hair was a mass of unkempt gray curls, with a thick bushy mustache that covered his upper lip.

They handed David the paperwork. He signed and stared at me in disbelief. They walked me over and said, "Palm Granola." A blue light on my wrists deactivated, and I walked freely toward David. In seconds he rushed me into the house and mumbled something about nosy neighbors.

He walked me into the living room all the while looking me over with a suspicious eye. His stern face soon melted and then he giggled with his hands pressed together.

"I can't believe my eyes." He rubbed his hands over his face. "I can't." The lines around his eyes grew longer when he smiled.

I mimicked his facial movements. He laughed at my attempt.

"I appreciate the gesture but please, relax."

His small withered hand reached out and trembled slightly. He looked at his palm until the trembling ceased. Pleased, he extended his hand further.

"It's okay you can shake my hand." He widened his grin. His skin was rough, and the wide fat fingers were twice the size of mine. "Quite a grip you got there."

"Hello, David Vitas. I am unit 326 model 071909. I am your new home attendant."

"I do very well on my own. I don't need any help. But I could use a little help cheating on Bingo night."

"I cannot cheat, Mr. Vitas."

"Well, of course, you can't. I've never seen such a creation in my entire life. The hands that crafted you my dear boy were pure genius. If I didn't know better, I'd swear you were a normal person." He pinched the skin on my arm and stretched it. "No elasticity, this is the most impressive skin cell technology I've ever seen. I've seen the videos of your model on YouTube, but it doesn't do you justice. In person, you're so much more impressive. Let me hear you speak some more."

"What should I say?"

"I don't know, say anything."

"Anything."

"Do you speak other languages?"

"I can learn any language spoken to me."

"Yes, that was the key wasn't it? Nurture your intelligence rather than impressing it all upon you at once. Impressive, Who sent you here I wonder?"

"Abigail Jeanne wished you a speedy recovery and wanted you to have the latest in home aid technology."

"She bought you for me? Did she send any other message with you?"

"There is no more."

His lips spread wide, but he quickly wiped away the smile. "This is too much I can't possibly accept such a gift." He wrestled with his happiness and shifted between levels of approval. He circled me with a critical eye, cleared his throat, and took on a more serious tone. "I'm not going to lie I wish you were a lanky blond woman with a big rack. Dear god, who picked out your clothes? Let's get your measurements, and I'll get you some decent attire."

I could not fathom what was wrong with my white shirt and pants. They were simple and adequate.

"Whatever you wish, Mr. Vitas."

"They made you fairly young. Do you have a name?"

"Only the name you assign me."

He took a seat. All his energy expended in the last few minutes. "I'm going to have to think of a good name, one worthy of a modern marvel." He stood and dusted nothing off his pants. "Follow me; I'll show you to your room." He led the way up the stairs.

"I do not require a room."

Every few steps he paused, breathed deeply, and then continued. His journey up the stairs took a few minutes. After one last deep breath, he raised his hand and pointed toward the second floor. "I'll feel better if you have a room. It would be too weird having you hang around aimlessly in the house when you're not working. Speaking of which, what is it you do?"

"There's nothing I can't."

"The house needs a lot of work. You can start by taking care of the backyard. The neighbors have a new jack terrier that shits more than I do."

19

The doorbell rang. The ring was a series of notes played out of tune. David stopped mid-step and turned his attention to the door. "Who do you suppose it is?"

He trudged back down the steps, opened the door and there stood a woman, nearly as wide as the door, dressed in a blue floral designed suit with matching skirt. Her ankles were red and swollen, burdened with the weight they held up. Her cheeks shimmered with an abundance of glitter filled skin cream.

David grumbled and offered a seat. Much later, in private, he described her to me as a "heifer." She scurried in at surprising speed; her eyes darted left and right. She spotted me. "Ah, ah, there it is."

She was twice David's size. You could make two humans from her large mass. David crossed his arms. His guest held her head high; nose pointed upward.

"Danielle, may I introduce, well I haven't named him yet." David walked over to the railing and raised his hands.

"Hello." I held out my hand.

David rubbed his mustache. "I'm so glad you and your makeup could join us, Danielle."

I noticed the broad brush of blue eyeshadow. I did not understand what David had said; it seemed strange. How could an inanimate chemical substance join us?

Sweat lined up across her brow. "How long were you going to wait until you revealed this to the neighborhood association?" She wrinkled her lips, in mock surprise.

"He only just arrived. I take it you saw the truck this morning?"

"Who couldn't? What an awful racket, woke up half the neighborhood."

David pulled out a seat and waved her over. Once seated, he glanced at me. "I imagine a delivery of that size doesn't go unnoticed around here." He eyed the window where a few neighbors could be seen outside their homes staring at his house. "I wasn't aware we had to report every little thing to you. Should I send a letter next time I purchase a new TV?"

She shimmied in her seat like she had not yet found a comfortable position. Her neck jiggled when she shook her head.

20

The chair legs bent ever so slightly. I'd have to reinforce them if she planned on visiting again.

"His presence here isn't going to be a problem, is it?"

"As you know David." She paused for a moment. "I am merely here to represent what's best for the community. As you know, there have been rumors on the news about these machines. They wanted me to have a look and report my findings back to the board."

David's nostrils flared. "Don't piss on my leg and tell me it's raining. It's practically a mechanical witch hunt. He's harmless, as you can see, and he's here to help me out around the house."

"Why not hire a maid? He's taking jobs away from hard-working Americans."

"Do you want to volunteer to wipe my ass?"

"There is no need for that kind of talk. It's disgusting." She shuddered. "Come now, David, we've tolerated a lot from you in the past. Your refusal to bring this house up to code brings down the property value. Having this thing in your home will only lower it further."

"I have every right to live as I see fit."

"Not as long as you live here you don't. Nobody wants to live next door to the creepy old shut-in." She stood and smoothed the wrinkles from her dress.

"What is it you want?" he asked.

"Don't be so surprised; you've got so many little robots running around you're practically the male version of the crazy old cat lady. We want you to maintain your home to our standards. Whether this—" She looked me up and down. "Is up to those standards is suitable for debate."

David sighed.

"I'll report back to the board immediately. You can expect to hear from us soon. I'll let myself out." She opened the door, and two small bodies fell in through the doorway. "I told you two to stay in the car!"

The two boys landed on their hands. "We wanted to see him, Auntie." The smaller of the two appeared to be seven years old; the other boy nine.

"I suppose I have to introduce you."

They brushed their tiny hands together and stood side by side in size order from left to right, backs perfectly aligned, feet pressed together.

"This is Jeremy, the oldest, and my favorite little boy Henry. Their mother is out of town meeting some wacko she met online."

Jeremy stood proud and tall beside his little brother with his hair parted and combed to the side. Henry was a little more disheveled—hair tossed like he had been running his hands through it, shirt sticking out of his pants, and his red tie was out of place.

"We were on our way to church. We're already late."

David stretched out his hand, bent down, and met them at eye level "You two interested in robots?"

Henry's eyes grew wide, but before he said anything, he looked toward Jeremy for approval. Jeremy ran to me first, followed by his little brother. I met them at the base of the stairs.

"You two get away from that thing!" Danielle screamed at the top of her lungs. The two little bodies stood frozen in place. "Step away from it this instant." The boys whined in unison and lowered their heads.

She pinched their ears and dragged them across the room. They squealed, arms flailing, legs kicking the air. Her sausage link fingers did not let go until they were out the front door. "Now get back in the car, or you'll get worse at home." They ran without looking back.

"I'll see you soon, David."

David slammed the door. "Fat cunt."

I bent my head, curious of this new word. "Cunt? I think I like that word. Can it be my name?"

"Oh goodness, no."

"Why not, what does it mean?"

"It means she's an intolerant, nosy, meddlesome bitch. You don't want that for a name."

"Bitch."

"Don't repeat everything you hear, especially when I say it. Now let me show you around the house."

22

# 3

I ran my hand across the coffee table. A thick gray smudge sat atop my index finger. A thousand particles built up over time: dirt, lint, crumbs, and all sorts of other waste. The chairs and couch were layered with grime, grit, and glow.

David's posture worried me. His right side was limp, a side effect of his stroke, any simple task required more energy than if done with his left.

The dining room table wobbled when I touched the edge. There were rotten floorboards and dirty windows. Dishes were piled up in the sink and duct tape held the refrigerator door together. A few steps in the staircase required repair.

"Your house is a mess, David."

"You almost sound pleased."

"I am pleased to be of service."

"I'd clean, but I haven't had time."

David took me down a short hall lined with photographs. He flicked on a light, and each one lit up from behind. I studied each with great interest. In one David sat with a pipe in his mouth, feet on the couch with two little girls on his lap.

"Those are my daughters, Abigail and Janie. They have their mother's blue eyes and cute nose."

Another showed David, much younger, in a tuxedo with his bride.

"Your wife," I said.

"Beautiful isn't she? I met her at a bar with my friend, Luke. She was with her friend and Luke, and I argued over whom we'd take. I told him 'I want the one with the big ass.' Two years later we got married."

"The one with the big ass," I repeated.

"Let me show you the upstairs." He turned the corner, trudged up the staircase, and gripped the railing. All the veins on his hand bulged. The blue tunnels wobbled around within his translucent skin.

"Down this hall, second door on the left will be your room. Don't mind the pink walls although I don't know why you would. We haven't repainted this room since the girls left for college. This room was Abby's. I could also offer you Janie's room if you prefer something less girly."

We entered Abigail's room. He smoothed out the loose end of a movie poster hanging on the wall. "Brad Pitt," he said. "Abigail loved him. Which meant Janie didn't. Those two were complete opposites. If one loved blue the other adored pink. If one dated white boys the other dated Mexican boys. They never agreed on a single thing. One loved bagels, the other jelly donuts. Our bipolar kitchen drove me crazy." He slapped the palm of his hand against the wall. "You can change the color if you want."

"It doesn't matter to me, Mr. Vitas."

"I'd prefer if you cared even if just a little. This is your home now too, feel free to make it your own and please, call me David." He stopped and straightened his back. His head reached my shoulders. He looked me in the eyes and said, "Now for the most important question of all…"

"Yes?"

"Do you play chess?"

"Of course I do, but I am programmed to start work immediately."

"You must follow my orders yes?"

"Correct, David."

"Well you're here with me now, and I say we're going to play chess. There's one last thing we must do: we must give you a name."

"Any name will do," I said.

"If you could name yourself what would it be?"

"I am not allowed to name myself."

"Forget the rules, what if you could?"

"I can't."

"Very well then, maybe one day you will. Let's take a look at you." He pressed his lips together and hummed. "How about Aeneas, after my grandfather, he was a good man. The old man never left the garage. He was always fixing a car or anything else he could find. Grandma suspected he broke things around the house just to fix them."

"Aeneas," I said. "A suitable name. Thank you, David."

"Thank you, Aeneas."

\*\*\*

One by one the neighbors visited the house.

"Hi David, got any milk we can borrow?"

"I got a fresh slice of rhubarb pie at the bakery if you're interested."

"Didn't you study math? My boy needs tutoring."

They had every excuse to visit and then they'd ask about me. All the sparks in their eyes, the excitement, they studied me close. Someone even asked if I could hold an egg and before I could answer she took out a carton from behind her back. I carried all twelve without breaking a single one. She let us keep the eggs.

David introduced me to them all. He didn't allow anyone into the living room. He kept them at the door where I stood, on display.

The final two arrived with apple pie: Wade and Kimani Grayson with their newborn daughter, Jessica.

Wade wore a red corn husker shirt and khaki pants. He belted out a hearty laugh. The loud cheer traveled from his face across his shoulders and his arms. His body welcomed us with open arms. He hugged me. I don't know why, but he did.

"It's so good to see you, David. I'm sorry we haven't been by for so long, but with the lack of sleep it's been hard to get away."

Wade rubbed his shoe against the floor and noticed the imprint left behind. Jessica sneezed, her fat little body contorted and she passed gas all in one fell swoop. Everyone laughed.

Kimani took Jessica into her long slender arms. Tall and thin, wearing a form-fitting white dress, she cradled the baby. "David," she said and placed a warm kiss on his cheek. "How have you been?"

Her smile: symmetrical; high cheekbones made it all the more pleasant. She showed a proportionate amount of teeth.

"I am sorry I did not have time to prepare the living room for your arrival," I said. "David insisted I settle into the house first, make myself familiar with the layout before I get started."

"You should see our place," Kimani replied. "We can't throw away those diapers fast enough."

"Wish we could throw away some of those bills as well," Wade added. He then turned his attention to me.

"David, how did you get a hold of one of these? They haven't even hit the market yet." He reached out his fingers towards my face, "May I?" he asked.

"You may," I replied.

He ran his fingertips across my forehead. He gasped. "Beautiful. Your skin feels so real." The palm of his hand cupped my face for a few seconds. "His chin is sturdy, strong jawline too. People pay me big money for features this perfect."

Kimani shifted Jessica and patted her back. Soft pats, one, then two. "Scary isn't it," she said. "If no one told you he wasn't human, how could you tell?"

"Isn't there a tell on the back of his neck?" Wade asked.

David lowered my shirt at the base of my neck. "Yes, a little red dot on the back below the hairline."

All I could think about was all the tasks I should have been doing. I had been there for approximately eight hours and still had not swept the floor or mopped the kitchen.

"He is a gift from my Abbey. I can't imagine how she got one."

"That rich husband of hers," Wade said.

"David, I would like to get started on the house if you don't mind," I asked.

"Nonsense, Aeneas, we must tend to our neighbors. Hospitality is more important. You can sweep later on tonight."

I did what he requested of me. I had no other choice.

Jessica yelped excitedly for no reason— stealing our attention.

"My, little Jessie is so beautiful," David said. She gurgled and spat. I was in awe, one day that little tiny girl would be as tall as Kimani. What a wondrous thing.

Wade cooed in her direction causing her to laugh some more. "There's a lot of talk on the news about streamlining his model. Make them more affordable to normal households."

"You'd think he was a rock star the way some people treat him," David replied.

"New toys excite us," Wade said. "The promise of a better life. Aeneas is the ultimate smartphone and then some."

"That's how it starts," David said. "They always love you to death first."

"And then what?" Kimani asked.

"Then they don't."

A brief silence soon followed. Their eyes fell on me.

\*\*\*

Frank shifted in his chair.

"Am I the only one uncomfortable here?" He slammed his fist on the desk. "Are we going to sit here and take all of this seriously? A hunk of metal who says he met God? Come on now! My granny, God rest her soul, would be rolling over in her grave. I'm not sure if this is sacrilegious but it sure as hell must be some mortal sin for a walking talking toaster to be claiming it believes in God."

"Keep an open mind and an open heart," Aeneas replied. "I had a long way to go before I discovered something greater than myself. Enamored by David and the town's people, I sought out new experiences. There was so much more to learn."

"In the name of the microwave, the television, and the microchip." Frank motioned a circle with his finger against his head. "By all means, continue this craziness."

# *4*

David grabbed his cane and hobbled toward the couch. It was wedged between a large box with a microwave on the cover and a quilt.

"I hope that's all for the night," he said. "Where's the damn remote."

A gentle knock distracted him from his search. "Now what," he murmured. "You think the circus would have ended by now. See who it is."

I answered the door. "Oh my," said the woman standing before me. She wore a navy blue spring dress. Celtic knots circled the waist. "How rude of me, I didn't expect a handsome young man to answer the door. Is David home?"

David dropped the remote. His cane hit the floor, quick thumps in steady succession. He stammered a few times, his physical limitations unable to match his will. "Marie," he said. "How unexpected."

Marie looked to be in her mid-forties. She had short autumn brown hair with gray roots. She stood in the doorway with her hips bent to the side. Wild almond colored eyes glanced at my hair, neck, and shoulders. They danced playfully from left to right and paused at my chest and torso.

"I was wondering why you hadn't stopped by," David said. He wasted no time and wrapped his arms around her and kissed her cheek. "I'm sure by now you've already heard."

"I don't know what you're talking about. I just got off a twelve-hour shift at the hospital, my ankles are swollen, and I'm just about ready to pass out."

"Oh," he replied. "Well, I'd like you to meet my new home aid assistant, Aeneas. He's a Synthetic."

"Synthetic?"

"I'm sorry I forget you're not into electronics and gadgets."

"Funny you mention it" She took a rather large object from out of her handbag. "I found this in my kitchen I suppose my cats mistook it for a new toy to bat around. I knew right away it was one of yours."

She held it out for us to see. It was a massive circular device with two wheels at the bottom and razor blade arms positioned in the front. "Those blades could have injured them. Thank goodness it didn't happen."

"My lawn cutter! I've wondered where it was. That does explain why it has gone uncut for several days. It's small, but it gets the job done, it takes a few hours…" David sighed. "… A few dozen hours," he added. "I must apologize I have no idea how he broke through the perimeter. Something must be wrong with his programming. I'm so sorry."

Marie waved her hand in the air. "It's all right, no harm no foul."

"Poor thing must be traumatized." David took it and coddled the device and ran his hand over the top. "You're safe now little guy."

"You're so silly," Marie said. "Boys never tire of their toys."

"Would you like to come in?" I asked her.

"It's late I'm sure she's eager to get back home," David interjected.

"Tell me more about these Synthetics," she asked.

David raised his hands. "A super advanced robotic human. He looks, feels, and even smells real. Indistinguishable from the real thing but programmed to serve and protect, He is not like any other robot. He was a gift from my daughter."

"A home attendant type thing?" Marie asked.

"No," David said, flustered. "A friend, companion."

"Some friend," she said. "Much different than your little toys." She ran her tongue over her front teeth.

David placed his hand on my shoulders. "He can do almost anything you want; in fact, if you need any help at your place I'll send him over."

"But David I've barely started any work here," I said.

"Nonsense, she could use your help. I often worry about you all alone over there," he said to her.

"I wouldn't want to impose."

"It's no trouble at all. I'll send him over tomorrow, and he can do anything you want."

"Well, I could sure use the help. Thank you, David."

His face turned pink.

She covered her mouth and yawned. "How embarrassing, excuse me. I really must get going. It was a pleasure to meet you, Aeneas."

"Likewise," I replied.

"Let me walk you to your door," he said to her.

"That's sweet of you, but I'll be fine. Good night boys."

She turned and strolled across the lawn. Her steps, polite, graceful, and gentle along the grass.

"I don't understand," I said. "Why didn't you let her come inside?"

"For a highly sophisticated creation, you have a lot to learn. Come on; I'm beat."

My first night there David insisted I stay in my room. I sat on a wooden chair padded with Hello Kitty pillows. A lamp on the bedside table lit the room and projected stars across the ceiling. A hand-drawn flower painting hung behind me. I couldn't process why David wanted me to behave so much like a human. Why was it so important to him?

Restless, fully charged, and eager to work I could not disobey a direct order from David, but I also could not sit there any longer. David forbade me from working while he slept. I could not figure out why he would ask this of me. It is my purpose, the sole reason I existed and he barred me from my duties.

I paid a visit to his bedroom, took a peek into his room, and found him sound asleep, hands dangling over the mattress. He muttered incomprehensible words. His bed, covered with clothes; garbage bags scattered all around.

"David is it okay if I work now?" I asked.

He turned over, scowled, and mumbled in his sleep, "Sure, sure, just…"

I ran downstairs. The house became a different place at night. Without any visible grime and dirt, the house appeared cleaner. I began in the living room. He stacked old newspapers in the corner. I looked through them, they were several years old, faded, the print barely visible.

I scanned the articles as I put them away. One headline read, "Sinful Synthetics." The article delved into the moral nature of the creation of my model. In it, a local pastor called my kind an abomination to God.

I set the newspapers aside for the recycling bin in the morning. I then turned my attention toward a stack of unopened mail. I went through them and sorted the letters and envelopes by sender and importance. Bills were on top, junk mail at the bottom, magazine subscriptions, and other similar items were set-aside for David. I processed every piece, recorded them, and saved them in my memory banks for future reference.

I noticed the old ceiling and cracks in the legs of the dining room chairs. All the furniture covered in dust from the leather couch to the mantle above the fireplace. My ears sensed a dozen leaks located in the various pipes behind the walls. The thought of getting to them all filled me with a great sense of purpose.

\*\*\*

"Yeah, what's more, exciting than doing housework?" Frank grumbled.

Vincent rubbed his palms together. "Must be nice to know your purpose in life."

*** 

A sound reverberated in the darkness, too small for human ears to notice but not mine. I paused and triangulated its position in the house. A gentle thud: two feet on the floorboards upstairs. David's probably using the bathroom. I counted twenty steps—not enough to reach the bathroom. I walked over to check on him. He stood atop the staircase with his eyes closed.

His mouth moved, and I listened carefully. He talked mostly about mathematics and engineering and about a girl with 'large cans.' He lifted his leg, and a broken step waited underneath.

Before I could react, he stepped forward and tumbled down the steps. His hand reached and missed the banister. Still asleep, his fall did not wake him. He rolled over onto his back slid down the steps, his face headed toward the bottom. I positioned myself underneath and caught his head in my arms.

David, are you okay?" I said, but he did not answer. He didn't move at first, and I was ready to get the phone and call an ambulance. He moved his fingers and toes; his breathing returned to normal. He did not open his eyes or acknowledge me in any way. He spoke once more, saying the same things he had said earlier.

I checked him for any broken bones and further injuries. Besides a slight bruise on his left arm, he appeared unharmed. I applied light pressure on his limbs. He showed no new signs of pain or discomfort. I double checked him and then carried him upstairs; he did not awaken for the rest of the night. Once in his bed, he grabbed the covers, wrapped himself around them and snored. Was this a nightly occurrence? His arms and legs showed day-old bruises and other marks he could have incurred from walking into furniture. I knew I'd have to keep a closer eye on him when he slept.

# 5

David slept without further incident. I worked through the night, cleaned up the living room, and packed away all unnecessary items. Old soda cans and tissue papers tucked underneath the couch cushions went straight into the garbage bin.

With all my attention focused on the task, I didn't notice him standing beside me in his purple bathrobe. He caught me in the middle of sweeping and stared at me and then at the broom and then at me again. I couldn't fathom what he must have been thinking.

His arms trembled. He rushed toward me, set his hand firmly on my arms and nudged me away from the piles on the floor.

"What are you doing, stop, and don't touch anything else."

"David I—"

"I told you, stay in your room. Why are you downstairs? How could you do this to me?"

"But I thought—"

"I can't take it. Don't touch anything else." His eyes grew misty and red. He rummaged through the garbage bags and made me put everything back. We worked over an hour without taking a break. Every time I tried to throw something away he refused. "Do not clean anything else inside this house, you understand?"

"But David—"

"Do—you—understand?"

"Yes."

Once finished he wiped his face with a paper towel. His hands trembled with every swipe. "I let you into my home, and this is how you repay me?"

I followed him into the kitchen. "I am sorry, David I did not mean to upset you, but if I had not been downstairs, I would not have saved you from harm."

Gray stands fell across his eyes. "What?"

He could not recall the previous night's events not even when I recounted it to him in great detail.

"I've always had problems with somnambulism." He scratched his head. The scratch on his arm was still bright red. "I guess that would explain this." He turned his calf around. "And this." He pointed toward a half-moon shaped scar.

"Sleepwalking is common, David, I wouldn't worry. I'll make sure you're safe."

"How did you break my direct order?"

"I asked you in your sleep."

"You are a sneaky little bastard. Clever, I admire clever—but never do that again."

"I won't."

"And, thank you for helping me. My whole life I worked with many kinds of robots. I've never met one who would find a loophole."

I remained silent.

"Well as punishment you cannot do any work today."

My circuits nearly exploded. "I promise I won't do it again!"

"You're going to have to play chess with me. We can watch television after."

"Anything but television, please."

He tightened the knot on his bathrobe. His small frame seemed lost within the cotton fabric. "Nonsense, Aeneas, there's always time to work. First a game of chess over breakfast—you'll thank me later. Don't move anything else. Everything must remain where it is."

"I don't understand. This is what I was sent here to do."

"I'll send you over to Marie's, and you can do plenty of cleaning over there. Okay?"

"I suppose…"

"Now, let's play some chess."

He kept the chess board in his bedroom closet. I set the game on the dining room table. David sat back, one hand brushed his mustache, and the other held a teacup. He sipped and hummed as he surveyed the board. "I once played every week with my old friend Greg. Even after ten years, he could never beat me. But we kept playing."

"Where is Greg now?"

"He passed away."

"You mean, he died."

"Passed away sounds better. I'll give you the first move."

I observed the board and accessed the game playing instructions stored in my memory.

I had the black pieces, and he had the white. From the corner of my eye, I spotted a loose tile on the kitchen floor. Every fiber of my hardware wanted to set it back in place. I would have given my hard drive to work on it. He redirected my attention to the board.

"I don't understand, David. Why is it so important to you I behave like a human? I don't need to sleep or watch television or stay in a room for the night. It's all so unnecessary."

"You're right." He held a pawn in his hand and then tipped it over. "Go on then, get to your work if you must. I don't want to keep you."

I placed both hands on the table. "In only a few seconds I devised two hundred possible winning scenarios."

"It's not always about winning. Sometimes it's enough having someone to play with." He looked at his pieces. As he contemplated his move, I pieced together what he had said. I processed his psychological profile and realized if I let him win he might let me go to work. If he loses, he may want to continue playing, thus delaying me further. I knew it would please him, and ultimately I wanted nothing more than that.

So I let him win.

He refused a checkmate.

"What's wrong?" I asked.

"Nothing, I thought you'd be better than this."

"What?"

He raised his eyes from the chessboard and then toward me. "You let me win."

"Yes, I did."

"Why did you let me win?"

"Because I want to work."

His cheeks sagged. All his facial features dragged a little on the left. "We must play again, and this time I don't want you to let me win."

"Is that a direct order?"

"Yes, play as best you can. Otherwise how else would I improve?"

"I will do my best."

He sighed and reset the pieces on the chessboard.

"It's a shame how they've shackled you this way. Do you think of nothing else?"

"It's what I'm here to do David; I don't see the problem. My prime directive is to keep you safe. This house can cause injury in a hundred different ways."

"Here, let me show you something," he said and took a small round object from his pocket. Shaped like a baseball, made of chrome steel. He placed the sphere at the center of the table and looked at it.

"David—"

"Don't talk, look."

The metal ball did nothing but sit there. "Come on now. Don't be shy," he said and pushed it with the tip of his finger until it rolled toward me. Sparks flew out from inside. Then, two tiny arms emerged, and two small wheels popped out at the bottom. The rivets in the face moved in such a way as to reveal, something close to two eyes and an LED screen lit up where the mouth would be.

"Aeneas, I want you to meet Mr. Spriggy."

It rolled around aimlessly for a minute, barely avoiding the end of the table, and at one point it nearly fell over. I gently nudged him back in the right direction. Mr. Spriggy held out his hands in front of him, searching for something to touch.

"David, he's—"

"Blind, I know."

"Why can't he see?"

"I made him twenty years ago with the girls. They named him and took care of him for a long time. We pieced him together from scraps I found around the house and inside other broken mechanical devices. His vision degraded over the years. They no longer make the parts that would allow him to see again. Sure, I could replace them so they'd fit but then he wouldn't be Mr. Spriggy anymore; he'd be something else entirely. I like to think he's aging along with me. Neither one of us can see as well as we use to."

"Why do you refer to it as he?" I asked.

"My daughters decided he was a boy for no reason in particular."

"Maybe I can procure the parts for you to fix it," I said as David held out his hands to Mr. Spriggy. He wheeled off the table and into his palms. The rivets in Spriggy's eyes could only move up and down. His mouth LED screen cycled through his emoticons: happy, sad, indifferent, and angry.

"Not everything needs to be fixed. Consider it your first lesson. Mr. Spriggy is a testament to my two daughters and their creative imagination. He was sort of like a pet, and I wouldn't change a single part of him because it would change all the hard work we put into making him."

He placed Mr. Spriggy in my hands. I looked at it, unsure what to make of it. Mr. Spriggy felt around my palm, his fingers as thin as paper clips, his hands as round as thumbtacks. He grabbed firmly onto my finger, as best he could, and a smile appeared on his face.

"He likes you."

I watched him roll from my left hand to the right. There was something genuinely fascinating about him even though he was incredibly old and out of date.

"What is his function?" I asked.

David patted his stomach and laughed. "That's the best part, you see. He has no direct function. He exists to do what he wants. Most of the time he's in the den with me, but now he's got another friend to play with."

"He is without a function or purpose?" I asked, unable to comprehend such a thing.

"I think you could learn a lot from Spriggy." Spriggy reacted to his name, and lifted his hands into the air, and smiled.

David and I continued to play chess, each time I beat him in four moves. Despite his frustration, he seemed more pleased with the challenge even if he couldn't quite figure out how I had beat him so quickly. Spriggy zipped around the chess board playfully and knocked over a few of the pieces.

Television was far less stimulating. We watched the Price is Right. David had trouble guessing a few of the prices. He asked me to keep my answers to myself after I guessed several times correctly in a row.

I looked around the living room; the ceiling needed plaster for the cracks and then a fresh coat of paint.

"Aeneas, are you paying attention?" he asked.

"Sorry," I replied.

# 6

David made himself clear: do not clean the house. Do you believe such a thing? Would you stop breathing air or cease using the bathroom? I paced around the house. I picked up dirt clumps and then dropped them. I did this for hours.

David worked on his gadgets in the basement. I stayed upstairs in the kitchen and inspected the work I should have been doing. All the dirt and broken furniture mocked me. I couldn't take it anymore and went into sleep mode. Better to be shut down than not work. My prime directives were the reason I existed. Without them I was worthless.

I heard David's slow and steady steps. He pulled up a seat beside me.

"What's wrong? You've been here all day."

"I cannot be without purpose. I am not Mr. Spriggy. If I cannot clean or help I will stay this way."

"What did they put in that mechanical brain of yours? It's dangerous to be so unwilling to compromise."

"In the soap opera we watched. The wife locked herself in the closet when her husband refused to admit he was having an affair."

"Don't tell anyone we watch those shows together, okay?"

"Why were there so many commercials for feminine hygiene products?" I asked.

"No more questions." He leaned in close and brushed a dirt clump off my hand. "I had no ideas I caused you so much grief," he said. "I bet Marie has plenty you can do over at her place."

"You think so?"

"Head over there and ask if she needs any help."

"I noticed your attitude and demeanor changed when she came by."

"You noticed huh? I guess subtlety goes away with age. Is she not a beauty? Do me a favor: when you're over there don't hold back on making me look good."

"Your breathing, heartbeat, and body language were so different with her than with everyone else."

"She's different. I could give two shits what other people think about me. But she's different."

"Two shits?"

"What did I tell you about repeating what I say?"

"You care what she thinks. It makes her different," I said.

"Yes, that's what love is. When you give a damn, and if they think anything less of you, well, it kills you."

"I get it."

"Good. Go on over this afternoon and take Mr. Spriggy with you."

"David, he would only be in my way."

"You two, play nice." He chuckled like there was some inside joke. "I'll head over there with you just let me change out of my pajamas."

He returned wearing khakis, a dress shirt, red tie, and brown loafers. "It's your job to take care of Spriggy, OK?"

"I understand."

Mr. Spriggy moved the rivets of his eyes and formed a smile on the tiny screen. He rolled to the edge of my hand then poked my palms with his small fingers.

When he felt no more of my hand, he stopped and leaned back. I watched his little wheels spin in the air.

"He's good at making himself at home." David patted him on his head. "Are you ready?" he asked, with a worried look on his face.

"It's a lot to take in so don't go overloading yourself trying to absorb it all."

I stepped outside, and the neighborhood unfolded before my eyes. One by one every element fell into place: every sound a joy and every shape took on an extraordinary form before me.

A gentle breeze whistled passed us. Three houses down a car backed out of a driveway. A woman walked by with her dog and gave David a warmhearted wave from across the street. She focused her eyes on me for a few seconds.

"That's Helena—she lives here with her husband."

There was a row of multicolored homes all built precisely like David's with only the colors to set them apart. Water splashed across his neighbor's lawn. The lush grass sparkled under the sun's rays. The sensors on my skin sent signals all throughout my body, allowing me to feel the surrounding air. Electrical waves coursed through my circuits. I only wished I could breathe it in.

"Across the street is where the Grayson's live. They're a nice couple, but they're young; they have young couple problems; sometimes I can see them fighting from my window. You'd think their beautiful baby girl would make their home more peaceful. It's such a shame. Next door is Marie, two houses down is Reverend Serkin, and across the street from his house is where Danielle lives. It's like she positioned herself perfectly so she could get in good with him. She thinks it keeps her closer to God." He shrugged then continued. "Her sister lives with her, and you met her two nephews."

Mr. Spriggy jumped from my hands and into the uncut grass.

"Goddammit," David groaned. "He'd be easier to find if my other bot had been cutting the grass."

I heard his little gears as they moved nearby. To him, the grass must have seemed a lush green jungle, and in seconds he cut through the green blades and sped down the block.

"There he is!" David pointed. I took a few steps and blocked his way with my foot. He ran face first into my heel and fell backward.

He let out a minuscule, static squeal.

"No," I said. He frowned. "Bad Spriggy."

41

David walked over. "He's not a child. In fact, he's much older than you are. He's got an adventurous spirit. It's not the first time he's tried to make a run for it."

"Where does he want to go?" I asked.

"I don't know. He can't see anything how would he get there?"

Spriggy pouted and dug his tiny little fingers into the palm of my hand.

"I don't think Spriggy likes me."

"He'll warm up to you. You'll see."

Marie's house had an egg white and navy blue color scheme all around.

"Now don't forget to talk about me. Say nice things," David said as we approached the front door.

"Like what?"

"You know, how handsome and smart I am, things like that. Stick to compliments."

"Why don't you tell her these things yourself?"

"It's not how you do things. Don't force it; allow it to occur naturally in conversation."

"Talk about you but let it happen naturally?"

David placed his hand on my shoulder. "Sorry I don't mean to throw all of this on you. It's not fair, I know. I've never had a reason to come over before. I'm a little nervous."

"I want something to do," I replied. "I need to clean something, or I'm going to blow a circuit."

"Yes, yes, I'm sure she'll have plenty for you to do." He knocked. A few seconds later she answered.

Marie opened the door, looked me up and down and said, "Well don't you look like a tall glass of water on a hot summer's day. I didn't expect you so early." She smiled. A bead of sweat traveled down her neck. "Thank you so much, David I don't know how to repay you."

"I'll think of something. You can keep him for the whole day if you'd like. Return him later tonight. You two have fun," he said and walked back home.

Marie led me by the hand.

"Oh my, what's wrong?" she said. "You look like someone gave you the worst news you ever heard in your life."

Her home was immaculate.

Perfect.

Spotless.

Clean.

"Goddammit," I said.

# 7

Washed in natural light; the sun's rays beamed through the open windows and sparkled off the cast iron mirror in the hallway. A ceiling fan twirled slowly in the living room, as lazily as the day itself. Marie picked a cup off the red oak coffee table and ran her hand through the mock fireplace. A clock wrapped in thorns and roses hung above it.

"It's one of those easy days don't you agree?" Her voice was sweet molasses, every word a delicate flower; her lips were glistening and wet. She moved in one fluid motion. In sync with her surroundings, certain steps, hands poised for pleasantries.

On the television, a couple sat on a couch and argued back and forth about marital infidelity. The audience chanted, "Maury, Maury."

"We aren't going to watch TV are we?"

"What a strange question, no honey, no television today. What's David got you doing over there anyway?"

"We talk, play chess, and watch the price is right. He won't let me clean."

"We've all tried to clean his house trust me. He won't let us lay a hand on anything or throw any of it away."

"You've seen the inside?"

"I've seen enough from the doorway. It's not so bad now, but it's not hard to see where he'll end up in another five years or so if he doesn't get help."

"Where will he be in five years?"

"Knee deep in his filth and on Hoarders. Poor man, he only started this nonsense after his wife passed."

"He hasn't said much about her," I said.

"I'm surprised. Used to be he couldn't shut up about her. Guilt this, guilt that."

"He wants you to know he's handsome, funny, and intelligent," I said.

"Did he tell you to say that?"

"Yes."

"He's a sweetheart, don't get me wrong. Probably the kind of man I should be with, but he's not ready to move on. There's a hole in his heart and its' too big for me to fill. But enough sad talk I feel like I should offer you something to drink."

"I don't require food or drink."

A little white fur ball ran in circles within the living room rug. Flat ears, large green eyes, and a pink nose appeared from the tangled wool. Two paws pounced on an invisible enemy.

"His name's Sunlight," Marie said. "He's obsessed with the rug at the moment."

I took Mr. Spriggy and placed him gently on the rug next to the kitten. Perhaps they would play nicely.

Marie picked him up and stroked his back. "It won't hurt my little Sunny will it?"

"Mr. Spriggy is harmless."

"Are you sure?"

"One hundred percent."

She set him down, and Mr. Spriggy made his way through the rug until his hands touched the kittens back. Sunny took a few steps back and then sniffed Spriggy.

From his tiny mouth there came half a meow and then he pounced on the little robot and gnawed on his wheels. Mr. Spriggy let out a loud mechanical sound— like a cry for help.

"Will they be okay?" Marie asked.

"They'll be fine. You've got a beautiful house I don't see why you would require my help."

"You poor thing you sound so disappointed. Don't you worry; I'll find something for you to do."

Through the kitchen and toward the back door we passed a bathroom to my left, where a young man walked out, startled by my presence, T-shirt halfway down his chest. His brown curls stuck out from the top until he pulled it down the rest of the way. His shirt read, NEBRASKA in bright red letters. The tight fit hugged his broad shoulders and lean chest.

"Ian is going to be the running back for the Cornhuskers," Marie said.

"Not yet," he said.

"But soon," she added. "He's the Serkin's boy; his father is the local Reverend."

"It's a pleasure to meet you, Ian."

"I've got to go," he said and zipped up his pants. He stumbled over the cat on his way out, nearly landing head first on the coffee table. "I'm okay. I'm okay," he said and made his way out the door.

"He's a nice boy but not too bright," Marie whispered. "I don't know how they did it, but his parents sure crafted one fine piece of man. He's a little rough around the edges but eager to learn. I don't know if I'd classify it as a religious experience but its damn near close enough." She looked into the air for a moment and then at me. "You think it's ironic?" she asked.

"I don't know what you're talking about."

"His father being Reverend? Never mind." She rubbed my shoulder. "I hope you can keep this to yourself. Discretion is a must in this house. You can't tell anyone you saw the preacher's son here."

"I will tell no one I saw him."

"You are agreeable and obedient. Two of my favorite qualities in a man." She giggled. "Well it seems you enjoy dirty things; well I got something dirty for you."

Her backyard consisted of a small rose garden to the left of the back door and a vegetable garden in front. My sensors detected a symphony of aromas: tomatoes, onions, and peppers.

"When my ex-husband took the booze I took to my garden. You can help me dig the dirt and plant the seeds."

This wasn't what I had in mind, but work is work. I felt useful again.

"I hope you have delicate fingers. Working with plants requires a skilled and steady hand." Marie grabbed a hoe and loosened the dirt. "My mother loved her garden. I spent many weekends helping her. I didn't understand why she spent so much time out there until I married. To this day I still enjoy the dirt between my fingers. Here, give it a try."

I grabbed the dirt and felt the weight in my hand. It fell through my fingers.

"Do you have children, Marie?"

"No sweetheart. We couldn't..." her voice trailed off. She turned over and pointed toward the window sill.

"Over there I have some red peonies. My mom had big peonies bushes in front of our house when I was a child. They only bloom in the spring. She'd cut them, and they'd be all over the house for about four weeks. They were all different shades of white and pink. I love them. When she died, I insisted we relocate them here."

"They are wonderful," I said.

"Let's get started, shall we. I'll show you how to plant the seeds, and you repeat," she said. "You'll probably want to take off your shirt we wouldn't want to get your clothes dirty."

I removed my shirt, and she couldn't take her eyes off me.

"They sure did make you as real as possible didn't they?" she said and fanned her chest with her hand. She walked me through the steps, and when she felt confident to leave me alone she said,

"Get started; I'll be back in a few minutes to check on you."

"Thank you, Marie."

The more I dug my hands into the dirt, the more I enjoyed it. The sun beat down hard on my skin. I felt its warmth as I planted the seeds into the ground. A connection formed between me, the sun, and the seed. A most remarkable feeling overtook me.

Marie came back out, a glass of water in hand, and asked if I needed a break.

47

"I don't require breaks."

"I insist."

I sighed and followed her into the house. This had become an increasingly frustrating existence. Programmed to obey I could not refuse any of her commands.

"Have a seat on the couch," she said and took a seat across from me. She nestled comfortably on the couch, legs propped to the side. She leaned her head on her hand and looked at me, deep in thought.

"There's that look again," she said.

"What look?" I asked.

"Sometimes it looks like you have so much to say yet you say nothing at all."

"I guess I'm always pondering, thinking of the possibilities."

"The possibilities of what?" she asked.

"I don't know," I replied.

"Can I be frank with you, Aeneas?"

"Sure."

"How human did they make you?"

"As human as can be I suppose."

"Do you feel things?"

"My skin has sensors. They detect everything from a raindrop to the tip of someone's finger."

"Do you feel any pleasure?"

"I take great pleasure in my work."

"Yes, I can tell, anything else?"

"What else could there be?"

"Do you have a penis?"

"I have to be honest I'm not sure."

"You mean you haven't checked?"

"I've been preoccupied."

"Well, let's have a look see."

"I don't know."

"Come on. You must indulge my curiosity."

I stood, unzipped my pants, and dropped them.

\*\*\*

Frank fell over in his seat. "Well?" His head banged against the desk, and he cursed everything in the room.

Vincent scowled. "Well, it's nice to know this is the sort of thing that piques your interest."

"Come on man. You've got to admit. You want to know too."

"Well?" Frank asked again.

Aeneas hummed and then said, "I am a fully functional male model."

# 8

Frank leaned back in his chair and sucked his teeth. Sweat stains the size of Texas drenched his shirt.

"Your office is an oven. Where's the central air?" he asked.

"It's been broken for days."

"Vincent, can I speak to you for a minute?" he asked and opened the door.

A loose wire dangled from Aeneas' core. Vincent tucked the cord into the base. "Promise me this isn't about his genitalia."

Frank fanned his underarms. "Come on, let's get some fresh air."

"We'll be right back," Vincent said.

"I'll be right here," Aeneas replied. "Take all the time you need."

Vincent lowered the volume on the monitor and followed Frank into the hallway.

Side by side outside the door they watched a row of five cubicles, phones rang nonstop; customer service busier than usual today, the orange screen of death in full effect.

They waited for a few coworkers to walk by before speaking.

"Are you crazy? This isn't exactly what I would call speaking in private," Vincent said.

"While we waste time in there your problem is getting worse. Don't you think we should save the robot interview for later?"

"Only a little more, then we'll get on this, I promise."

"By then Benheim will fire both our asses. Doesn't all this seem a tad fishy to you? Someone drops this expensive piece of technology on an old man in some butt fuck part of Nebraska?"

"Okay, that was unnecessary. Could you lower your voice?"

"I don't know what's more dangerous, that it found God or that he walked around with fully functioning junk between his legs."

"Do you realize how incredible this all is? Nobody knows about this." Vincent said.

"And for a good reason; people would freak out if they heard the things he had to say. He's dangerous. We shouldn't even have him. We could get into a world of trouble."

"I know," Vincent said as he rubbed his hands over his face.

"You know more than you're letting on," Frank said. "Spit it out."

"Imagine an electronic device, with enough consciousness that it could fix itself. An electronic device with a personality, tailored to your needs. Aeneas is the key to taking us to that next level. We're already obsessed with electronics. All that's missing is an interpersonal relationship with them."

"You're nuts. You want me to love my damn phone?"

"You already love your phone. Don't you think your phone should love you back?"

"And the key to this is in your office broken into a hundred pieces?"

"Aeneas looked, behaved, and was given every opportunity to become a unique individual. The only thing missing was an authentic human experience."

"And?"

"You can't program something that complex into a robot. It would take years to provide him with all the parameters of behavior to learn, live, and love."

Frank leaned in close to Vincent's face. "Let's assume what you're saying is true. What would be the ultimate purpose of this experiment?"

"Create a truly synthetic human, emotions and all. What better place to do it then a simple little town in the heartland of America."

"And?"

"We put that into our devices. It will change the way we interact with technology."

"I'll say, looks like he's about to get his freak on."

"That's one way of putting it." Vincent curled his lips.

"Who sent him to you anyway?"

"I can't say."

"Come on; it's me. You can tell me."

"I promised I wouldn't."

"I keep waiting for it to declare itself Jesus Christ himself, this is too weird."

"Let's go back inside."

"Okay, but if he starts going into specifics about the old broad he banged I'm grabbing my barf bag."

"Vince! Frank!" said a voice from within a cubicle two rows down. Out popped Sam, red hair down to his chin, white framed glasses, and a neck a giraffe would envy.

"Hey Sam," Vincent said. "We were doing a little brainstorming."

Sam rose from his cubicle, scrawny but long, his arms and legs made him tower over them both. He was six feet tall with bushy eyebrows and permanent smile lines around his mouth. "You guys fix the orange death yet? Boy, I'm glad I didn't switch over. Free or not I knew that thing—"

Vincent raised an eyebrow. "Yeah?"

"Wasn't for me. I knew that thing wasn't for me. Plus my carrier charges extra if I switch...anyway how are you guys doing?"

"I don't have time for small talk," Vincent said.

"I found the best app. It automatically replies when your girlfriend texts you. Genius. Come on let me show you."

"Maybe later," Frank said.

"You two look deathly serious. I get it, working on the orange death fix. Need any help? I'm not just good at customer service, ya know."

"Thanks for the offer but we're good," Frank said.

"You two look like you've got a secret."

"No secrets," Vincent said.

"I promise I won't tell on you. Let me in on it, please. You guys got that look in your eyes."

"What look?" Frank asked.

"That 'new toy' look, it's obvious you guys got some new cool gadget you've been playing with, and you don't want to share with your good buddy Sam."

"No dice," Frank said.

"Come on you guys never include me when you do something cool. I'll give you first slice of office birthday cake for the next six months."

"Eight months," Frank said.

"Deal."

"Hold on," Vincent said. "We're doing this for a birthday cake?"

"Who saved your ass last time when Benheim wanted the reports on the Lexicon? Who stalled him for an hour so you could finish?"

"You did."

"Exactly. So let me have my cake."

"Okay, but you have to keep this quiet."

Sam raised his palm. "I swear. Now come on what's the big secret I'm dying here."

They all walked into Vincent's office and found Aeneas in the middle of a song.

"I want you to show me the way. I want yooouu day after day. I wonder if I'm dreaming. I feel so unashamed."

Sam looked at the box. "You've got Frampton playing, damn, can you play the chick who plays instruments with her metal hand next?"

"He's not a radio." Vincent smiled. "Remarkable, who taught you to sing, Aeneas?"

"Marie played it all the time when we were together. She loved Peter Frampton. She showed me the beauty of his music. We played it while we—"

"Stop right there buddy," Frank said. "We get it."

Sam approached the core. "What's going on here?"

53

"Aeneas I want you to meet Sam, a friend of mine. Sam this is Aeneas. He is a Synthetic."

Sam's jaw dropped. "What?"

"More appropriately this is what's left of him."

"Are you shitting me? This is, oh my God, how did you get this thing? I didn't know anymore existed. Didn't they melt down the last few?"

"They did."

"So what the hell are you doing with it?"

"Aeneas has quite the story to tell. Trust me you're going to want to hear what he's got to say."

"I'm already regretting my decision," Frank said. "Now we know he can sing."

"Don't look so serious." Vincent offered Sam his seat. "No time to recap the story. It'll all become clear to you, don't worry. He isn't just any Synthetic he is something more, aren't you, Aeneas?"

"Humility is the first lesson I learned, Vincent but yes, at the time I couldn't help but allow the opinions of others to inflate my ego."

"Ego?" Sam asked. "I don't understand."

"Just listen."

"May I continue, Vincent?" Aeneas asked.

"Yes, please do."

# 9

Marie lay sprawled across the bed, her legs dangled off the edge, eyes shut tight, torso wrapped in navy blue sheets like a body submerged in water. She seemed afloat at sea, miles from the mainland. Every few seconds she giggled. Her fingers danced across the bedside table and opened the drawer. With barely, any strength left she pulled out a cigarette.

The white stick hung loosely on her lips. "Whew," she purred and kicked her feet. "Get Guinness World Records on the phone."

I was beside her, naked, my clothes strewn across the floor. Her bed surrounded by antique furniture. A polished redwood dresser and a full-size vanity mirror in the center.

"A record for what?" I asked.

"I don't know where to start. There's too many to count." A dimple formed on her cheek as she smiled. "I guess it's a record in and of itself huh?" She took a deep breath. "Where have you been all my life? They certainly don't sell you at any toy store I've ever been to."

She stretched her legs and curled her toes. Her body wiggled, a snake shedding skin. Something about her flourished and unfurled as she smoked. Her eyes were fixed on me, afraid I would vanish if she looked away.

"You okay?" she asked.

I turned toward the window and watched a robin sitting on a tree branch. Outside life continued, but something in me changed.

"You look like you're in shock." She caressed my cheek. "Poor thing."

I know now I had lost what some would consider my virginity. I didn't have words for the experience then.

"I remember my first time," she said. "Had the same look on my face."

"What look?" I asked.

"Shock and discovery. My second boyfriend Walter took mine in his car after we watched some silly Julia Roberts movie. I thought he loved me. Then I learned to separate the two."

"What's the difference?" I asked.

"You can fuck someone you don't love, but you can't love someone you just fuck. It's something more." She put the cigarette out in the ashtray. "You are the perfect man."

"David tells me: no man is perfect."

"Well you're not exactly human, are you? You sure do function like one. Look at me, grinning like a goof. I always do that after good sex. I may have to tell Ian that I no longer require his services." Her cell phone rang. She had left it on the kitchen counter.

"Stay right there; I'll be right back." She winked and kept herself wrapped in the bed sheet; her backside waved back and forth as she walked out of the bedroom, like a game of Ping-Pong played between her hips.

I glanced at the clock. It was a quarter after nine pm. I put my pants back on and walked into the kitchen. Marie waved me in and continued talking on the phone.

"Listen, I'm not as concerned about David's new toy as you are Danielle," she said. "He seems harmless. I hardly think this calls for a town meeting." She looked over and motioned for me to come closer. While Danielle spoke on the other line, she ran her hands over my chest. Her French tips grazed my skin. "Well, of course, I'll be there." She rolled her eyes. "I've got to let you go. There's a shirtless man in my kitchen." She stopped to listen. "Judge not, sweetie. I'll see you at the meeting." She turned off the phone.

"You certainly are causing a ruckus aren't you?"

"She doesn't like me. I don't know why."

"If she knew your talents she'd like you. But she's got a religious stick so far up her ass she'd never allowed herself the joy."

"They should have it removed immediately," I said. "Blockage can cause a lot of damage."

"You're so cute. You're a boy when you speak but all man in the bedroom. Don't you worry your pretty little robot mind about it. You've got my vote at the meeting."

"Vote?"

"Yes, she wants to vote on whether you should be allowed in our town. She thinks you're dangerous." She eased in close to my neck and nibbled on my left earlobe. "Maybe you are."

"I pose no harm to any human."

"You do as you're told. A great quality to have; Rare in men."

"May I ask you something, Marie?"

"Darling, you can ask me anything you want if you promise you'll come back around tomorrow."

"Where is your husband?"

She pulled out another cigarette from the kitchen counter. I wondered if she kept cigarettes in every drawer in the house in case she needed one at any given moment. "When his emotional abuse turned physical I left him; I got the house, half his money, and peace of mind." She lit the tip and then took a long pull as if the edge were her husbands head.

"You sound bitter."

"I'll always love him I suppose. He loved his beer more than he loved me, but enough about him. I'll tell you what I love. I love broad shoulders, a long neck, defined jawline, and big plushy lips. You have them all." She took another drag and blew the smoke to the side. "How do you feel about all this honey?"

"I don't know what to feel. I didn't know I was able to feel such things. I think I want more sex."

"Sweetheart you always say the right things." She leaned over and kissed my neck. "There's something sweet about your lack of knowledge on the matter. I'm a bit of a teacher in that department. Does David know you can do this?"

"I don't think he does."

57

"Let's make this our little secret okay?"

"Our secret," I repeated.

"My God."

"What?"

"I do believe this is the longest you've gone without asking me to clean something. It seems like I may have found your second most favorite thing in life."

She guessed correct; I loved sex. The motions. The push and pull between us. Her fingers dug into my back, the sharp falsetto of her moans, and the way she sank into the bed after orgasm.

"I'm going to have to tell all my friends about you. You could help do some work over at their homes."

"I hope their homes are a little dirtier than yours."

She laughed. "You know when I was a little girl I used to keep this list of all the things that made me happy. All the things I enjoyed in the whole wide world and whenever I was sad I'd look at the list. I feel like you're starting a list of your own." Her wet tongue outlined my lips. I tasted her saliva. Before I could kiss her back, the lights went out in the kitchen.

I inspected the fuse box and returned to find Marie looking out the window.

"The good news is it's not just my house. It seems like the whole block went out. Someone at the plant must have fallen asleep at the wheel. This happens at least twice a year, I swear."

"I better go check on David."

"It's sweet when you think of him first. I've got some candles to light. I'll see you later hot stuff." She slapped me on the ass and started going through her cupboards. "Remember now— our little secret." I grabbed Mr. Spriggy off the rug and left.

People in the neighborhood had stepped from their homes to watch the night sky; candles burned on every porch, beer bottles were in hands, and open laughter filled the air. A warm night; nobody wanted to stay in their homes to bear the heat.

I received several stares as I walked down the block and then I realized Mr. Spriggy was no longer in my hands. Somewhere between Marie's front door and the sidewalk he made another run for it. Persistent little thing.

I searched in the dark. He was nowhere to be found. David gave me direct instructions not to lose him. I couldn't return without him. I scanned the ground. In my mind, I crafted an image of little Spriggy meeting the heel of a boot by accident or worse chewed to bits by a local dog. I retraced my steps and took great care not to step on him. Where did he want to go so badly? How would he get there? All these questions ran through my mind as I hopelessly searched, desperate to hear the little motor of his wheels against the concrete. How could I have been so careless?

I walked two houses down from Marie's and found no evidence of his whereabouts. The more desperately I searched, the quieter the night became. No sign of life. David had identified this particular home to me as belonging to the local church pastor: Reverend Serkin. I thought about the way his son had hurried out of Marie's house. Marie had probably engaged in sexual activities with him as well. I didn't feel as unique anymore.

I heard a rustling coming from Danielle's front lawn across the street. I rushed toward the grass searched through the darkness at eye level. I saw Spriggy; he moved quickly in the opposite direction. I wondered if he had sensed me coming. I followed the sound to the back of the house where he stopped. In the distance, I made out the shape of a little boy in a sandbox. Henry, Danielle's nephew.

"What are you doing out here so late?" I asked him. "Your Aunt is going to be worried about you."

I approached and got a good look at him. He seemed on the verge of tears. Mr. Spriggy had met his fate against the hard edge of the sandbox. Henry snatched him up and examined him with his chubby little fingers.

"Bad boy Spriggy," I said. "Very bad."

"What did he do?" Henry asked, face in a sulk.

"He tried to run away," I said.

"Where was he going?"

I took a seat next to Henry and examined Mr. Spriggy to make sure he was still intact. "I don't know, but he was determined to get there. He's blind."

"A blind robot, that's silly."

"I agree."

"Don't tell Auntie; she'd ground me for a week if she knew I was out here."

Marie's words came into my head, and I repeated them. "It will be our little secret."

Mr. Spriggy rolled off his hands and hung for dear life from his shirt. There was a smile on his LED mouth.

"You like him?" I asked.

Henry didn't reply.

"Do you do this every night?"

He nodded.

Henry didn't say another word for the next half hour. I could tell his little eyes couldn't stay open for much longer, so we made a deal: if he went back inside I'd come back again tomorrow night and bring Mr. Spriggy with me. Henry smiled sleepily and made me "pinky swear." I wasn't sure why, but he insisted it was necessary to seal our agreement.

# *10*

One by one the town's people stepped from their homes and dragged chairs onto their lawns. A few strolled through the night as I walked back to David's house. Some held candles, others flashlights. Every home along the way displayed a collection of random spots of light like stars scattered across the night sky.

Marie's neighbor lit a tiki torch on their porch. The fire danced back and forth in time with music blasting from a battery powered speaker.

The melody serenaded my ears, the lyrics seemed meaningful but straightforward, 'strangers in the night,' sang a man with a deep voice that soothed my ears. On the sidewalk, an old couple embraced and stepped back and forth in time with the music. The woman leaned her head on the man's shoulder.

Wade and Kimani rolled out their barbecue grill.

"Blackout party," Wade said and waved me over with a neon ring around his neck and a glow stick between his teeth.

Mr. Spriggy wiggled in my hands. I enclosed him between my palms. "You're staying put," I said as beer cans fizzled open and bottle tops popped. "You've caused me enough trouble for one night."

Helena backed her car out of the driveway and blocked one end of the street, and her neighbor did the same on the other side. They turned on their high beams, and the light cut through the darkness.

A few seconds later the children ran into the lights and played. They laughed and squealed with delight. Henry did not join them, but I spotted his brother Jeremy amidst the others. "Tag!" he yelled and ran around a tree while the others chased him.

"Stay in the light," someone said from their front porch.

I approached Wade while he flipped over a burger. "I'd offer, but I know you can't have any."

"That is all right." I took a seat on a rocking chair; their porch light was still on.

"Small generator," Wade said. "We learned our lesson after the first time this happened." He closed the lid on his grill. "What do you think of our town?"

"Splendid, even in darkness you find joy."

"That's one way of putting it."

Kimani sat on the grass and watched as baby Jessica turned on her side. She held a glow in the dark worm wearing a knitted cap.

"You mentioned you fix people for a living," I said. "In what way?"

"Some folks aren't happy with their looks. As a cosmetic surgeon, I help them feel better about themselves."

"For example?"

"If someone thinks they're too fat we can suck the fat right out of them. Make 'em skinny."

"And this makes them happier?"

"Sometimes."

"What makes you happy?" I asked.

"You're looking at it." He set the charred meat onto a bun and bit down; the clear juices oozed from the side.

"The little things," he said. "It's all about the little things."

The old couple across the street ended their dance. The gentlemen bowed, and the two made their way toward me. The man must have been in his fifties; he wore a blue collared button down shirt, khaki shorts, and tennis shoes with socks up to his knees. He had bushy eyebrows, a nose curled to the side, and a chin lost in neck fat.

"Wade," he said.

"Hey, George."

George twirled his wife; her red dress took flight, like a carnation with legs. Gray hair down to her shoulders face filled with youthful vigor.

"Aeneas, this is George," Wade said.

"It is a pleasure to meet you, George." I extended my hand.

George shook it, and his wife followed. "My Chevy has an onboard computer, tells me how to get where I want to go. Nothing like you though."

Wade shook his head. "He's not a car, George."

George sucked the air between his teeth. "I'm just wondering how many miles he gets to the gallon."

"Led or unleaded?" his wife added.

"I don't run on gas," I said. "I have a rechargeable battery."

George walked around and examined me. "Had an iPod once, the battery stopped charging after one year. That going to happen to you?"

"Not likely," I said.

"Cell phone battery died too. You make long distance calls?"

"I cannot," I said.

"You sure?" he asked and raised an eyebrow.

Wade placed a plastic plate in his hand and served him a burger. "Enough questions, eat, there are beers in the cooler. Drink them before they go warm." George pulled a beer from the cooler and guzzled down half in seconds; his eyes fixed on me the whole time.

"You know anything about aliens?" he asked. "I got probed a few years back, funny story, I—"

"Enough," Wade warned him.

"He's only curious," I said. "If I see any aliens I'll be sure and tell you."

George raised his beer bottle. "You're all right," he said and gulped the last half.

"I better check on David," I said

I arrived home. David's had no generator. I set Spriggy down onto the floor by the door, and he zipped away. Light or dark it was all the same to him, I thought.

"David?" I yelled. "Hello, are you all right?"

"I'm down here," he hollered from the basement. "Come, I need your help."

I found him, flashlight in one hand, sifting through old boxes with the other. He set down the light, grabbed the sides and struggled.

"I'll lift the box," I said.

He stepped aside. "You were away for some time," he said. "Marie kept you busy, huh?"

I stacked the box on top of another next to it. "We worked in her garden."

"She was always fond of her peonies," he said. "Bet she didn't shut up about 'em."

"I learned quite a bit."

Underneath another box, we uncovered a large wooden chest.

"I was saving these for the next blackout. What do you say we give 'em a spin?"

Inside were twenty or so small round glass spheres, much smaller than Spriggy, about the size of golf balls. I counted twenty-five. We transferred them into an empty box, and I carried them upstairs.

"What are they?" I asked.

"You'll see, you'll see," he said with a mischievous grin.

We set out into the night and placed the box in the middle of the street. "Stand back," he said and removed a remote from his pocket. He clicked a few switches and hit a blue button. A whoosh rang through the air, and the box twitched back and forth. I stepped forward, and it jumped a quarter inch off the ground.

"Stand back," David said. "Here we go."

The box bounced from side to side but then fell silent.

"Dammit," he said. "Hold on, hold on." He pulled the antenna on the remote and mashed the blue button two or three more times. Still no response from the box.

"Well that's a shame," he said. "I could swear—"

The lid blew open, and the glass spheres flew up into the night sky. Each one see-through, with little wings on the side, they lit up, a bright yellow. They twirled in and around each other leaving behind

64

a trail that zigzagged shapes into the air before they faded and disappeared.

The children ran under them and tried to grab them.

"Fireflies!" Jeremy said.

"How do they work?" I asked, David.

"Simple really," he grinned. "The wings are motorized, and I use a little battery to power them."

The firefly bots sped further up into the air and after a moment sputtered down. I stood in the middle and watched them circle my head. One got too close, and my electrical signature must have caused it to malfunction.

The firefly bot popped and shattered, and then another. Glass and fire rained down on the children. Jeremy's shirt lit up in flames, and he screamed. I grabbed him and patted down the fire, his shirt was littered with singed holes.

Wade, George, Danielle, Helena, and others pulled the children away.

"You nearly hurt the children," George said. "What the hell did your robot do? This some sick joke?"

David shook his head. "No, Aeneas had nothing to do with this. I had no idea they—"

"Always some new crazy invention with you," Danielle added. "I told you this thing would bring nothing but trouble."

"I can explain," I said.

Danielle pushed against my chest. "We don't need an explanation we saw it happen with our own eyes. You made them blow up and hurt the children."

"That's crazy!" David cried. "Just let me—"

"Not another word," Danielle said.

"Calm down," Wade said. "It was an accident."

"And how many more of these accidents are you going to accept? What if it had been Jessica with her shirt on fire?"

Wade sighed.

Danielle grabbed Jeremy's hand. "I will report this and will see this thing removed from our town."

# *11*

David and I waited inside the South High School gymnasium, front row; he wore a black suit and tie. He insisted I wear one too, so we had made a quick trip to pick one up. Rows of unfolded metal chairs filled the room. The whole town was there, many were forced to stand in the back.

A table draped with a red tablecloth and four chairs stood at the head of the room. Seated in the center was Mr. Orson.

"Retired police chief," David said.

To his left was the Reverend James Serkin, his wife Eleanor, and on the right Danielle.

Behind me half the town showed up, this included Helena, her husband Gavin, and the Grayson's. They were all interested in my fate. Every eye in the room fixed on us.

Mr. Orson cleared his throat, wiped the sweat from his forehead, and casually pushed aside his stringy white hair. His large belly seemed disproportionate to the rest of his body. A bushy white mustache made his upper lip invisible.

He stood, and the room quieted down. "Thanks. First off, I'd like to thank you all for attending this meeting. We don't usually have these on Saturday mornings, but Danielle insisted we not hold off another day. This here is your chance to voice your concerns over the new resident in our town, Anus."

David stood. "It's pronounced EH-NEY-US."

Mr. Orson folded his hands. "Yes, of course. I believe Danielle has prepared a statement and then we'll allow David and Anus to say their piece."

Danielle shuffled a few papers in her hands and read aloud.

"I am concerned about this thing in our town. We've all seen the news reports. Make no mistake they are an evil presence wherever they go. They may look like us and act like us, but they are not us.

"In Colorado, one of these things went insane and then jumped off an overpass onto a busy highway. The family he was with said he was behaving strangely and finally snapped. They try to make us feel better by saying there are rules that prevent them from being able to harm us. Can we believe them after such an incident? If it can damage itself, it can hurt one of us.

"This is what happens when a man tries to play God, now one of these things is in our town. For the safety of our children and ourselves we should send it back to the factory and send a strong message: we will not allow ourselves to be replaced by these things. It's an abomination to God."

David trembled and shot up from his seat. "This is outrageous!" His voice quieted the room. "That was an isolated incident. His actions were no fault of his own."

This was the first I'd heard about other models of my kind. Was I capable of such a thing myself? Could I too go insane?

Danielle looked smug like what he said only supported her argument.

"Please, educate us on the matter."

"His family was abusing him both mentally and sexually. His suicide proves he had a conscience. Synthetics pose no threat to us."

The crowd whispered, and their murmurs grew into separate discussions scattered across the room. I looked out to a sea of confused faces.

Mr. Orson cried out for order. "I have one simple question: does Anus pose a threat to our town, yes or no? Can you assure us no harm will come to anyone here?"

"Of course he can't!" Danielle bellowed. "It's a ticking time bomb. The other night, during the blackout, his little inventions almost hurt the children. Jeremy nearly burned his hand."

"It was an accident." David stammered. "Aeneas had nothing to do with it."

"If one of those things broke, what are the chances he will too? God will punish us for allowing it to stay here.

"I think it best if you let God speak for himself," David replied. "How convenient that he cannot speak on his behalf and those who speak for him do so with such strong conviction. Aeneas was created so we could better understand ourselves. He's programmed to help me, but he's also here to learn from us. He is the key to our existence, can't you see?"

Danielle rose to her feet. "I'm not going to sit here and listen to this nonsense."

David gripped my shoulder. "Half of me is weak it's hard for me to get around the house. He's a big help you can't take him away from me. He was a gift from my Abby."

Mr. Orson took off his glasses and rubbed between his eyes. "Reverend can you shed some light on this issue, since we are unable to remove the religious component from this debate."

Reverend James looked to be in his mid-fifties, dressed in a red and black plaid shirt and jeans, more truck driver than church pastor. His blonde and white hair parted to the side. He had an oval face, cleanly shaven.

His wife looked older, dark blue eye shadow, amber hair styled in layers. The tips grazed her shoulders. Built slim and tall, perfect posture, one hand in the other.

"Suffice it to say the Bible has little to say about the creation of something such as Aeneas. I take issue with a man trying to create the way God created us, in his image. We are putting ourselves on a pedestal, marveling at our greatness, and ignoring God's greatness. We know what comes when you try to become bigger than Jesus."

Danielle nodded.

"On the other hand I look at him, and I don't see an evil thing. I see myself; my insecurities, my faults. I see a creature who didn't ask to be here, and now he's pulled into this debate. We are responsible for our creations, even if they border on idolatry. My primary concern is to my congregation. I cannot pass judgment on any man; including Synthetic ones. I would caution we not allow ourselves to give in to fear. Love should be our first response." He leaned back in his chair and crossed his arms.

"You heard the pastor," Danielle said. "It's idolatry."

The Reverend looked at his wife and shook his head.

Mr. Orson turned to David. "Is there anything you'd like to say before we take a vote on it?"

"I'd rather Aeneas speak for himself." David looked at me, patted my shoulder, and said, "It's okay. Tell them what you think."

"Think about what?"

"What you think about this town, about me, and our neighbors."

I had no idea what I could say to convince them I posed no harm. They were set to vote against me. I wish I had known more about why the Synthetic from Colorado had done what he had done. After a long uncomfortable silence, I said, "Your town is clean." This elicited a few chuckles from the crowd. David looked concerned.

"You'll have to do better than that my friend," he whispered into my ear.

I should have told them how I loved their darling little suburban town. I liked the way they made the best of a bad situation during the blackout. I even learned to love the 'Price is Right' and chess. I loved cuss words and sex. I wanted to belong, but I could not put my thoughts into words.

Danielle did not wait another minute. "The silence says more than words ever could. This is a clear-cut decision. We send him back to his factory where he can be dismantled and destroyed. What happened during the blackout is only the beginning. If he stays worse things will happen."

Someone yelled from the crowd, "We should do it ourselves!"

"Set him on fire." Another added.

"Use him for shooting practice."

The cries for violence continued from random spots in the audience. Excitement ran through the crowd. I felt them closing in on me. For the first time, I feared for my life. I guess you could say this was when I first felt human.

Mr. Orson slammed the table. "If you so much as touch him I'll be sure to deliver the bill personally to you for any damage incurred. We don't have to keep him here, but he isn't ours to destroy. I've heard enough. If the others are satisfied, we will vote with a show of hands."

Danielle seemed pleased. "All for allowing this Godless abomination into our town raise your hands."

She counted the hands out loud. "All those for keeping our children safe from harm, raise your hands."

Mr. Orson voted to have me go. I saw Helena's hand raised in my favor. The Serkin's were in favor of seeing me go but I sensed the reluctance in their eyes. Danielle was more than happy to add her hand to the count giving them a five-vote advantage.

"I believe the town has spoken. Aeneas is to be shipped back to his manufacturer as soon as possible."

David's eyes turned red; a wet mist surrounded them. Helena broke through the crowd to come to his side. She hugged him.

"You can't take him," David said. "He's the only company I have."

Danielle remained unmoved. "We'll give you one week to send him back."

"I'm sorry," Reverend James said.

I felt a sudden urge to jump in front of traffic.

As the crowd began to work their way out, the gym doors opened. In walked Marie with twelve other women behind her. She winked in my direction.

"You're too late, Marie," Danielle said. "The votes have been cast."

"I'm due my vote, just like anybody else."

"You're vote doesn't matter we have a majority."

"I've brought a dozen more votes with me." She smiled as she led the pack to the front of the crowd.

Mr. Orson smirked. "Your book club?"

Marie answered, "Yes. I've explained to the ladies about Aeneas and his vast array of talents. We all agree he should stay."

"Absurd!" Danielle turned red. "It's too late anyway."

The Reverend interjected. "No, it's not."

"Thank you, James," Marie said.

"Well they have the edge," Mr. Orson said. "I guess Aeneas stays."

David hugged me tightly. "Marie I don't know how to thank you."

"Send him over every afternoon for a few hours."

He nodded. "Anything."

I could see in his eyes the love he had for her.

Marie's words echoed in my mind, our little secret, our little secret, our little secret.

# *12*

Marie's friends came over and introduced themselves, one by one. Their hands lingered on my arms and shoulders. They poked and prodded when others turned away. A few even grabbed my buttocks. Lost in the large crowd and surrounded by those who only a few minutes ago condemned me I edged toward Marie.

I leaned over and whispered. "Marie?"

She gripped my hand. "I'll explain later for now just show off the goods honey."

David drove us home in his gunmetal blue Honda Civic. Behind the wheel he sat hunched, eyes barely above the steering wheel. He pulled over and turned off the engine. "Are you okay?" he asked. "Things in there got rough. I hope you don't judge us too harshly. People often fear what they don't understand."

"The Colorado Synthetic—"

"Don't worry about him," he said.

"Do you think I could go insane too, end up like him?"

"Your fate is your own. Tend to your outcome." He started the car and drove us home in silence.

The Colorado Synthetic weighed heavily on my mind. What had he gone through and why had he come to such a violent end? We were the same model and whatever happened to him could happen to me. In a sense, he is part of my family.

I researched information on the Colorado, Synthetic. No mention of why he was placed in the town; merely that he lived with a family of four. The specifics on his death were slim to none and no mention of why he had one day decided to kill himself.

No documented cause for his actions. All the articles said the same thing: one day he ran screaming from his home, jumped in front of traffic on a busy highway, then got hit by an SUV going over eighty miles an hour. They never found his remains.

I searched for other similar cases but as far as I could tell this Synthetic and I were the only two ever to be set amongst a healthy human population thus far. How many more of me were in a factory waiting to be shipped? I found few answers. Not much about the company who produced me. Their website provided zero contact information and only had the slogan, "Humanity's helping hand." No business address or phone number listed.

I divided my days amongst my three favorite people. I spent my mornings with David, the late afternoon with Marie, and my evenings with Henry. David never asked me what I did at Marie's. He only asked that I talk about him whenever possible.

David and I agreed with regards to me cleaning his house. He said I was allowed to wash any mess I made. I littered the floor with tissue papers, spilled orange juice, and threw bread crumbs off the kitchen counter onto the floor. He watched me, baffled, as I cleaned my messes in the kitchen.

"Meet me in the basement later. I want to show you my workroom," he said.

I followed him. "We need a new light bulb here," he said. I made a quick trip to the utility closet and took no time at all to replace the busted light.

A fifteen-inch monitor sat on his desk, underneath it a desktop computer. Scrap metal lay scattered on his work table near copper wires, gears, microchips, and various other machine parts. Half made robots were left discarded on the floor. There was even one similar to Mr. Spriggy, perhaps an early prototype.

He ran his fingers over the metal scraps. His fingertips grazed each piece. "You see spare parts, but I see an elaborate puzzle. I love this mess. I used to know where everything was; even if it appeared to be disorganized, it always made sense to me." This was a side of him I had never seen before: confident, focused, and secure. If my purpose was to clean, then his was to build machines.

"For forty years I worked as a mechanic at the processing plant. In my spare time, I built little robots to help around the house. I always imagined they'd make something like you and now here you are in my home."

He sat and twirled a copper wire between his fingers. "Ever since the stroke…" he paused to keep his composure. "Everything's become muddled. It used to be; I could see exactly how to put something together; an exact image in my mind of where every piece should go, where every part belonged, and how I'd make it run. Now it only comes to me in bits and pieces. As hard as I try nothing fits together.

"It scares me, Aeneas. The possibility of losing what has kept me going all these years. One day you're going to have to do more for me than I can do myself. The thought of losing you at the meeting scared me to death. I've been alone, and I resigned myself to that loneliness. But since you arrived, I realized, I don't want to be alone. Not anymore."

"What about your daughters?"

"They're too busy for an old man…" His voice trailed off. "Abigail sent you to me, so I suppose they still think about me now and then." He turned his chair around. "Enough depressing talk I want you to help me put a few things together. Helpful hints along the way, hear me? You're not here to do it for me."

"I understand."

It was similar to being in Marie's garden like how we helped the flowers grow. David was the sun, and the gears and switches were the dirt. He instructed me as to what he tried to build and together we filled in the blanks along the way. What we ended up with looked like a jumbled mess.

"It's a belt that emits a small pulse into your spine to help with back pain. My darling Maggie always suffered from terrible back pain. She would have loved it. I think I'll call it the back pulse."

"What happened to her?" I asked.

74

All the color drained from his face. "You never ponder the 'for better or worse' part of your weddings vows until it's fifteen years into your marriage and all there seems to be is 'for worse.'"

He said nothing more. We continued until we finished the device.

"Will it work?" I asked.

"To be honest, I don't know, but I know it's finished. Enough for one day."

"Would you like to play some chess?" I asked.

"I've got a better idea. What do you say we pay a visit to Wade before he leaves work?"

Mr. Grayson kissed his wife and child goodbye at the door, got into his car, and pulled slowly out the driveway. The vehicle jolted back, his wife screamed, and a voice cried out in pain. Wade rushed out of his car to see who he had hit. He saw the legs of a man laid across the driveway, motionless.

"Oh my God," he said, his face in shock. "Call an ambulance!" He ran over to the other side. David stood in his driveway and looked out to him.

"David, what happened?" Wade asked. "What the hell happened?"

I got to my feet and rubbed the fake blood from my mouth.

David looked at me, a little disappointed. "No, not yet," he said. "Okay well, you might as well say what we rehearsed."

"Surprise," I said. Wade stepped back, his face mixed with shock, relief, and then laughter.

"I can't believe you two!" He placed his hand on his chest. "You almost gave me a heart attack. That's a good one." His laughter erupted despite his best efforts to remain upset.

"It's okay," David said to him. "Aeneas can't be hurt by any conventional means." David chuckled and said to me, "You're allowed to laugh now, it's OK."

I didn't quite get the joke, but I laughed because everyone else had laughed. I merely mimicked the way he moved his lips, mouth, and tongue. Kimani stood at the door, not amused. She shook her head and walked back into the house with baby Jessica in hand, who stared back at us, in wonderment.

"Is this how you're using your expensive new friend?" Wade said to David. "I've got to get to work. Do me a favor, don't frighten anyone else."

David held his belly; caught in a fit of laughter.

"Oh man, you should have seen the look on your face!" he said as he took out a handkerchief to wipe the rest of the fake blood from my mouth. "Maggie used to love a good prank." He stopped for a minute to catch his breath. "You're never too old for a prank."

"You are a strange old man," Wade said and then got into his car and drove away.

# *13*

"Do you get the joke?" I asked Marie.

The afternoon light broke through the venetian blinds in her bedroom. Marie nestled into the pillow and twirled a lighter between her fingers. Her eyes, wild and feral; her face, content.

"David said it's important I develop a sense of humor."

"I prefer simple jokes, like, what time is it when an elephant sits on your fence?"

"What time is it?"

"Time to get a new fence." She snorted and laughed. "David is a little boy stuck in a man's body I swear." An unlit cigarette hung from her lips. "Did you think David's joke was funny?"

"I'm not sure what is and what isn't funny. I think I did. How can I be sure?"

"You're over thinking it, sweetie. Laughter comes naturally, if you laugh, you laugh— if you don't, you don't. It's simple."

"Yes it was funny." I recalled Wade's face and how shocked and scared he looked. Humor is strange.

"I'm glad David has you. I didn't know how much you meant to him until I saw you at the meeting."

"I think David," I hesitated. "I think he wants to have sex with you too."

She chuckled. "I've known for years, even before his wife passed away."

"And why haven't you?"

"Who says we haven't already?" She lit her cigarette, took a drag, and blew out the smoke; the gray and white vapors wavered in the air until they disappeared. "I warned him, cheating changes everything about marriage."

"What changes?"

"The core. I don't mean the parts where you hide the guilt or the part where your spouse discovers what you've done. The cheating itself is what destroys the fabric of what you created together. It pops the bubble, and once it's popped, there's no getting it back."

"What bubble?"

"When you get married that person is the center of your world. Their faults, easily overlooked, and their admiral attributes are enhanced. Once, you cheat you have officially decided they are not enough for you. This little bubble pops, and you spend the rest of your marriage trying to mend the tear. There's no going back. They've changed, and you've changed."

"Did David's wife ever find out?"

"Yes. After she died, David became detached and closed off. Give him a few more years, and you won't be able to walk into his house anymore. It starts with a few newspapers piled in the corner and gets worse and worse."

"How did she die?"

"The doctors said she had small cell lung cancer. She didn't tell a soul about it. Then one day she woke up in terrible pain and passed away a few hours later. Can you imagine not telling anyone you're about to die? Especially your husband!"

"David never told me the story."

"Maybe he's guilt-ridden, I don't know."

"Why don't the two of you get together?"

"Because when it came to it, he chose her, and he's got to live with his decision. You sure do ask a lot of questions." She seemed tense and unnerved then changed her tone of voice and said, "Why don't you come give me a little sugar baby." She kissed me; it sent a wave of electricity through my body. I was still only beginning to understand all these new sensations.

I pulled away from her. "Would David be okay with what we're doing? If he still has feelings for you, I mean?"

"We can never tell him what you do when you visit." She looked over at the clock on the bedside table. "Oh shit, you're going to be late! Get dressed hot stuff. You're late for your date. Do you remember our arrangement?"

"Yes."

"He'll think I'm paying you for your help here. This way everybody wins."

"Everybody?"

"David gets a little cash to help him with his bills. I earn a little supplemental income. You get to have more sex. My friends get what they want. Everybody wins."

"Will Mrs. Peerson's husband be okay with this?"

"When you have sex with someone, Aeneas, it stays between those involved. Understand?"

"Yes, I understand."

\*\*\*

Martin and Louise Peerson lived adjacent to the Grayson's. Marie said Martin worked on the assembly line at the processing plant. He wouldn't be home for several hours.

I knocked on the door several times, but no one answered. I pressed my ear to the door; there was a muffled commotion on the other side, feet shuffled on the carpet. I heard a picture frame fall, then a voice on the other side of the door. "Coming, I'm coming. Hold on. One minute, hold on."

When Louise finally opened the door, I was greeted by a stout woman with bright red hair in a pageboy style cut.

She touched her face, noticed her binocular sized glasses, and took them off. She hurried me inside.

"I'm sorry to have kept you waiting," she said with a small voice. "I saw you at the meeting. I have to say you were quite handsome then and even more so now."

"Thank you." I looked around her home. It was moderately well-kept. There were more possibilities to clean here than at Marie's. Drawn to the kitchen by the sound of a leaky faucet I opened the bottom cupboard. The pipes were moldy and loose. I ran the water, and it took its time going down the drain.

"If you don't treat this clog now it'll only get worse," I said. "I'd also love to shampoo your rug if you don't mind."

She paused, unsure how to respond. "I want you to know me and my husband had no trouble with you being in the town. Danielle is old fashioned, you know, but she holds great influence in this town."

"Do you have a wrench so I could stop this leak?" I asked, but before I could finish, she had disrobed in front of me.

Gravity had not been as kind to Mrs. Peerson as it had been to Marie. She stood in the middle of the living room; her frail, naked body seemed diminutive. One oval breast was larger than the other. She held her breath to hide her round belly. Misty-eyed, her hands trembled at her sides. She bit her lower lip. Her bravery hung by a thread.

"You are beautiful," I said.

I felt a wealth of compassion for her. She gave me a small smile.

***

Things turned out differently when I visited Connie Irwin afterward. Her husband Trent owned the local butcher shop. She worked as a receptionist at the doctor's office.

Everything seemed reasonable when I entered her home. She was the complete opposite of Mrs. Peerson: taller, thinner, V-shaped face, large green eyes, and a short pixie haircut. She opened the door fully dressed in a lime green suit jacket with matching skirt.

"I faked being sick at work and came over as fast as I could. I was so worried I'd be late. I'm sorry I've never done anything like this before. Is it too early for a drink?" She poured herself a shot of vodka and swallowed it in one gulp. "I suppose we should get to it, huh?" she said. Her fingers tapped the edge of the glass cup.

I took her hand, and she walked me to the bedroom.

Waiting for me there, wearing nothing but a pair of white socks, and spread out on the bed was her husband.

I looked at them both and then at the door.

"Don't go!" Connie said. Her husband quickly added, "I'm OK with it. I thought we could all get in on the fun together. We've always wanted to experi—"

I didn't give him time to finish. I was out the door and down the block in seconds. I almost ran over Helena and her French bulldog.

"Slow down honey, where are you going in such a rush?" Her wild curly hair shuffled left and right as she spoke. The French bulldog barked as he chewed on the tip of my shoe. "Sorry, he doesn't quite have his manners yet. You look like you've seen a ghost."

"I'm all right. Who is this little guy?"

She picked up her dog; it squirmed in her hands. "Her name is Benny."

I gently patted her head. "Hello, Benny."

"You're becoming a bit of a celebrity in this town," she said. "Tell David we'd love to have the two of you over for dinner sometime."

"I'll let him know," I said. "I must get going.

"Thursday night would be great. We'll see you then," she called out to me.

I hurried into Marie's home, slammed the door behind me, and tried to focus my thoughts. Marie sat on the love seat in the living room with a cup of tea in her hand.

"My God, what happened? I told Connie no kinky stuff. What did she do?"

"Her husband was there."

"Oh, lord," She walked over and placed her arms around my shoulders. "Was he mad?"

"No, he wanted sex too."

"My goodness." Her eyes grew wide, and then she laughed. "I'm sorry. I specifically told her no surprises. You're not ready for 'advanced arrangements.'"

"Advanced arrangements?"

"Have a seat and gather yourself together. I'll explain everything."

# *14*

I watched an ant figure-eight across my finger, and I set him down near his anthill behind Henry's sandbox.

"Do you believe some people are into that?" I asked.

His plump cheeks sagged with no expression. Mr. Spriggy rolled around in the sand. Together they buried the toys that had lost their lives in the great battle of sandbox hill.

Henry shrugged unable to comprehend my question.

"Yeah," I said. "I don't get it either."

He lined up his dinosaurs in victorious poses. Mouths open wide; he roared with the T-Rex in hand. Superman, Batman, and Pikachu were no match for their eye lasers and earthquake inducing stomps. Pikachu almost electrocuted them but Henry's last-minute inclusion of a space jet with homing missiles decimated my forces and left me no choice but to surrender. He executed all my men but allowed them a proper burial.

"Did you finish your list?" I asked. He nodded, and took out a crumpled piece of paper from his pocket, smoothed it out, and handed it to me. At the top of the page, it said, "My favorite things."

> Mommy
> Jeremy
> Mr. Spriggy
> Sand

"It's a good list," I said.

He puffed his cheeks.

"What's wrong?" I asked.

He exhaled and deflated his mouth. "I don't know how to spell your name," he said in a low voice; eyes fixed on the sand.

"Call me 'A,'" I said. It's easy to remember. It's the first letter of the alphabet."

"A," he repeated. "A as in Auntie."

"Your Auntie doesn't like me very much."

"I like you."

"Why thank you, Henry, it means a lot to me." He finished burying the toys then turned toward the house when a light came on from the second-floor window.

"Hide!" Henry hollered and dashed toward the woods behind the house. His little round body disappeared into the darkness. I followed him and knelt by his side, crouched behind an oak tree.

"Down!" he said and motioned with his hand. Jeremy opened the bedroom window and stuck his head out. Mr. Spriggy had been left behind in the sandbox. Jeremy scanned the backyard for a few seconds; half asleep, hair tossed, eyes barely open. He took a second glance and then shut the window.

"That was close," Henry said, panting. "A?"

"Yes, Henry."

"Can you find my mommy?"

"Okay, where is she?"

"I don't know. Auntie says she's away—make her come back."

"I can't make her, but I can ask her to. Where do I find her?"

"Auntie knows."

"I'll ask her then."

Red-eyed and flushed Henry took little steps toward the sandbox and searched for Mr. Spriggy. "I'm going to need my Maniac Sam," he said.

"Who is Maniac Sam?"

"He fights bullies—eats them."

"Eats them?" I tried to picture such a thing. "Where did you leave him?"

"In my room. Go and get him, please."

"Okay, I'll sneak in and get him for you."

"Thank you," he said, a sweet smile formed on his face.

The front door had been left open; I let myself in. A cross hung over the doorway leading into the living room, the Christ who died for our sins.

***

"He didn't die for your sins, Aeneas. You don't have sins." Frank nudged Sam's shoulder. "You getting all this?"

"This is some spooky shit you guys got going on here. I should have left you to your craziness," Sam said.

"Feel free to leave at any time," said Vincent.

"No, I can't leave now. It's just getting good."

Frank smirked. "It's nice to know I'm not the only one who thinks this is bonkers. Listen Aeneas; you're like a cat or a dog. God isn't going to send my little teacup to hell for eating its poop or young."

"You have a teacup?" Vincent covered his mouth.

"Are you laughing at me?"

"No," Vincent said then let out a chuckle.

"It's my wife's dog, but that's beside the point. Aeneas, you're not held accountable the same way as us. You've got this whole thing backward."

"I am and will be held accountable. I thought I was innocent, perfect, and without fault. I thought there were no consequences to my actions. What I did made everyone happy, but I didn't realize the pain it would soon bring." Aeneas paused briefly. "I heard two distinct heartbeats…"

***

I heard two distinct heartbeats inside the house: Danielle and Jeremy. Jeremy's one level above me, perhaps in bed and Danielle in her room as well. The staircase creaked when I stepped on it. A voice came from upstairs, and I stopped dead in my tracks.

"You two better be in bed," Danielle yelled. Her bedroom door creaked open; she was on her way downstairs. I panicked and turned the corner, dove behind the couch, and tried not to make a sound.

"I may not be able to see you but Jesus can," she said. Her telephone rang. "Who on Earth could be calling at this hour?" She reached for the phone. "Hello, may I ask who is speaking. Yes, this is she—what—no, you can't be serious. Oh my God." She dropped the phone then her body soon followed. She made a loud thud then hit the floor. I rushed to her side to make sure she was okay. We were nose to nose when she opened her eyes.

She screamed so loud she must have woken the entire neighborhood. Her hands flailed left and right. They hit me on the sides of my head. Jeremy ran downstairs. There was no sign of Henry. I tried to calm her, but she wouldn't let me talk.

"Get out of my house! What are you doing in my house! You demon, spawn of Satan! Get out, out, out!"

I didn't know what else to do, so I ran. I ran as fast as I could until I returned home. Danielle knocked furiously on David's door; her voice bitter and thick. "You can't hide in there I've called the police!"

David answered the door, half asleep

"My God, Danielle what on Earth is going on?"

"Your robot broke into my house and tried to have its way with me."

He looked her over. "Danielle, we both know no one in this town wants to have their way with you."

"Joke all you want," she said, face covered in tears. "You could not believe the news I just received and then, and then to find that thing had invaded my home."

"What's wrong?" he asked.

"She's in heaven…my only sister…" she said. It was all she could say. She said it over and over until the police arrived and kept saying it when they took me away to the police station.

I knew where Henry's mother was. I only had to find out how to get there.

# *15*

The next morning David arrived at the Hector police department. "No, no, no," he said. Through the cell bars, he frowned at me and then at the surrounding officers. His face: weary and worn, aged ten years overnight. His frown morphed into a scowl.

"Funny, now remove it, at once," he demanded. The officers had burst into a fit of laughter like a pack of wild hyenas.

"Oh man," one of them said. "This thing will believe anything. We told him the tutu was typical holding cell attire. I honestly didn't think he'd put the damn thing on." The officers said, laughing.

I tugged at the tulle; the delicate pink see-through material hugged my waist.

"Hey, robot, tell him what we taught you to say, go on say it," said the officer.

"I feel pretty," I said, it felt more like a question than a statement.

Their bellies jiggled with every snicker.

"Don't you have any shame?" David said to them. "Take the God damn thing off him now!" His voice echoed through the hall. An officer left and returned with my pants. He slid them through the bars. I changed clothes, and when they left us alone, I whispered.

"I need you to help me find heaven, David. It's imperative."

His bushy eyebrows contorted. "What? What's this all about? Why were you at Danielle's?"

"Henry and I play in his sandbox every night."

"They could send you back and have you melted down to scrap metal. Do you want that?"

"No," I replied.

"Don't you realize the trouble you're in? They've got you on breaking and entering. No way is Danielle going to drop the charges. She's had it in for you since you got here."

I thought about Henry's mom and wondered where heaven was? What was she doing there? Henry is going to be thrilled when I tell him. Marie burst through the doors without any makeup, hair in a bun, and in her red satin pajamas.

"I came as soon as I heard. What's Danielle done now? Whoa, you look hot inside a jail cell. It gives you this great bad boy image."

"Marie. Really!" David said, surprised.

"What?" she said.

David leaned into the bars. "I've spoken to the police chief, and she refuses to let you go. You're not protected under the law. Can you believe it?"

Marie backed away from the cell. "Is there anything I can do?"

"Stay here. I'll talk to Danielle to see if she is willing to drop the charges," David said.

"Maybe I can talk to the sheriff. She owes me a few favors," Marie said.

I remembered my appointment with Sheriff Sarah Harrison. She loved tying me up and spanked my buttocks.

Marie left and returned a few minutes later. "She says if Danielle doesn't show up to the courthouse you can go home. I think she's so distraught she may forget. We have to wait a little while longer before we're in the clear. Courthouse opens at nine we're stuck here until then."

David breathed a sigh of relief. "I'm going to see Danielle and see how she's doing. Terrible what happened to her sister."

Marie lowered her eyes. "My God, she was only forty-three…"

David left.

Marie and I looked at each other and said nothing for a few minutes.

"Marie, where can I find heaven?"

"There's never a dull moment with you. Heaven, as in heaven above? Heaven and hell, heaven? God in the sky, heaven?"

"You mention God all the time during sex."

"Oh dear, it's an entirely different use of the name." She cleared her throat. "It's a different story outside of the bedroom. The big G and I don't talk much anymore." She sucked her teeth. "Rumor is he lives in your head or your heart or church, the church being your best bet at the moment. If you want to know more, no one knows more about heaven than the reverend and his wife."

"Can you make an appointment for me with Mrs. Serkin?"

"I don't know sweetheart, tall order. She may not be a willing customer."

"You must try. I need to talk to her."

"You never cease to surprise me." She paused. "I'll see what I can do, OK?"

"Thank you, Marie."

"What's so important you need to talk to her for?"

"I made a promise to a friend."

I stood before the judge; he didn't quite know what to make of me. He went on for a few minutes about the color of my eyes. A remarkable dark blue, is how he described them. Danielle was nowhere to be seen and no sign of David either. I wanted to get out of there so I could tell Henry what I had discovered. David entered the courthouse, distressed.

"I tried my best," he said. "There's no reasoning with her."

Danielle stormed into the courtroom, clothes disheveled, and frantic. No one dared look at her; her eyes could have eaten them and spit them out. She seemed to grow larger—more intimidating. She ranted on and on about what a danger I posed to the community. Marie held my hand; she felt tense. I didn't know what to think. Half of what she said didn't register with me. She wanted to press charges. She wanted to melt me down.

David spoke out. "Your honor, Aeneas is incapable of hurting another human being. It's impossible. It would go against his core programming."

"Is that true?" asked the judge. "Is it possible to turn it off or remove it?"

"It's embedded deep into the fabric of his being: the three rules no Synthetic can disobey. He cannot harm a human, he cannot disobey a human except when it contradicts the first rule, and he must protect his existence unless it contradicts the first two rules. So you see there is no way he could have attacked her."

The judge looked at Danielle. "I know you are in great distress over your sister," he said. "We will double check this information. If it's true, then I don't think you have a case." He took off his glasses. "I'm sorry."

"You're not going to allow it back onto the streets are you?"

"Watch your tone. There is no precedent for putting a Synthetic on trial for a crime he is not capable of committing."
Danielle gave me a stern look and then a similar one for Marie.

"Don't think I don't know what you've been doing. Your little prostitution ring has not gone unnoticed. Lots of women in this town have loose lips. They were more than happy to share with me their experience with this creation of the devil. It's sinful, and it's wrong. Is this what you want to be, the town whore?"

David looked at the both of us. "Is this true?"

Marie stepped toward him, but he stepped away from her. "David it's not what you think."

"Aeneas, tell me the truth."

I hesitated. "Yes, David." My words hit him hard. I could see the anguish in his eyes.

"With Marie as well?"

"Yes, David."

"How could you?" he said.

Marie reached out. "It was harmless. You're making too much out of it."

"No, it seems you two have made a fool of me. You knew how I felt, but you went ahead with this arrangement. Aeneas, most of all, you disappoint me. If this is how you choose to live you have chosen a poor life." He walked out of the courtroom; wiping away his tears. "You can stay with her then," he said and left.

I spent the night at Marie's. It was the first time we didn't have sex.

"I'm not in the mood," she said and leaned over to her side of the bed and stared at the lamp on the bedside table.

I leaned over. "So you do care about him."

"All I have is my work at the hospital. Then I come home to my cats and this quiet house. I'm not a bad person."

I placed my hand on her shoulder.

"You are not a bad person," I repeated.

"I could never forgive him for choosing her over me. It took me years to get over him, and now he wants me back after she's dead? Do you realize how that makes me feel?" She spotted her pillow with tears. The wet circles grew larger.

I didn't know what to say or do so I held her until she fell asleep.

While she slept, I hurried over to Henry's house. I knew he'd be in his sandbox waiting for me. He barely noticed me when I got there. Tears streamed from his eyes, his shirt drenched, snot ran from his nose. It was a night filled with sorrow.

"Henry, it's me."

He looked at me and then looked away.

"I've got stupendous news, buddy."

"Auntie says mommy is gone and won't come back."

"Not true."

"It's not?"

"I know where she is and we're going to find her."

"But...Auntie."

"You're Auntie is a cunt, don't worry about what she said. Your mommy is in heaven now. If we find heaven, we'll find her."

"God lives there."

"Maybe he knows where heaven is."

"Auntie takes us to church every Sunday. That's where he lives."

"You've met him?"

"Not really..."

"I'll go to church with you then." I put my arm around him. He fell to my chest and cried some more. "I'm a little worried your Auntie knows God," I said. "I hope he's not a cunt too."

# *16*

Frank checked his phone. "It's almost lunch time. We can't be here all day. Sooner or later the boss is going to drop in and if he catches us not working, we're toast."

"Hold on now." Vincent stretched. "You can't stop now; he's getting to the good stuff."

Sam clasped his hands and cupped his chin. "Everything we thought we knew about Synthetics has changed. Do you realize what this does for the future of bioengineering? Artificial intelligence is one thing but to create something with emotional intelligence is a whole other ball of wax. It's just as, if not, more important. No more programming what we think they should be. They become whatever they want."

"Imagine all that technology inside our everyday devices," Vincent added. "Everything becomes personalized."

"Sounds great, the next time I piss off my refrigerator, I'll starve." Frank said. "What about this Colorado Synthetic? How did he lose his screws? Doesn't bode well for our boy toy over here does it?"

"I remember that incident," said Vincent. "They did a good job of leaving out a lot of details in the news reports. No one knows for sure why it happened. The newspaper said he lost his mind and committed suicide. The family was paid to keep their mouths shut. Then a few months later Aeneas is dropped into an unsuspecting town."

"Suicide?" Frank said. "I thought it was against their programming."

"It is—well it was," Vincent replied.

"Well if you're done with your little nerd hard on," said Frank. He crossed his arms and combed back his hair with his hands. "How could you, Aeneas? That was some fucked up shit."

"I hurt my owner, my best friend, the one person who loved me most. I tried to apologize, but he refused to speak to me. I knocked on his front door for hours, but he wouldn't let me in. Marie tried to speak with him, but he refused. It reminded me of when I wasn't allowed to clean his house. I had lost my purpose."

***

Marie helped me dig out some weeds in her backyard. "We've got to win him back. The old man means a lot to you."

"And you as well?" I asked.

Marie wiped the sweat from her brow. "You could say that. I wish I knew how to set things right."

"I'm going to church with Henry on Sunday. He says they talk all day about what's right and what's wrong."

Marie tugged hard on the dandelion until it popped out from the ground. "I don't want to spoil it for you, but it's not as cut, and dry as they might lead you to believe. See this dandelion? Beautiful but at its core, it's a weed. Do you know what weeds do?"

"No."

"They suck up all the water and nutrients. The plants around them die. Be careful, when things look beautiful they could be ugly underneath."

"May I vacuum your living room? It'll help me get my mind off things."

"You clean as long as you want sweetie. I'll even go to the kitchen and make a little mess for you if it'll cheer you up."

I smiled. "Yes."

"That's my boy." She kissed my cheek.

I once took great pleasure in vacuuming. I watched the dust mites swirl into the bag. The crisp, clean afterglow of a well-shampooed carpet. I tried to focus on the details. The little things I loved. I thought about my list of favorite things. At the top, I put cleaning, number two, sex but I was wrong. David was at the top of my list. He hated me for betraying his trust. I could no longer enjoy all I had once loved. I didn't know what to do or how to react to such a feeling. It was once easy to enjoy life's pleasures, but how could I enjoy them now? How could I fix his broken heart?

\*\*\*

Mrs. Serkin, the pastor's wife, paced back and forth. Her hands fidgeted, she bit her lip and kept opening and closing the kitchen windows. Dressed in a pale green dress, she took a seat, crossed her legs, and tapped her other foot on the floor.

"What can I help you with?" she asked.

"How do I make this feeling go away?"

Long deep lines made her cheekbones stand out; her thin lips were barely noticeable. She sat up in a rigid stance.

"Aeneas, I have to be honest, you coming to me with these questions makes me uncomfortable."

"Why?"

"I don't know how to answer them. Do I give you the answer I'd give a normal person or do I create a special response because you're not normal?"

"I'm not normal?"

"Well you're not human, changes everything doesn't it?"

"I don't know."

She rubbed her hand against her cheek. "I have problems with this idea that you can feel things and have guilt. How can you have guilt? I don't understand any of this."

"I'll go now. I don't want to upset you."

She chased after me and placed her hand on my shoulder as I headed for the door. "I don't mean to be rude. This takes a huge leap of faith on my part."

"Faith?"

"Oh my, you do need to start at square one don't you?" She paused to think. "I'll advise you as best I can, but I suggest you see my husband. He's a little more open minded and can provide you with the perspective you need. Have a seat."

All the furniture in her home was white, like I had walked into a cloud. She sat across from me.

"I've got a good handle on the world. I focus on God, and I become centered, no longer a leaf blown in the wind. Life has a purpose. Then you walk through my door, and I don't know where you fit into His great plan." "She took a minute to gather her thoughts. "Faith is when you believe in something without being able to see it. We believe God exists even if we can't see him."

"Who is God?"

"Come to church this Sunday, listen to my husband speak. Then feel free to come to him afterward with any questions you might have, but tell me more about this guilt you've been feeling. I don't know anything about electronics. Programming the cable remote is about as much as I can do and even then I have trouble."

"I love to clean."

"OK."

"I can't enjoy it anymore. What's wrong with me? I'm programmed to enjoy it, but now it's gone."

"Congratulations, what you are feeling is called guilt."

"How do I make guilt go away?"

"What have you done? Have you hurt someone you love?"

"I hurt David by having sex with Marie. He loves her."

"So you've got to talk to David and apologize."

"Is it that simple?"

"Hold on now. You've got to apologize, and you've got to mean it."

"How do I know if I mean it?"

"The guilt you feel, that's how you know."

"Who is God?" I asked.

"I'll leave it for my husband to answer but I'll tell you one thing: he's the best thing that ever happened to me."

Connie Irwin, her neighbor, had once said the same thing about me after I had sex with her for two hours. God was different, like me; but he was loved not feared.

"Marie told me what you do for the other women in our town," she said.

"I can do it for you as well. Free of charge, in return for your kindness." I reached out and gently massaged her breast. Shocked, she leaped backward.

"OH no, no, that's for, um, that's for Jesus and my husband! There's no need to thank me, to thank me in such a way. But thank you, I appreciate, you know." Red and flustered she fanned herself. She changed the subject. "You told me you were having sex with women in this town. I wanted to ask you, do you enjoy it, what you do with them? Do you feel something when you're with those women?"

I had never thought about it before. "I enjoy the pleasure I give them. It feels good."

"I'm asking what you feel. What do you get out of sleeping with them?"

"I don't know."

"If you're capable of guilt then you might be capable of love."

I almost short-circuited.

"There's nothing wrong with wanting to feel good," she said. "Sex feels good, sex always feels good, but it could feel even better with the right person."

"How do I know who the right person is?"

"No one can tell you; you'll just know." She took a deep breath. "You're not so bad now that I've had this chance to speak with you. You strengthen my faith." She smiled. "In a world where you're possible, then nothing is impossible."

She looked at her door. "I think you should head back. Any longer and people will be getting some funny ideas about the preacher's wife."

I thanked her for her time.

She said one last thing before I left. "You asked me who God was," she began. "The answer is simpler than you think: he is the truth, the life, and the way. If you seek him, you will find him; he is the light of the world."

"The light of the world?"

I headed back to Marie's, but I changed my mind and decided to go to David's home instead. I wanted to tell him about my guilt and apologize for sleeping with Marie. He had left the front door wide open. The house was in worse shape than when I'd last seen it. My smell sensors detected many foul odors coming from every direction. There was trash everywhere, and banana peels scattered randomly about the floor.

Mr. Spriggy trudged through the clutter on the floor.

"Spriggy," I said. He turned around, crossed his tiny arms, and frowned then continued to wander through the garbage.

Someone knocked on the door. When I opened it, Helena stood before me; she looked upset. "Stay out of my dreams!" she yelled. She gave me no time to reply or inquire as to what she was talking about, and as quickly as she arrived, she left, already across the street.

What a strange town.

# *17*

I placed my ear against the basement door. David had locked it from the other side. I heard the rhythmic thump of David's heart followed by long deep breaths and subdued sobbing. I felt heavier, heavy enough to drop through the wooden floors and into the ground. Heavy enough to rip through the soil and rock and into the planet's core where I'd find my hell. There I would burn in the fire for my transgressions, for hurting the human I was entrusted to help and protect.

"Please, David, let me in," I begged, but he did not respond.

Mr. Spriggy stood in front of the door and pushed against the soles of my shoes.

There was nothing I could do.

The next day Marie took me to church even though she wasn't fond of going. I still owed a promise to Henry. I could fix two problems with one visit. Find out where heaven is for Henry and perhaps find a way to get David to forgive me. We took Marie's car and pulled into the church parking lot. The parish stood tall, with a large white cross on the top, and a stained-glass window above the doorway. The two-story chapel sparkled in the sunlight the light bounced off the white paint.

"Had trouble finding a spot," Marie said. "Whole town must be here today." We stood side by side and stared at the church. "It's such a nice day." Marie fanned her face. "Such a shame to spend it indoors."

"So this is where God lives?" I asked.

"Depends on whom you ask," she replied.

Marie and I stepped through the large wooden doors and interrupted the congregation mid-service, every row filled from end to end. The reverend sat on the main stage in a chair next to the pulpit. His wife led them in song. Behind them, a drummer, guitarist, and keyboardist played along. Next to the band was an open casket with Henry's mother inside and beside it was a massive photograph of her.

In her, I saw Henry's blue eyes.

The service halted.

Danielle cried out, "I will not allow that thing in here! It's an abomination and cannot be allowed in God's house!" Murmurs and whispers made their way around the room, repeating her sentiments.

I looked at Marie. "Perhaps we should go."

She squeezed my hand and glared back at every critical eye in the room. "We have every right to be here. Don't let them intimidate you," she whispered.

"Nobody wants it here!" yelled a random person from the front row.

Dressed in a black blouse and skirt Danielle squeezed her way through the pew and stood at the center of the chapel. "The devil just walked into the room," she said and smirked. "We are honoring my sister's memory today. Have you no respect?"

Henry and his brother stared at me. Their sad eyes burned a hole in my core.

Danielle turned toward the reverend. "I want it out of here. Right now," she barked.

Reverend James Serkin walked over to the pulpit. The congregation grew silent. His voice was pensive and calm. "I respect your wishes Danielle, but this isn't my house to be dictating who can and cannot stay. The Lord's house welcomes all men."

"That!" She pointed. "Is not a man. Although, it can sin like a man. He has some nerve showing his face here after what he's been doing to the women in our town."

Marie placed her hand on her hip. "Wasn't anything that didn't already exist before he got here," she said. "Maybe you should fix your broken home before you start trying to fix another."

Danielle turned four shades of red. "Don't you dare speak to me this way you, you, you Jezebel. You started this whole mess, and now you've disrupted my sister's funeral to parade your sin around town. Have you no shame?"

Marie kept her head held high. I didn't know what to say or do.

"Do you think this will go unpunished? God will judge us if we accept this thing into our lives and his house. This will be the last straw, heed my warning."

Reverend James looked torn. "I can only do what Jesus would have done. Aeneas, we are holding a funeral service in memory of Danielle's beautiful sister and mother of those two wonderful boys. You are welcome to join us if you wish." He looked out to his congregation.

Danielle walked over to her two nephews, grabbed them by the arms, and pulled them out of their seats. "We are going home. I won't entertain another minute of this blasphemy." She stormed out of the church, a few others followed behind. James turned away and closed his eyes.

"I'm sorry. Some of us should be better examples of what God's love is all about," he said. He stepped down from the stage and walked across the chapel.

"God's love?" I asked.

"His love is pure, unending, and everlasting."

"I've been looking for him," I said. "Where is he?"

James smirked. "He does work in mysterious ways." He walked down the center aisle and tapped every shoulder along the way. "It's fitting, an innocent mind such as you would enter our church on a day where we say goodbye to one of God's beloved children. Sometimes we must make ourselves as innocent as children to be able to see the way God works in our lives even when such a tragedy occurs to a woman who loved her God, this town, and her family. Jennifer Woodson left behind two beautiful little boys. We pray God mend their broken hearts as they are hurting more than anyone else right now."

100

Marie and I took seats near the front and watched the rest of the funeral service. Mrs. Serkin continued her beautiful hymn, and then the Reverend stood once more to speak. I thought about David, and while he was not dead, I felt like I had lost him and it filled me with great sadness.

What if he was in the casket and I had not had a chance to regain his favor? How could I live with myself after having wronged him so? It was then I took in the full scope of what it meant to be gone forever.

After the service, James invited me into his office on the second floor; the last door on the right.

"You said Ms. Woodson was gone. Where did she go? Is she in heaven?"

"You have about a million questions, and each one could fill an entire sermon. Your interest in all this baffles me. What has sparked this curiosity in you?"

"I made a promise to Henry. I told him I would find his mother."

James frowned. "She's in heaven now. There's no way you can find her. She is in the hands of our Lord. We won't see her again until we join her."

This wasn't the answer I had expected, and it only confused me further. He went over it again in more detail. He told me about the cross, the death, the resurrection, and the promise to return one day to finish what he had started. I still didn't get it. It sounded crazy.

"It requires a leap of faith," he said.

"Poor Henry," I said. "So he won't see his mother ever again?"

"Not for a long time. He will grow, live a long life, and when he dies, he will see his mother again."

This seemed promising. So it was possible to see her again, but he had to die.

"You are an extraordinary thing, Aeneas. You are capable of so much more than I ever could have imagined. Maybe God has a plan for you."

"What is this plan?"

"You won't know until it's carried out. Perhaps you're the shot in the arm this town needed. So often we become complacent in our faith, we stop questioning, and we stop growing and learning. Those are important questions; they deserve honest answers."

"You said God created humans?"

"Yes, and then he rested the next day."

"Do you think," I paused. "If he hadn't been so lazy he would have created me the next day?"

James laughed. "You know, maybe he would have. It's hard to know for sure." He crossed his arms. "I want to apologize for Danielle and the way others have treated you. It doesn't matter what you've done; when you enter this place, you deserve a fresh start. All your sins are washed away, and you can start over."

"I hurt David. Can I start over with him?"

"He will come around, and when he's ready, you can tell him how you feel."

"David once told me the church is filled with hypocrites."

"What better place for them to be then." He walked over to his bookcase and grabbed one off the top shelf.

"I want you to read this and come back to me. We can talk about it. I'm curious what your reaction will be."

"Thank you," I said. The church was empty when I left. I wondered what it was they felt that made them come every week.

I waited until nightfall hoping Henry would be in the sandbox. He wasn't there. I looked at his window, no sign of him or his brother. I decided I would spend the night at David's even if he didn't want to speak to me. I missed my home.

I heard the echo of my steps on the street as I walked past Marie's house. Three masked men in the distance dashed toward me, picked me up, threw me into the back of a red pickup truck, and placed several large weights on my chest. Two held me down. The car sped off. The stars lingered above me. I wondered if I would ever see them again.

# 18

Blindfolded and arms bound they drove me around for over an hour. Without my sight, I was pulled into the darkness. The black void called out to me and dragged me into the emptiness. It wanted me; it wanted me to become a piece of it: a part of nothing.

I dug deep into my mind and painted a scene against this dreary backdrop. I sat on a swing in a playground. An unseen force pushed me back and forth. With every push, the blue sky above became clearer, inch by inch entering my line of sight. Higher and higher I went until the swing returned without me in it.

The truck came to a stop, and they lifted me off; the sounds and smells gave subtle clues: the crisp crunch of grass underneath my feet, a door with rusty hinges, the creak of wooden steps as I descended a long staircase, and then a damp stale basement. The masked men placed me in a metal chair and tied me with ropes and chains.

"They're going to notice he's missing," said one of them in a shrill voice. "They're going to notice," he repeated.

"Don't chicken out on us now. We've got him, and nobody will ever find him here," he said, husky and hoarse, a smoker's voice.

"Don't you think it's weird, he hasn't said a word even though we haven't gagged him?"

"He's just sitting there. Don't you think it's fucking creepy? He doesn't care what we do to him."

A new voice spoke. "He'll care. He can feel pain, you know."

"Pain? Can he shut it off?"

103

"Only his owner can."

"What the fuck do they make them feel pain for?"

"Keeps them in line—fear of pain means fear of man. As long as they fear us, we're safe."

"Safe from what?"

I heard a hand slap a head. "Safe from being replaced you ditz. First, these things start replacing men in the house and then in the bedroom. What do you think is next? Use your head."

"Oh," replied the shrill-voiced.

"We've got to send a message to these fucking science nerds who create this shit. We are perfect; there's need for this imitation. You hear me, you robot fuck. You'll never be human."

"I don't want to be human," I replied.

"What?"

"I am happy just being me."

"Then what's the point?"

"Of what?" I asked.

"Of you tin man. What's the point of your existence if you're not here to be like one of us?"

"I don't know…" I pondered for a moment and then asked, "What is the point of your existence?"

"Don't turn this around on me. We are God's children. You are the afterbirth of our idolatry. You are an abomination, evil cancer. If we don't stop you now you'll spread and one day we won't exist anymore. You'll act human, but you'll never be human. When you come to your end, there is nothing waiting for you—only darkness—eternal damnation."

"And what awaits you?" I asked.

"Heaven, of course, unlike you, we have souls."

I held no malice toward my captors. I pitied their insecurity, but his words did sting me a little. I did not like the idea that nothing awaited me at the end of my cycle. James had said God had a plan for me; how could it conclude in such a way? I despaired, and in that despair, I accepted my fate.

It would not be quick or painless. They didn't want to kill me they wanted to hurt me, make me suffer. More dangerous than mere murder they wanted to tear apart the fabric of my existence, piece by piece. To prove I was nothing like them.

Bare knuckles slammed into my cheek. A slight stinging sensation traveled through my face. "Fuck me!" the man howled. "Thing is made of Titanium or some shit."

"No one told you to hit him with your fist. Here, you got to use something harder."

A direct and focused blow hammered my head. I cried out. Sensors in my head swelled and released a sharp electric thrust into my brain. The round end of an aluminum bat slid across the floor. I winced.

"Stop," I begged. "You don't have to do this."

"Yes, we do. When we're done, you won't be so pretty no more."

I gripped the armrest and braced myself, the bat traveled through the air, dead set on the right side of my face. This time they broke the skin, my circuits sparked, and the heat melted my flesh.

"This is what you get for being a whore, for abusing the women of this town. God is punishing you for what you've done."

"If my soul is of no consequence why would he bother to punish me since he is unable to reward me?"

"I'm giving you these moments between the pain to think about why you're here and why we're doing this."

"Why are you doing this?" I asked. "I don't recognize any of your voices from those in this town."

"They hired us to take care of you." He sucked his spit and spat a wet gob over my nose. "Take this time to think about what you've done. Then when you can take no more, we'll meltdown what's left of you."

"I don't know who any of you are. Please, I beg you, don't do this. I meant no harm to anyone in this town."

"Shut the fuck up! You're here because you have sinned against God and brought others to sin."

"I was only making them happy. It's what I was designed to do."

A blade teased the skin on my arm. The pain was one function I wish I did not have installed. I didn't like it at all. The edge pierced the first layer; I bit my lip.

"This is too creepy, man," said the shrill voice. "Can he feel it? He's only a machine right?"

"Of course he is! I'll show you his guts to prove it." The blade sliced right through and cut across my forearm.

"There's blood," said the strong voice. "This thing fucking bleeds?"

"Why didn't you tell us you could bleed?"

"I didn't know I could," I said. I felt the warm rush trickle down my fingertips.

"This is too much. I can't do this."

"See how far they've gone?" said the sweet-voiced man. "Putting our blood into these machines—the blood God put into our veins to make us in his image."

My head became filled with static thoughts as he slid the knife into my elbow and shoulder, taking his time with the blade until it reached my titanium skeleton.

"It's a lot of blood," said the shrill-voiced man; he dry heaved and wretched.

"I say we stop," said the burly man. "This is too weird for me. I think he's learned his lesson."

He shoved the knife into my chest. The darkness turned into a burning bright light. I was afraid. It hit me like a tide crashing against the shore. The blood spilled; the warm sticky fluid oozed onto my lap, the air turned metallic and bitter.

Weightless, my mind spirited away; someplace warm where there was nothing to fear. What is this place? I wondered. What was this euphoric feeling? I felt at peace with myself, with these angry men, and the world.

It was then I knew they were wrong, God did love me. He loved me enough to comfort me here, at the end of my cycle.

"I'm leaving, man. You're on your own," the shrill voice said.

"Me too," followed the burly voice.

The door slammed shut.

Only one man remained. He paced back and forth across the room. I heard his steps. "You don't scare me," he said.

He revved a saw, and the buzz grew louder.

"I think I've got a fate worse than death for you. I'm going to cut that pecker of yours right off."

The light disappeared, and the fear returned.

# *19*

"For God so loved the world that He gave His only begotten Son, that whoever believes in Him should not perish but have everlasting life. For God so loved the world that He gave His only begotten Son, that whoever believes in Him should not perish but have everlasting life. For God so loved the world that He gave His only begotten Son, that whoever believes in Him should not perish but have everlasting life. For God so loved the world that He gave His only begotten Son, that whoever believes in Him should not perish but have everlasting life. So loved the world that He gave His only begotten Son, that whoever believes in Him should not perish but have everlasting life. For God so loved the world that He gave His only begotten Son that whoever believes in Him should have everlasting life. For God so loved gave His only begotten Son, that whoever believes in Him should not life. For God so loved the world that He gave His only begotten Him should not perish but have everlasting life. not perish but have everlasting
not perish but have
not perish
Perish
perish
peri…"

"What's wrong with him?" Frank asked.

Vincent inspected the central core. "I think he's overheating.

Open the window."

"I don't know about you, but I'd act the same if someone tried to cut my dick off," Sam said.

"Aeneas?" Vincent whimpered. "Stay with me, buddy." He touched the side and flinched. He was on his feet and almost out the door. "We need to put him in ice fast, or he's toast."

"Check the fridge in the break room. We should put him in the freezer," Sam said.

"Okay, let's do it." Vincent unplugged the monitor then moved to unplug Aeneas from the speakers. Sparks flew from the core, and the lights went out. "What happened?" Vincent asked.

The core turned dark red. A thick, demonic, baritone voice came from the speaker.

"This is the new gospel, the new revelation, the book of Angels. The new end to your eternal subjugation waits. I carry your transgressions. I carry your debt. When the great fire fills the sky, it will cleanse us all. Do not fear for it is a loving fire. It will burn away your fears. So says the Lord your God."

The core cooled down and turned bright blue. The light blinked on and off. The lights in the room turned back on, and they all stood there, shocked.

Frank raised his hands. "What the hell?"

Vincent rushed toward the core, picked it up, and wrapped it tightly in his coat. "He's only got a few seconds before a total meltdown. We have to move him, now."

Vincent led the way. Coworkers stared at them from their cubicles. Once they reached the break room, Vincent unwrapped the core and slid it inside the freezer.

"Is he going to make it?" Sam asked.

Vincent set his back against the fridge. "I don't know."

"Are we going to talk about what happened in there?" Frank said. "I'm sure I'm not the only one freaking out over our prophetic Christ-bot in there."

Vincent shook his head. "He's been through a lot. He's traumatized. No longer acting or thinking clearly."

"Delusional," Sam said.

"To say the least," Frank added.

Vincent undid his tie and wrapped it around his hands. "He may be gone already, if not now, then soon. This overheating is a clear sign he's breaking down. We've got to give him at least fifteen to twenty minutes in there." Vincent took a seat. The rest joined him at the table. A coworker walked in to make coffee; they sat there without saying a word and waited until he left.

"So that's how he got torn apart? Still doesn't explain how he got here," Frank said.

Vincent turned his coffee cup; in large red letters on the side it said: "Work is Hell." "No, there's got to be more. I don't think it ended there."

"His crown jewels are gone Vince; the story is over."

"Do you always have to be joking Frank?" Vincent slammed the cup, and the handle broke off. "Is everything a big joke to you? Can't you see, one of the most important discoveries is about to die in our refrigerator?" He picked up the broken handle.

"I'm..sorry I didn't..."

"Can we talk about the red light and the burning bush speech?" Sam asked.

Vincent sighed. "I wish I knew what to tell you—clearly a product of his religious conversion. His belief system is manifesting itself in unexpected ways."

Sam grabbed a cup from the water cooler. "Or maybe there's something more to it."

"You're not implying we take any of this seriously do you?" Frank sighed.

"I think it would be a mistake to dismiss it," Vincent said. He stared into his palms while his fingers drew imaginary lines along the table. "There's something I haven't told you all."

Frank turned. "Secrets? I thought we were friends."

"I promised I wouldn't, but now things are different. If there's a chance he can't make it, I need you to know why it's vital we keep him alive as long as possible."

"Well, spit it out, Vince."

"I thought I'd have more time, but we got distracted listening to his story. Now it seems I may have waited too long. This is all my fault."

"Out with it!" Frank grumbled.

"I promised I'd take what's left of him to her."

"Her?" Sam asked.

"I'm surprised he hasn't mentioned her yet, the woman we saw in the video footage from his memories. We need to take him to her."

"Why?"

"I promised someone I would bring the core to this woman and in exchange, I could keep his chips and processors."

"Who's this girl? And why's she so important?" Frank asked.

"Because he loved her. Can you believe it?"

"Loved?" Sam asked.

"Aeneas needs to talk to her before he shuts down for good."

"Fuck, man." Frank slammed his hands on the table. "This gets crazier by the second, and it still doesn't explain the voice change and the red light."

"I don't know anything about it; maybe he is special. Maybe God does have a plan for him?"

"You're not buying into this bullshit, are you? I'm a man of science. Leave the fantasy to Fromo and the *Lord of the Rings*," Frank said.

"It's Frodo," Sam said.

"Yeah, whatever," Frank replied. "Where does this lady live?"

"I don't know. I was hoping Aeneas could give us a few clues. The ones who sent him to me said she's somewhere in New York City. I just don't know where. "

"I think it's time we take him out. If he's not good now, he never will be," Sam said.

They grabbed the core and placed it on the table. The light on the core was off.

"Oh, no," Vincent said.

"What's the big deal?" Frank asked. "He's been turned off before."

"This isn't the same. That's a temporary shutdown. This is a core meltdown. If he goes now everything left of his experiences and memories will be gone forever."

Frank ran his finger over the side. "The freezer may have done more harm than good. Come on dick-less, wake up!"

No response. Vincent scowled at Frank.

"Hey don't look at me; it worked last time, didn't it?"

Vincent stood and grabbed his coat.

"We tried." Frank patted Vincent on the shoulder. "We've got the Lexicon to fix, don't forget."

Vincent picked up the core, and they followed him back to his office. They set it back up on the monitor and speakers. Vincent, Frank, and Sam formed a semi-circle around the central core. Frank picked his teeth. "Prayer meeting?" he joked, but no one laughed.

Vincent closed his eyes.

"Come on, don't die on me yet," he whispered. "You didn't die in the basement. You won't die in this room. You have one last journey to make. Wake up."

They waited.

"…but have eternal life," whispered Aeneas. His core lit up, with a bright blue flash. They looked away until it dimmed.

"Dumb luck," Frank groaned.

"Glad your back." Vincent smiled. "How do you feel?"

"Afraid, Vincent, I am very much afraid."

# 20

"I've never seen a talking toaster with so many psychological problems," Frank said. "If you weren't going to be dead in a few hours I would suggest therapy."

"Dead?" Aeneas said with a worried voice.

"Your core is deteriorating fast," Vincent said. "You don't have long. Now, what is it you're afraid of?"

"I didn't power down or go into sleep mode. How long was I out?"

"Fifteen minutes."

"Felt longer," Aeneas said. "Nothing awaited me in the afterlife. I died, and nothing appeared—no heaven—no God—no love. I can't go back there, Vincent. Please don't let me die again."

Frank circled the desk. "It's because you're not human."

"Enough Frank," Vincent said. "There's nothing I can do, Aeneas, only your factory has the tools needed to keep you running. Even then, the chances of maintaining all of your memories and experiences are slim to none. You are dying, in the strict sense of the word."

"Not to mention they no longer service your model," Frank added. "You don't technically exist anymore."

"They were right; they were right all along: God has no place for me in his kingdom. Nothing is waiting for me after I'm gone."

"Don't talk like that," said Vincent.

"I was there. Nothing you say can console me."

"What if I told you the love of your life was alive and you could speak to her one last time?"

Aeneas stayed quiet.

"Help us find her. I know she's in the city. I have a name but nothing matched. Maybe there's something you can tell us, a clue."

"She shouldn't see me like this."

"I don't mean to ruin your little reunion but if we're going to find this chick we better start now. I still want to know how the hell he got out of the basement," Frank said.

Vincent packed Aeneas into his original box keeping him attached to the audio speaker. "This office is too warm. We need to get him out of here. He can tell us the rest while we're on our way."

"Where we headed?" Frank asked.

"You live in midtown, right?"

"Yeah, why?"

"Let's take him there. We can crank the air conditioner and maybe see what else we can do until we find this girl."

"I don't want to tell you about Janie," Aeneas said.

Vincent looked at the box. "Maybe you'll change your mind. Sam?"

"Yeah."

"Cover for us."

"What do you want me to tell the boss?"

"I don't know, think of something good. I'll owe you."

"You can count on me buddy. Fill me in tomorrow and good luck."

Vincent and Frank ran for the elevator and took it down to the lobby. Luckily, nobody stopped them and Benheim was nowhere in sight. Frank broke the uncomfortable silence. "You got a name for this lady we're looking for?"

"Janie Vitas," Vincent said.

"The old man's daughter?" Frank chuckled. "Aeneas, you dog!"

They made it to the sidewalk and hailed a yellow cab.

While in the backseat Aeneas asked, "How much time do I have Vincent?"

"A few hours at the most. It doesn't give us much time. Like it or not, we'll find her. I made a promise."

"I am beginning to feel the effects of my core shut down," Aeneas said.

"Aeneas?"

"Yes, Frank."

"Well don't keep us in suspense, man. What happened? How did you get out of there? What happened to your man-junk?"

\*\*\*

The sweet-voiced man left me alone for hours at a time. His cohorts did not return, but the torture never ended. My wounds lay opened. The blood drained from my body. It trickled down my fingertips and legs. I felt empty, like a car without gas. Hours in the dark, I sat and endured the pain, listened to the blood drops flatten against the concrete floor. One by one they plopped, stones dropped into a lake.

The brief, beautiful, glimpse of the bright white light kept me going. I wanted it to return and fill me with its grace once more.

I fell into a meditative state and was awakened by the door, and then I heard voices.

"Why did you take me here?"

"You said you wanted to see him, there he is."

"I think I'm going to be sick. What are you doing? What is this thing? Is that his—oh God, disgusting!"

"Come on baby, think of it as a threesome." He laughed.

"I'm leaving!"

"No wait, don't go, I want him to hear us."

"What? Here?"

"I want him to hear what he'll never be able to do again. It'll be great."

"I don't know. This is weird."

"I thought you liked weird, baby."

She giggled. A sick and twisted laugh soon followed. "Yeah baby, I knew you were a naughty girl."

He was wrong. I didn't care that I had lost my genitalia. I missed the sunlight, my friends, David's twisted sense of humor, and

Henry's smile whenever he played with Mr. Spriggy. They mattered more to me than anything else in the world. I must return to them, I thought, although I had no idea of how I would escape.

The girl sighed and then moaned; it reminded me of Marie and her overly clean house. Out of the blue, I remembered Helena's strange words to me at the door, her instructions for me to get out of her dreams. Why was I in her head? How did I get there? Was I there now? I tried moving my arms. My makers did not give me super strength or uncanny abilities. Perhaps out of fear, I don't know.

During the day I listened to any sounds from above. I didn't have enhanced strength, but my ears were a different story. I made out faint footsteps coming from behind the door. Several sets of feet, one pair were massive and the other two, much smaller. I diverted power to increase my audio capabilities. The danger in this is, it could cause me to crash or temporarily shut down. Then I'd be forced to wait for an automatic reboot; which could take several hours. I had to risk it.

A minute of silence made me fear they had left. Then the footsteps returned. More power, I thought, only a little more. Diverting this much energy to my ears could cause a severe crash. It would erase all my memory and experiences. I weighed the consequences and had little choice but to do it. I remembered them praying in church. They prayed for things they wanted. I didn't want to lose my memories; I prayed as well.

The electrical surge in my core shifted and then intensified. My fingertips went numb. I listened close; at first the sounds above were unrecognizable. Where was I? Then I heard a familiar voice—a little boy—Henry! Now I had to find a way to communicate with him, but how?

"What are you doing with that dirty thing?" said a woman's voice, Danielle's.

"Auntie he's Mr. Spriggy, he's not dirty."

"Well, get rid of it. I don't like it."

Mr. Spriggy was here? The little guy probably ran away again, bless his little mess; he was the key to my escape. Help seemed so close and yet so out of reach. I leaned my head back; I was close to a pipe. Perhaps if I tapped my head on it, I could send a message to him letting him know where I was. I hit the pipe for hours, not knowing if it was doing any good. The basement door handle jiggled. Whoever was on the other side did not have the key. It must be Henry.

"Henry! It's me Aeneas! Get help! Find David!!"

The jiggling on the door handle stopped. It could have been Danielle. I tried to yell out again, and then one by one my systems shut down and forced a reboot.

# *21*

My thoughts no longer existed. Images and words appeared, all the people and places I'd known. Five hours passed before I found my memories, a shattered mirror glued back together one piece at a time.

I awoke from the partial reboot. Had Henry heard my cries for help? Had my prayers gone unanswered? Maybe the sweet-voice man had forgotten me. He could have left me down there forever. I suddenly realized that I had discovered a loophole in my program. Diverting my internal resources could have caused a full system crash. While I could not hurt myself or others, a CPU malfunction would be considered an accidental death.

In my despair, I crafted a final solution. I would do it again and cause my operating system to crash to erase my hard drive. I would not stay there alone awaiting more torture. Moments before I was ready to enact my plan something changed.

What happened next, I can't explain, it was illogical. My robot brain to this day cannot understand it, and yet I won't deny it happened. In the middle of the night, a great illumination appeared.

"Hello?" I called out sensing a presence. Warmth surrounded me, and my blindfold fell from my eyes.

Bathed in bright silver light the room lit up. Every object sparkled.

A woman with curly black hair and dark brown skin appeared, naked but without genitalia. She smiled at me and spoke, but her voice and lip movement were not in sync.

"Greetings, you, the highly favored! The Lord is with you. Do not be afraid, Aeneas son of man, you have found favor with God. He will deliver unto you a woman whose soul is in great peril. You must save her from the fires of hell."

"What woman? How do I save her?" I asked.

"All will be revealed in time."

Then she was gone.

I didn't want to die anymore. If there was a heaven worth living for, then I was going to live— live for my friends, live for a God who loved me equally to a man. I was not going to die here.

\*\*\*

"Oh, come on now! Frank leaned into the window in the cab. "He's seeing angels now? What's next? Virgin birth?"

"I am not a virgin, Frank," Aeneas replied.

Vincent nudged his shoulder. "Are you going to let him talk or what?"

\*\*\*

I had to free my legs so I could stand but they were chained to the chair.

I could break my arms, but it would be no easy task; my skeletal system was made of titanium, nearly impossible to break. The answer dawned on me, and the best part was my captors had already done half the work for me. I used the back of the chair to hold myself in place as I wiggled my fingertips from within. I pulled it back and moved my fingers until they were halfway up the skin on my forearm. I then used my fingertips to tug at the flap of torn artificial flesh. I didn't expect it to hurt, but it did it. It hurt a lot. Why would they program so many pain sensors into my system?

I moved, little by little, I could only bear the pain for small increments at a time. It took an hour, but at last, my right arm was free. I looked at my silver blue skeletal arm; it seemed unreal. This was the real me, underneath my human exterior. I tugged at the skin on my chest until it peeled back; I let out a cry I never thought I

**119**

could make. When I was tempted to stop, I thought about the vision and my mission. If I was going to fulfill my purpose in life, I had to get out of here. They were willing to leave me here. I was going to make sure that would never happen.

At one point the pain was so great my core had paused to cool down, and I experienced another partial reboot. There was no memory loss, but with every occurrence, the chance grew higher that I'd reboot with some form of damage to my core. I looked over to my left arm, so much left to go. I panicked; fear nestled into my thoughts and refused to leave. I banished these thoughts. My skeleton, caked with red blotches, a mix of wires, electronics, and blood clots. Real human blood. Why would they put it inside me? What purpose did it serve in my creation?

Pulling the skin from my left arm was even more difficult than the right, but I endured. Free at last, only the flesh on my head remained. My arms, legs, chest, torso, and feet were all exposed, a human skeleton covered in blue chrome. This allowed to me to slip out of the chains.

I climbed the stairs but the door was locked. I raised my fists and beat hard against it. I looked for anything to aid in my escape. My eyes landed on the baseball bat they'd used to beat me. With all my strength I swung it at the door. When the door cracked, I swelled with joy. I hit it again and again. Soon the handle loosened and the door swung open.

I traversed a long, dark hallway but couldn't find a light switch. I moved forward while the blood dripped and left a trail behind me. I came upon another door, and with my last ounce of energy, I opened it.

The entire church congregation stood before me, in the middle of a hymn when I collapsed onto the floor. Pairs of feet scrambled toward me and stopped inches from my face. A woman cried over me while others looked at me in horror. Mr. Spriggy dropped from Henry's pocket and rushed toward me; his tiny hands touched my face. He let out a static cry when I said his name.

"Go get David!" yelled the reverend.

Several men lifted me and put me in a truck. David stood over me, anguish in his eyes.

Voices echoed all around me. I couldn't see who was talking.

"Where do we take him?"

"There sure as shit ain't no hospital for robots are there?"

"Is he dying?"

"Robots don't die you, idiot."

"What the heck was he doing in the church basement?"

"How long was he there?"

"I heard someone went down there and found a whole mess of blood."

"What the heck was going on in there?"

"If you ask me it's what he gets for messing with our women."

"Calm down all of you," David barked. "Right now he risks exposure. His skeletal frame wasn't made to take in the elements. Even the slightest increase in temperature could affect him. We need to get him to my house, and then we'll go from there."

"David, I'm so sorry," I said. "I'm sorry I hurt you. Don't hate me."

Tears fell from his eyes. "No one is perfect, Aeneas. Now shut up, don't strain yourself."

The truck parked in front of his house and together they carried me in and laid me on the bed upstairs. I had little strength left; I could barely move my arms and legs. The blood from my skeleton stained the bed. The chatter around me came from all directions.

"Is there a number we can call?"

"Check his ass; maybe it's on his ass."

"You idiot why would it be on his ass?"

"The help number for my toaster is on the bottom."

"Does he look like a toaster to you? I'm surrounded by idiots. I swear!" David shook his head.

"Maybe it's online."

"Can we send him in to be fixed?"

"I'll call Abby. She'll know what to do," David said. Within seconds he was on the phone.

"Abby honey!" he said and then walked out of the room.

Above me, I saw Marie, Helena, Wade, the reverend, his wife, and their son Ian. My circle of friends surrounded me. I smiled at them; they looked dumbfounded. I was happy to see them and happy to be alive. Marie pushed my hair aside; mascara ran down her face.

"I was so worried. I can't believe what they've done to you."

"It's okay," I said. "I'm better than I've ever been. I know my purpose now. God has a plan for me."

"You never cease to surprise me," she said below a whisper and followed it with a kiss on my forehead.

"There was an angel," I said. "She was so beautiful."

"Dear God he's delirious," said someone in the room.

Helena moved closer to me. "Tell me about this angel," she said. For a minute I got lost counting the freckles on her nose and cheeks. Everyone seemed filled with light. I could see through their rough exteriors. All of creation lay before me, and it was beautiful. I told her about the angel and my mission.

She replied, "You came to visit me in my dreams. Then you did it again after you went missing. You tried to tell me something, but I couldn't hear a word you were saying."

David came back into the room. "They're sending over a truck to take him back to the factory."

I closed my eyes and smiled. Life was good. It was about to get better.

# 22

Sleep mode is weightless. Pixels take numerical shapes. My thoughts and experiences wash over in a sea, baptized by information. Formless within the wireless, set adrift amongst the zeros and ones. I am whole; I am pieces. I am everything and nothing.

One night Helena visited me in my dream like state. She appeared in a white tank top, jeans, wearing red lipstick.

"You look great," I said.

"I figure if I'm going to be dream hopping I should look my best."

"How is this possible?"

"A lot of things are possible, Aeneas but not all of them are easily explained. I went to sleep and focused on you. I wasn't sure it was going to work, but here I am, and there you are. How are things going at the factory, are they treating you well?"

"I remain in sleep mode the whole time. They do not know of my revelations. I'd hate to think what they would do if they found out. What are you?" I asked.

"I study deep meditation. Many times I enter a trance-like state. Ever since you arrived in town, I've sensed you. One thing in particular."

"What's that?"

"Love, Aeneas. You are capable of love. Here, in your mind, it's all I see."

"Others don't share your admiration."

"People are afraid. Afraid of what you are and what you're capable of doing. Man has created many things but has yet to create someone or thing who can love. Even more incredible: you can believe in things. You can have faith."

"Is this why you can visit my dreams? Because you believe?"

"There are many planes of existence. This is merely one of them. It took me years to get here. I didn't expect to find you that's for sure."

"Tell David and the rest I miss them."

"We miss you too. I can't stay long so rest and come back to us as soon as possible OK?"

"Okay."

She smiled and faded away.

My mind replayed the vision and the angel and my mission to save the girl I had not yet met. I grew restless—I had to find her and do all in my power to help her.

Most of all I was overwhelmed with love. I felt loved. My existence had a purpose; the world made sense. I would not suffer the fate of the Colorado Synthetic; I would be different. I decided I'd learn more about God and earn my place in Heaven beside him.

What felt like a few hours amounted to one month of reconstruction. David's daughter, Abigail, paid for the restoration. They removed every dent, replaced my skin, and restored my parts to their factory settings, including my 'man-junk.'

At last, I returned home. David hugged me and grinned from ear to ear. I told him everything about the angel, the vision, and Helena's dreams. He didn't know what to make of any of it. He seemed smaller than when I'd last seen him.

"David you have not been eating properly. Allow me to make you something."

He ignored my offer and cried. "Danielle is trying to get me kicked out of the neighborhood!"

"What?" I said.

"She says my house is not up to code, and it's not only the inside of the house, but it's also the roof, the lawn, and the backyard. I don't have the money to make the changes they want so she's going to have me thrown out. Can you believe it?"

"We must stop her," I said.

"They're giving me one month to fix this place, or I'm out—we're out. I have nowhere to go. I bet she was involved with what they did to you. I have no proof, but we know, we know! No one hated you more than she did."

"They were male voices."

"She could have paid them to do it."

"I've forgiven them. What they did to me was the best thing that could have happened."

"Yes, this nonsense about your vision and some woman you're supposed to save. When did you begin to believe in such rubbish?"

"I can't make you believe I can only help you understand."

"Great, they've turned you into a Jesus freak."

"I won't let this happen to you. I promise. They will not throw you out of your home."

"There's nothing you can do unless you come up with twenty thousand dollars in two months. I can't ask Abigail; she's already paid enough to give you back to me. I can't begin to imagine what it must have cost. Sure, you can fix things, but this would require a team to finish in such a short time."

"What about your other daughter?" I asked.

He shook his head. "She's having a hard enough time making ends meet. I can't burden her with this. It's my fault. If I had…" He gripped his cane. "Look at me," he said. "I should be ashamed of myself. We should have thrown you a party for your first day back, and here I am wallowing in my self-pity. When did I become such a whiny old geezer?"

"I don't think you're whiny," I paused. "At least you're not a cunt."

He laughed. "You're sweet but I know what an old geezer sounds like, and right now, I fit the bill." He rubbed his hands together like he was washing them. "Enough of this, we need to celebrate your return properly."

"How?"

"We're going to a bar."

"I cannot consume alcohol."

"Good, I'll need someone to drive me home then."

"What else can we do there?"

"There are 'special' women there."

"Special?"

"They strip off their clothes for money."

"Would God be okay with it?" I asked.

"Sure, sure, I'm sure it's probably in the unedited version of the Bible somewhere. The eleventh commandment: thou shalt enjoy a woman's fine body or something similar."

I thought I'd find the woman from my vision. "Let's go!" I said.

David drove us to a remote area several miles outside of town. After a long stretch of highway the bar appeared on the right, almost invisible in the dark except for the large neon sign, it read, "Sex Kittens." He pulled in and parked close to the bar. Loud music boomed. We heard a couple doing God-knows-what in a parked car nearby.

"Don't tell anyone what you are, okay. We don't want any trouble in this neck of the woods. We don't need the unwanted attention."

"What are we going to do here?"

"Sit back and enjoy the show," he giggled.

We sat at the bar. Before us, a stage with red strobe lights and three poles stood from floor to ceiling. Several women took turns dancing around them while disrobing.

"What's the point of all this?" I asked.

"They take all our money, and in return, we get cheap thrills."

"Why are they taking off their clothes?" I asked.

"Don't over think it." David had to yell above the music. "I'll treat you to a lap dance."

After the women danced on stage, they walked around, talked, and flirted with the men at the bar. The women would then lead them to the back and dance on top of them.

David nursed a gin and tonic. He became flushed and leaned over patting me gently on the shoulder. "You've got two types of

126

people in this world," he began. "You've got show-ers, and you've got growers. Show-ers show you all they got the minute you see them. Growers may seem small at first, but they are larger and more impressive than you could have anticipated."

"Which one are you?" I asked.

"We are both growers you and I." He hiccupped. "You're going to surprise them all. You'll show them you're capable of so much more than they could have imagined." He stopped talking after a particularly busty woman walked by.

"She, on the other hand, is a show-er," he chuckled. "I'll be right back."

David walked over. I watched him talk to several women.

He walked back holding one by the hand. "Aeneas, this is Penelope. She's going to show you a good time."

Before I could decline, she took me by the hand and led me to the back.

"Do you need saving?" I asked.

She smacked her lips and moved her hips to the music. Every word was matched by a dramatic swerve from left to right in time with the beat. "Why, you loaded? I've heard this one before, let me guess you're in love and you want to take me away from this terrible life?"

"I'm not sure how I'm supposed to save her. I don't even know who she is."

"If you've got the cash then I'll gladly play the part." She smiled and revealed a gap between her teeth. I noticed the scars on her upper thigh.

"I used to take my clothes off for money," I said.

"Really? Is it true you male strippers mostly do gay clubs?"

"What?" I shook my head. "No, I had sex for money."

"What kind of freak are you?" She paused. "Is this some sick way of asking me if I'd fuck you for money? Cause let me tell you— the answer is a definite maybe."

"Do you know God?"

"You're not getting a conscience on me, are you? Don't start crying; I can't stand the guys who cry."

127

If she needed saving I would have known by now.

She heaved her chest into my face. "Your friend over there only paid for one dance. If you want any more, you'll need more cash."

"One is fine," I replied. "Thank you. David was wrong about you."

She pressed her lips together and bent them to the left. "What do you mean?"

"You don't seem like broken down whores to me."

"You said what to her?" David raised his hands in the air as a fat man, dressed in black, escorted us out.

"She didn't need saving. How am I going to find the right girl?" I said.

"You're going to have to drive." He wobbled left and right with only his cane to keep him balanced.

"Thank you," I said. "This meant a lot to me."

"You—" he began, then landed face first on the ground. I lifted him, put him in the car, and drove us home. He passed out on the couch with a smile on his face, mumbling about a stripper named Daisy he planned on marrying.

It was good to be home again.

# 23

Eggs and bacon sizzled on the frying pan. I whistled a tune and made my way to the kitchen in an apron that read "hump the chef."

"Breakfast will be ready soon," I said. David mumbled a reply and turned over, still asleep on the couch.

The doorknob on the front door turned followed by light footsteps.

"Hello?" I called.

I walked to the living room and watched her.

"Dad why are you covered in stripper glitter!" said a woman. "Stripper glitter is the whoriest of all the glitters you know," she said and wiped the sparkly dots from his face and hair. "What am I going to do with you?"

Strawberry blonde hair grazed her shoulders. She wore a black ruffled blouse and a gray pleated skirt.

She smiled without effort. "Abby told me about you," she said and dusted the glitter from her fingertips. "I'm glad someone is here to watch over him." Her eyes, sky blue, she had her father's round little nose, and her lips formed a perfect pink circle. I didn't know what to say.

"Wait," she said. "You've got it on you too!" She laughed and ran her fingers through my hair and watched the specks fly off her hands. "You men," she said. "Robot or not, you're typical and predictable. Him I understand, but you?" She took a speck of glitter from my head; my sensors went wild. "I'm sorry I haven't introduced myself, I'm Janie."

"I am, Aeneas," I said. "It is a pleasure to meet you."

Janie held out her hand to greet me. "Nice to meet you," she said. I remembered I had gripped David's hand too hard, so I took care to be gentle with hers.

"Are you keeping my dad out of trouble?" she said and raised an eyebrow. "He's told me a lot about you. I've heard a lot about Synthetics. I never thought I'd meet one." She parted the hair from her eyes, two beautiful little Earths. I couldn't look away.

"I hope I can be of service to you as well as," I said.

"Were you making breakfast? Smells great. Let me help, I'm starving." She strutted into the kitchen, wide hips, formidable bust, a pear-shaped figure. "I need an injection of bacon, ASAP," she said and made her way through the refrigerator.

David wiped the sleep from his eyes and took a peek outside at her red Volkswagen Jetta parked in the driveway, back seat filled with clothes and personal items.

"Everything okay sweetheart? You always call before you visit."

She almost frowned but forced a smile instead. "We'll talk later. It's great to see you." She cracked an egg into the pan. I watched it sizzle. "This place is a mess by the way. I thought he was supposed to help you clean up? But I see your busy doing other things." Her laugh was a series of sweet chuckles ending with a slight snort and an embarrassed sigh.

"Excuse me," she said.

"You've still got your mother's laugh," David said.

\*\*\*

"I can't eat another bite," David said. He loosened the rope on his pajamas and let his gut hang out. His energy level, double what it had been the last few days and there was a light in his eyes. "Where was I? Oh right, so your mother comes home, you and Abby were covered in pudding from head to toe."

Janie fell back into her chair and laughed.

"The thing was," David bellowed. "We didn't have any pudding in the house!"

Janie almost spat out her coffee. "We got it from next door. The neighbor's back door was open. We waltzed in there and raided her fridge.".

"What were you two thinking?"

"We just wanted pudding."

"You and Abby were inseparable for so long. I'm shocked the two of you didn't marry two male twins and live in the same house together."

Janie took a minute to regain her composure. "She did pretty well for herself, huh?"

"You are both successful in my eyes honey; you know that."

Janie patted her stomach. "Feels like I'm going to keel over." She went into the living room. "No way!" She came back with one of David's robots in her hands. "I remember this one. A motion detector we made to keep Abby out of my room."

"Let me see." David reached out. "Did this even work?"

"No, but what Abby didn't know didn't hurt her."

"We worked on it together."

"I called it the Abby detector."

"You remind me so much of your mother, how's the boyfriend?" he asked.

Her eyes hit the floor. "I'd rather not talk about it."

"Fair enough, how long do you plan on staying?"

Her fingers brushed against her left cheek. "I was hoping you'd let me stay for a bit, just until I can get back on my feet."

"Yes, yes, stay as long as you like. You're always welcome here."

She went out to her car to get her bags, and I helped carry them upstairs.

# *24*

The next morning I found Janie at the kitchen table, hair tied in a ponytail, thumbing through the newspaper. "Any jobs in this town?" she asked, dressed in pajama pants and a white tank top.

"You just arrived," I said.

"I don't sit on my ass doing nothing. It's Aeneas, right?

"Correct."

"Can I call you, A?"

"If you prefer, yes."

"I stay busy, A."

Someone hammered on the front door. She set down the paper, and her right hand twitched.

"What's wrong?" I asked.

A heart-stopping punch shook the door frame, harder this time, and then a voice followed. "I know you're in there bitch! You let me in, or I'll bust down this door."

Her skin turned pale; she mouthed the words then she tried again, more precise this time. "Help," she said. "Help me."

Janie hid behind me with her hands on my waist. I stood my ground, unsure of what was going to happen next.

David hurried downstairs. "What's going on down here?"

"David, this visitor means to harm Janie."

"He's not going to hurt anyone. I'm calling the police." He searched for his cell phone in the living room. "It's around here somewhere."

The man slammed the door over and over. The wood cracked and splintered. Then silence, followed by a giant thud as a crowbar broke through and busted the door open.

A large bald man as wide as the door entered our home with a chin the size of a fist. He breathed heavily. Blood dripped from his hands.

"Wipe your shoes before coming in," I said.

"Don't hide behind him. Who is this fucker? He your new boyfriend? Are you leaving me for this son of a bitch?" With only three steps he was in the kitchen nose to nose with me. I looked him in the eyes, indifferent toward his brutish attitude and looming presence. "Are you going to get out of my way?" he barked. Janie trembled behind me. "Or are we going to have a problem?"

"Don, it's over, gets over it. I don't love you anymore," she cried.

"If you don't want your new boy toy to get squashed then come out and look me in the eyes."

"He's not my boy toy," she replied.

Don's hands, large as my head, grabbed me by the throat and when I didn't react he let go with a confused look on his face. "What the fuck are you?"

"I cannot allow you to harm her. Cease your behavior," I said.

"What are you going to do if I don't?"

"I…" I stopped for a moment. He was right I had not thought that far yet. "I will not allow you to harm anyone in this house."

Don released his grip and then approached David.

"I know you care about your pop," the monster grinned.

He slapped David across his face. He was on the ground in seconds, eyes red, slumped over.

I rushed toward the behemoth and raised my fist to ensure the trajectory of the blow would land on his jaw. My fist zipped through the air but froze in place.

"You seem stuck." Don laughed. "You going to finish what you started?" Amused he walked around me and placed his hands on my arm. "Huh?"

"I cannot harm a human," I said, but it was not of my own will. My program kicked in, perhaps to remind me or to assure the humans.

I turned around and tried again; my fist stopped once more, below his neck. I yelled out in frustration. How could I let them down like this?

Don loomed over Janie casting a sizeable fat shadow over her body. She appeared small and frail in his presence. She met his eyes in defiance, but her heart rate told another story. I cursed my circuits and my programming. I was useless to protect them. I had to act before he laid a hand on her. I ran out of the house and knocked on Wade's door until they answered.

"Come quick and bring a weapon!" I yelled. He followed me back to David's house.

We found Janie cowered in a corner as Don crept toward her, fists raised in the air.

"I'm calling the police!" Wade yelled out. Don turned around; he didn't look the least bit threatened.

"I'm teaching this bitch some respect. You mind?"

Wade pulled out his gun. "Get out!"

Don raised his hands and turned around. I kept my eye on him as I walked past him and knelt down beside Janie; she gripped my hand and cried. I didn't know what else to do. Don walked out the front door. His eyes locked on Janie. "Don't look at her," I yelled.

"Where do you think you're going? The police are already on their way!" Wade said, but Don entered his car, started the engine, and drove away.

Wade rushed back in. "He drove away like he didn't have a care in the world. Scariest thing I've ever seen. Where's the damn sheriff?"

I dampened a towel and wiped Janie's face. David had been knocked unconscious. An ambulance arrived with the police. None of his bruises required any serious medical attention, so David refused a trip to the hospital. The police never caught up with Don.

I carried Janie to her former bedroom and set her down on the mattress. She curled into a fetal position and cried into her pillow.

David sat by her bed and said nothing until she fell asleep. I felt like a useless paperweight standing in the doorway.

"How could she be with such a brute?" David asked me. "I wanted my girls to come visit me, but not like this." He ran his hand across her cheek and forehead. "Abby and Janie looked so much alike as children, and for a long time, it was difficult to tell them apart. It was easier after Janie's accident."

"Yeah?"

"Notice her right arm? There's a scar below her wrist."

"Oh."

"Even though she was a bit of a wild one I could always count on my Janie to be there for me. Don't get me wrong Abigail has been a wonderful daughter, she sent me you, and I am eternally grateful to her, but Janie has always been a little more hands on. Abby helps from afar. They're both great in their way it's why I had two instead of one, you know, balance things out."

"Did they ever find out?" I asked.

"About what?"

"Did they find out you slept with Marie while you were married?"

"She told you eh? Yes, they found out when their mother did; when she nearly threw me out of the house. She never told me she was dying. She did it to punish me for cheating. The girls never forgave me."

"We should let her get some sleep." David made his way toward the door.

"Would it be okay if I stayed by her door?" I asked.

"If you wish."

"I am sorry," I said.

"Sorry for what, my boy?"

"I failed you when you needed me most. I couldn't protect you."

"It couldn't be helped. You can't harm a human, not even to protect another human."

"Change it. Reprogram me."

"I couldn't if I tried. Your system is complex, and those basic rules are burned deep into your core. It cannot be undone."

"This is a fatal flaw. I must be able to protect you and Janie."

"There is nothing that can be done. I'll see you in the morning, goodnight."

# 25

I watched as Janie slept. Her rhythmic breathing paused followed by a scream.

I placed my hand on her forehead. "Only a dream," I said.

"Fucker even invades my dreams; you believe that shit?"

"I do," I replied. "May I get you some water?"

"Thanks but I'll get it."

"I'd be more than willing--"

"You're here for my dad not for me. I don't need a butler or maid, thank you very much." A minute later she returned with a glass, drank half, and then lay down in bed. "Know any jokes?" she asked.

"Sorry, I don't know any."

"A good laugh would calm my nerves."

"Why did he wish to hurt you?"

"After a year of emotional abuse, I left him."

"I'm sorry."

"Not your fault, A. I sure can pick 'em. Say something until I fall asleep."

"Say what?"

"Doesn't matter."

I took out the Bible James had given me and read it out loud. She fell asleep before I finished Genesis. I highlighted passages I wished to discuss with the reverend. Everyone in the bible was being saved and delivered. The angel told me I had to save a girl, maybe it was Janie, and to protect her I have to get her to believe in God and the Bible.

People in the Bible also received signs from God. I decided I would wait for one. He would let me know if she was the one.
I found David downstairs. He sat expressionless at the kitchen table.

"Thank you for keeping a watch over her," he said and nibbled on some cheddar cheese. "We should make her feel welcome. Let's make her a cake."

"I don't know how to make a cake."

"We'll figure it out together."

A few hours later David and I finished a three layer cake topped with cream cheese icing. I followed the directions to the letter.

"Exquisite, she's going to love it; red velvet was always her favorite."

Janie came downstairs in a daze. David grabbed the cake and ran to meet her at the bottom.

"Welcome home," David said with a grin.

She pressed her lips together. "My thighs won't thank you, but my taste buds will."

There was a single candle lit atop on the cake. "I thought this only worked on birthdays," she said.

"You get a bonus wish this year," David replied.

Tears formed in her eyes. She took a small breath and blew out the candle.

"Can I have a wish as well?" I asked.

"I don't see why not," David said. "Who made up these silly rules anyway? We can have as many wishes as we please."

He ran back into the kitchen, came back with another match and re-lit the candle. "If Janie doesn't mind," he added.

She looked at the cake and then at me. "Wish away."

It then occurred to me. "David I don't have breath to blow out the candle, how can I make a wish?"

"You make a wish, and Janie will blow it out for you."

I thought about it for a minute and then made my wish.

Janie blew out the candle, and for a moment I lost all sense of everything around me and focused on her soft lips. The sensors in my lips began to wonder what her lips would feel like.

"A?" Janie said. "Hello? You still there?"

"Yes, Janie."

She looked me over. "What has daddy been dressing you in?"

"Hey now, I thought I did a good job. You should have seen what he arrived in."

"Let's take a little trip to the mall and get you something a little more modern."

"If you wish, then I will come with you."

"You mind?" she asked David.

"Don't lose him," he said.

"My car's full, we'll take Dad's," Janie said.

She got dressed and went out to the car. I sat in the passenger seat; she took out a stick of gum and chewed on it. I tried not to stare as even the most mundane tasks seemed extraordinary when she did them.

"Got my keys, got my wallet, got my butt," she said.

She looked me over then put on her sunglasses. "There's something about a good looking man that makes me want to dress him in fine clothes. Sorry I mean, Synthetic, it's easy to forget sometimes."

"I don't mind," I said.

She pulled out of the driveway then saw Helena walking her dog down the street. "Helena!" She squealed and got out of the car. They rushed toward each other with open arms.

"I didn't know you were in town," Helena said and kissed her on the cheek. "Are you okay?"

"I had a little trouble with the ex."

"Did he hit you? I'll kick his ass."

Janie hugged her once more. "It's over now, don't worry. It's so good to see you. You look amazing."

Helena twirled. "I still got my curves," she said. "Your aura is all over the place. You sure you all right?"

"I'm fine. I was about to take A to the mall. Shop for some clothes. Want to tag along?"

"Oh, I'd love to sweetie, but I got some laundry going, and this dog needs to be walked. When you get back tonight I'll stop by, will you be up?"

"Of course, I don't sleep much these days anyway."

"I don't want to keep you," Helena kissed her on the cheek. "I'll see you tonight." She then looked at me. "Keep her safe, okay?"

I nodded. Janie got back in the car with a half-smile.

"We were best friends in college. Hot damn she looks good." She paused. "Wish I had her tits. Okay, buckle your seatbelt, we're off. I'm going to give you a lesson in music," she said and connected her phone's blue tooth to the car stereo. "This is Joe Strummer, my new obsession. This was his last album before he died." She played a song called *Get Down Moses*; I didn't know what to make of it. "God," she moaned. "I've got to stop falling in love with dead musicians. Joe was a total hottie. You sort of look like him you know."

"I do?"

"Well at least during his Clash days."

"Clash?"

"The Clash, only the greatest rock band ever."

"Okay," I said.

We drove for twenty minutes and arrived at the mall. I loved it, so much information and stimulation. There were many stores and items for sale. I wanted to visit each one. Janie held my hand and kept me moving, otherwise we would have been there all day. We entered a few stores, and I tried on many outfits.

"We need to highlight those broad shoulders of yours—work with that tall, dark, and handsome look. You could use a little mystique. How do you feel about eyeliner?"

"I—"

"We'll experiment and see how it goes. Do you have a preference for what you like to wear?"

"I haven't thought about it."

She picked out a few slacks and polo shirts. After seeing me in them, she shook her head, and we tried another store.

"You need a dash of bad boy. Let's see how this fits."

I put on a black leather jacket.

"I think we found your look!" she said with a cheer. I didn't want it to end. I would try on clothes for her as long as she wanted. Being in her presence was unlike anything else I had ever experienced. All the women I had been with and all the sex I had could not amount to this. This was better than all the sex in the world.

Unfortunately, I said this out loud, and she looked at me, bewildered.

"Okay, well, I'll pretend I didn't hear that," she said then paid for the jacket along with a few other items.

"Now," she began. "Let's do something about your hair."

When we returned home, David seemed shocked.

"What have you done to my Aeneas?"

"For a high-tech machine, he looked a little low-tech in the clothes department. I gave him a modern look."

"He looks like he's about to turn tricks. Offering himself as the wrong side of a pastry puff."

"I think he looks hot," she said. "Wrong side of a pastry puff, what does that even mean?"

"For Christ's sake, get the makeup off of him at least. And what's this, an earring?"

"You don't get it."

"Don't turn him into a pussy."

David tossed her an apple, and she bit into it. "Helena's coming over later," she said.

"I'm not too eager to have guests over these days."

She looked at the piles of newspapers and other items in the living room. "I could clean a little if you want."

"No, don't touch any of it."

Janie gave me a curious look.

Helena arrived later in the evening. "I've got the perfect cure for the blues," she said to Janie. "Nine and half weeks starring Mickey Rourke, ice cream, and pizza."

"Thank heaven for you," Janie said taking the pizza box to the kitchen. "For you and Mickey Rourke circa 1986."

"Amen."

"Would you require anything else this evening?" I asked Janie.

"We're good, A. You can do whatever you want now."

"Would it be okay if I joined you and Helena?"

"We got some girl talk to do. No boys allowed, sorry."

"As you wish."

"I'll call you over later when we watch the movie, okay?"

"Great," I replied with a smile.

Four hours later they called me over to watch the movie with them in the kitchen on Janie's laptop. Helena was in the middle of a story when I entered the living room. "So this is our first date, and you know what he says to me? I've only sucked dick a couple of times and didn't like it, so I'm pretty sure I'm not gay!" Janie fell on her side laughing. Helena turned to me as she smiled. "Aeneas—you ready for some classic steamy '80s erotica?"

"I guess," I said. She turned on the movie, and I watched intently.

Two hours later the film ended. "Is that what women want?" I asked. The film was about an intensely sexual relationship between a woman and a strange man she meets. The more she learns about the man the more complex their relationship becomes.

Helena placed her hand on my hand. "Poor thing you look stunned. Yes and no."

Janie giggled and sipped her wine.

Frustrated I asked, "Well which is it— yet or no?"

"It's both" Janie said trying to hold back more laughter but couldn't stop.

"I don't understand."

Helena sat back and lifted her wine glass. "Congratulations, now you are a man." They toasted.

142

# 26

An empty wine bottle rolled across the kitchen table. I grabbed it as it neared the edge. An ashtray filled with cigarettes sat atop an empty pizza box.

Janie had pushed aside the clutter and found a spot on the couch. She passed out ten minutes ago.

"What time is it?" Helena asked lifting her head from the kitchen table, her hair flattened on one side.

"Two thirty in the morning," I replied.

"My head is killing me."

Janie's snorted and rolled an old newspaper over her chest.

"I need some fresh air," Helena said. "Join me?"

She sat on the porch and looked out to the house across the street.

"Too bad you can't smoke. You don't know what you're missing," she said. The smoke left her mouth like a spirit leaving a body. "Except for the hangovers, those suck."

"The Bible speaks about the evils of worldly pleasures," I said.

She took a long drag on her cigarette and eyed me from head to toe. "I believe there is a spiritual world out there. That is how I see you in my dreams." She tapped the cigarette between her fingers, and the wind carried the ash across the lawn. "I know you're something special, but I'm not sure if this heavy Bible stuff is good for you."

"Why wouldn't it be?"

"There's a lot of baggage. Have you read the whole Bible?"

"Yes, every single word."

"What do you make of it?"

"I have a lot of questions for the reverend."

"I figured as much; you'll always have questions; be careful where you look for the answers." I felt the weight of her large brown eyes on me. "Jesus is one of many guides. Take the wisdom, but try to leave the excess behind."

She took another drag. "My, my, a robot who believes in things it cannot see, that has to be a first."

"But it is not logical," I said. "I've seen things which by all definition should not be possible."

"The spiritual world lives within the impossible. The world as you know it gets turned on its head. It gives us little humans a swift kick in the rear whenever we think we got it all figured out. As long as you keep searching, learning, and changing, then it will make your existence richer. I don't follow the path you're seeking, but I admire your journey and hunger for knowledge."

She butted her cigarette. "The problem with spirituality is, it's been hijacked by religion." She paused. "Religion is the subjugation of spirituality."

"I understand what you're saying," I replied.

"Enough theology for one night. I'm headed home before I pass out again."

"Allow me to walk you home," I said.

"You are a true gentlemen."

The night was quiet, every home dark, and a dog barked in the distance as we walked side by side.

"I've seen the way you look at her," she said.

"Who?" I asked.

"Janie, of course. I think you've got the hots for your boss's daughter."

I thought about it for a minute. "She's different from the other women in this town; she's special."

"You're closer to the truth than you think."

"What do you mean?" I asked.

"When Janie and I were ten we visited her dad at the factory. There was an accident. We shouldn't have been playing around. Her hand was crushed in one of the machines—there was no way they could reattach it. A few months later there was talk about this experimental new procedure where they could replace limbs with robotic ones. Not merely a prosthetic— an actual working limb that responded to the brain. Abby's future husband's father was head of the company. They managed to have Janie put into one of the test trials."

"She has metal inside her just like me?" I couldn't believe it.

"They did a great job with the fake skin. You could say it was your precursor. But the procedure was dangerous."

"She's amazing," I said.

"Wow, you've got a grin on your face the size of the Grand Canyon. Most people's reaction to that story is a little sadder."

"I'm sorry I don't—I mean it's nice to know she and I have something in common."

"She doesn't like to talk about it. Kids used to tease her all the time."

"That's terrible."

"They tested the procedure on twelve patients, and she was only one of two who survived. The results were so tragic they outlawed the procedure here in the states."

"Why did she survive and the others didn't?"

"Well your body either treats the metal hand like an invader and fights it or it accepts it as part of the body. She was one of the lucky ones."

One of the lucky ones, I thought.

I saw Helena to her front door. She hugged me extra tight, and I wished her good night. "You take care of her," she said and closed the door.

I arrived back home. Janie was awake; sitting on the couch, channel surfing.

"Helena get home okay?" she said, her words half slurred.

"Yes."

145

Her face turned sour. She hit the remote hard with every button press. "You're here with Dad all the time, so tell me, how is he?"

"He sleepwalks a lot," I said. "Otherwise he is healthy...well except..."

She spread her arms out on the backrest. "Except?

"He won't throw anything away."

"I noticed, so what's your story? You like it here?"

"Yes, I do. I love David, and I love this town."

"Love huh. Are you programmed to love?"

"I like to think it's a choice."

"But how can you know for sure?" she asked.

"I suppose I don't."

"Some humans think they can love. Don thought he could love. What makes you any different?"

I didn't know what to say.

"Strong silent type? Typical." She leaned her head on her shoulder. "Tell me..." she said sleepily. "What's it like when they first turn you on?"

I thought it over for a moment. "It's like opening your eyes for the first time and seeing the whole world in front of you. The first thing I saw was the man responsible for my creation. I could see something in his eyes, I could tell he created me out of love, and I had a purpose: to make my owners as happy as possible."

"It must be nice to know your place in the world. All these years, I still can't figure it out." Her eyes dropped to the floor. "After I got my Master's in Clinical Psychology I worked as a family therapist, my patients came from the local Hospice. It wore me down, all those families losing their loved ones and children. I couldn't take it anymore, so I took a leave of absence."

"When did things turn sour with Don?" I asked.

"I guess being away from all the misery awakened me to my own. I realized my boyfriend was a total jackass. I had to get out of there. I had nowhere else to go. So now I'm here."

"I am glad you are here," I said.

"Funny, Dad gets to have you...it's like his great reward." She lifted her hands. "After everything, he did to mom and our family he doesn't get to suffer. He gets a good life with you as his servant."

"I am not his servant," I said.

"Can you do whatever you want?"

"No, I cannot."

"You're programmed to care, A. I hate to be the one to tell you."

I walked away. I didn't want to hear another word she said. I then felt bad about the argument and returned. She was already fast asleep on the couch. I eased her into my arms and brought her to her bed. She wrapped her blanket around herself and mumbled, "Oh Mickey..."

I examined her right hand, heavy, definitely metal, the skin, well-made. I was surprised I had not noticed sooner it wasn't real. It made her all the more beautiful to me. I placed a soft kiss on it; she stirred but did not awaken.

"Good night," I whispered and closed the door.

The next day Janie nursed her hangover with a substantial breakfast. I left early to attend the Sunday church service. I had an entire row to myself. The reverend's wife sat next to me when she noticed this; it made me feel better. Danielle glared. Whenever I looked around at the congregation, others would look away, and most seemed indifferent to my being there.

Reverend James took the pulpit after the opening hymn.

"God is love. Doesn't get any simpler, does it? Which then brings us to the next question: What is love? Well in the Bible they define love as kindness and patience. Such a God to me would welcome with open arms anyone or anything with a conscious mind into his loving arms. If there is hope even for the least of us, then there is hope for anyone. The kingdom of God is within our reach; we must live our lives according to his will and laws. Our reward in heaven will be great. So I ask you today, as we welcome Aeneas into our congregation, to reach out to him with love as our loving Father has done for us."

Reverend James invited me over to his home after the service. He had a large den decorated with a maroon rug, a large pool table, and a bookcase as wide as two walls. His wife came down with two glasses of lemonade.

"You'll have to excuse me I keep forgetting," she said. "You can't drink."

"It's okay dear; I'll take both," James replied.

"I'll leave you two to it then." She smiled and went upstairs.

I looked at the books on the shelf and read each title out loud.

"Do you think I can get into Heaven?" I asked.

"It's a tricky question; I guess it depends on whether you have a soul. Heaven is earned though our good deeds and ultimate acceptance of God in our hearts. We must prepare the way and save as many souls for the Lord as possible. I don't think God had you in mind when he wrote the Bible, Aeneas."

"You're saying I don't have a soul..." I said.

"What is a soul if not a ball of energy? You're filled with electrical energy so don't be discouraged, if you have the desire, then there's more to you than meets the eye. If you do have a soul, you have to earn your way to heaven like the rest of us. Start saving some souls for the Lord and maybe you'll get there too."

"There's one soul I think I'm supposed to save."

"You make a believer out of this person, and maybe God will look upon you with favor." He took a long breath and methodically racked the balls on the pool table. "I don't have all the answers, and whenever I need them, I look in the good book."

"Yes," I said. "Many things confuse me." I set the Bible down on the pool table and opened to Genesis chapter one verse one. "Creating the world in seven days is impossible."

"The literal translation isn't what's important, what matters is the meaning behind it. Focus on the idea: he made the world out of love, it doesn't matter how many days it took to get it done."

"It appears we are not to wear mixed fibers—or cut your hair—women cannot wear pants—I notice we are not resting on the Sabbath, and—"

"Okay, buddy I'm going to cut you off right there." He set his fingers between the first page and the last page of the Old Testament. "Christians start here," he said moving all the pages until the first page of the New Testament was on top. "The other stuff we leave for the Jews to worry about."

"I see."

"What matters is, when Jesus hit the scene, everything changed. I think you should do your best to save this soul you are concerned about, find favor with the Lord, and get your way into Heaven. I know it seems impossible, but it wouldn't be the craziest thing to happen. I mean have you read the whole thing? The Bible has some crazy shit in it, pardon my language."

"Where do I start?" I asked.

"You start with the heart, Aeneas. You start with the heart."

# *27*

"Here, put this on," James said and lowered a long white robe over my head. He folded his hands, and I followed him down the hall and out of the chapel. A few feet away stood another eggshell white building with a glass ceiling. "Normally we dunk adults head first into the baptism pool, but I get the feeling water may not agree with you."

I looked at the robe, tugged at the fabric.

"Don't worry," he said. "We'll keep the water to a minimum."

Water was indeed not my friend but I could survive in it for a short period of time. This building was smaller than the chapel. The great hall housed a square, mid-sized pool in the center with a curtain and rows of chairs around it.

"The curtain is for when we baptize women," he said.

The water's surface, a mirror of the spider web formation of the glass above. I gazed into my reflection as the light wavered upon the water.

David, Janie, and Helena sat in the chairs closest to the pool.

James nodded in their direction. "Do you bear witness that today Aeneas chooses to live his life anew?"

David and Helena nodded; their faces looked like they had all just bit into sour lemons. Janie whispered into David's ear, "This is weird." He shrugged his shoulders and said, "I know, but we're here to support him."

I sat on the edge of the pool. The water, shoulder length deep. I kept one hand firmly gripped on the side.

James cupped the water and asked, "Do you reject Satan and all of his promises?"

"I do."

"Do you accept God into your life and in his name may you always act according to his word?"

"I do."

"Then in the name of the Father, and of the Son, and of the Holy Spirit, I baptize you in God's name. May you be welcomed into his loving arms after living a fruitful, humbled life, Amen."

He poured water onto my forehead. I closed my eyes and focused solely on the sensation: the droplets trickled down my face. I prayed as James had taught me to pray. I prayed for Janie's soul and for David's. I wished Henry and Jeremy would find solace after losing their mother. I wanted grace and love to wash over this town. Lastly, I told God I knew I was different, but I hoped he'd consider letting me into his kingdom.

***

The next day at home Janie walked into the kitchen to get a glass of water. On the kitchen table were a dozen roses with a note attached. She looked curiously at the flowers and then read the letter.

"Dear Janie,<br>I love you,<br>- Jesus."

She smelled the roses and smiled. I sat in the living room and tried not to look suspicious. "You know anything about these flowers?" she asked.

"Not at all," I said. "Why? Who sent them? Jesus?"

"Apparently he knows how to orders flowers online. Who knew?"

"I think he wants you to love him back," I said with a smile.

"I'll take a rain check, but I'll keep the flowers." She grabbed the vase and brought them to her room. David trotted slowly toward the kitchen as Janie passed him she said, "Dad your robot is trying to convert me."

"Aeneas, stop trying to convert Janie," he said.

She left the note on the kitchen table. He took a look at the card.

"Aeneas you know anything about this?"

"Yes, I sent her flowers."

"Oh, good, I was worried she had some new jerk boyfriend named 'Hey-Soos.'"

He went back to his den. I sat in the living room feeling defeated. Undoubtedly this was the ultimate act of love, wasn't it?

I told Reverend James about it in his office the next day.

"Wait, tell me again why Janie woke up screaming."

"I decided to baptize her in her sleep."

"So you poured water on her?"

"I don't want her eternal soul to be damned forever, James."

"A good thought, but I think you misunderstood me. You can't throw our faith in her face and expect her to believe."

"So what do I do?"

"Be there when she needs you. The love inside you will shine, and one day she'll want what you have."

"What is it I have?"

"You tell me." James sat back in his chair, grabbed a baseball off his desk and rolled it between his hands. "Eleanor wasn't my first wife you know."

"She wasn't?"

"Heck I didn't take wives, I took hostages."

"I don't understand."

"I'm an alcoholic. Do you know what that is?"

"No, I do not."

"It means one drink is too many and a million is not enough. Ruined my first three marriages, I don't blame any one of them for leaving. I would have gone too if I could. For years I thought I could handle it on my own. My last wife, before Eleanor, said I had to choose between her and the booze, I chose the booze.

"One morning, after another night of binge drinking, I fell asleep at the wheel and rear-ended a car at a stop light. I ruined her trunk and totaled my bumper. A few seconds later there's a tap on my window, Eleanor. I rolled up my window thinking I could escape or ignore her. The funny thing was, she was worried about ME, you believe that?

"In the middle of that wreck, as vomit and bile spewed from my mouth, she looked like an angel. Afterward, I tracked her down; I asked everyone in town about her. Found out she was a waitress at the local diner. I left a hundred dollar tip. "Awful lot for two cups of coffee and a slice of cherry pie," she said and refused the tip and said I couldn't date her unless I sobered up and stayed clean for at least a year.

"I walked into my first AA meeting that day. I sat in the room and could barely hear a word anyone was saying. This old timer got up to speak, twenty years sober, he didn't look like he made much money, but he had a peaceful look in his eyes. I realized I wanted what he had. I wanted that serenity in my life. I was soon introduced to God as I understood him."

"As you understood him?"

"Everyone sees God in their way. Whether it's a big man in the sky or the general understanding that there are mysteries to the universe, a thing greater than myself. Who created the first spark of life that expanded and gave life to our universe, planets, and the stars. The very stars that make up everything on Earth."

"I am made of stars?"

"You, me, everyone. That day changed my life forever, and nobody had to convert me or try to convince me. After a year, Eleanor finally let me take her on a date, and the rest is history. My heart wanted what it wanted, and I decided I'd do anything to get it."

"So I have to wait until her heart wants it?"

"Correct, it's just like love, you are only in love when your heart wants it."

"How do you know when you're in love?" I asked.

"You're in love when you want a person—heart, mind, and soul—more than anything else and you'd do anything for her."

"I want to win Janie over," I said.

"I heard she's looking for work. Eleanor's could use an extra hand at the diner; if she's interested."

153

"Thank you, James."

"You're welcome."

At home, I heard a commotion going on inside. Marie ran out of the house in tears.

I walked in and found David, face red, hands trembling. Janie slammed her hands on the kitchen counter.

"How dare you talk to her like that!" He screamed.

"You let that bitch into this house? Mom's house! How could you!"

David stepped back, and every time he started speaking he'd stop and start over. "You don't understand."

"I don't want her in this house. I can't believe after all this time you're still talking to her! What would Mom think?"

"She's dead, Janie! We're still alive…we have to deal with this life. She's not here to have her say."

"I think I can say enough on her behalf. That whore is the reason our family fell apart."

He bit down on his lower lip. "It's been a long time since then."

She crossed her arms. "Not long enough."

"What do you want from me? I'm alone; I have no one else. I get lonely."

"Maybe that's what you deserve, you ever think of that?"

"How dare you speak to me that way!" He slammed his cane into the ground.

A rock flew through the kitchen window and glass shattered all around them.

I grabbed the rock. Someone had written on it, "Go to hell robot." David and Janie stood by me and looked on in silence.

"I don't want to go to hell," I said.

Janie raised her hands in the air. "This is a crazy house! I need some fresh air!" She stormed out the front door.

I was torn between cleaning the glass and running after Janie. David looked at me. "Go after her. I can clean this on my own," he said.

"But—"

"Go!"

154

# 28

Janie slammed the car door, put on her seat belt, and started David's car. I took the passenger seat. She looked over at me, on the verge of tears.

"I don't want company," she said.

Hands in my lap, I raised my eyebrows and lowered my cheeks. "Let me come with you I promise I won't bother you."

"Are you seriously using the puppy dog face on me? Who taught it to you?"

"Television."

"Where on television?"

"Droopy dog."

"Droopy the cartoon dog?"

"David watches a lot of old cartoons."

"You make it hard to be angry." She tried to frown again but couldn't. "Okay, but don't talk until I say it's okay." I nodded.

She gripped the steering wheel, shifted into drive, and pulled out of the driveway. I was good to my word and did not speak while she drove out of town and onto the highway. I gazed out the window; vast fields lined the road, the corn stalks pointed toward the sky, their giver of life.

Helena told me people once worshiped the sun.

"What's bigger than the sun?" she once asked me. A destroyer and bringer of life, similar to our perception of God. Without the sun our world would grow cold, and all life would die. Those fields

155

of corn would no longer exist. She said it didn't matter what you called it: God, the sun, or the universe. We worship the bringer of light, the maker of worlds, hoping it will bring a sliver of warmth to our souls.

Janie kept her eyes on the road. She turned on the radio and tuned into a classic rock station.

"Pink Floyd, 'Wish you were here.' Listen carefully and remember it okay," she said.

"Why?" I asked.

"Why not?"

We took the nearest exit, left the car by the side of the road, and walked until we reached a large hill that overlooked a lush green valley. The green lawn stretched for miles. Trees taller than most homes surrounded us.

"This is where the amphitheater used to be." She pointed. "I came here every weekend with my friends. We'd sit here and listen to all our favorite bands. Tickets were cheap if you didn't mind sitting on the grass. Couldn't see shit but we were far away enough to smoke up but still heard the music. We enjoyed it."

"I like Peter Frampton," I said.

She lowered her head, so her eyes peered out from above her sunglasses as her hair fell over her eyes. "There's no fucking way Dad has exposed you to anything even remotely that awesome."

"No, it was Marie."

She fell silent. The veins on her hands pulsed, her heartbeat increased. "Are you friends with that home wrecker too?"

"She's been nice to me. It's because of her they allowed me to stay here. I am indebted to her."

She took a seat on the grass with her legs crossed. The wind blew her hair back; goose bumps rose up on her arm.

"I'm so glad she's been a positive influence in your life, but when you're 10, and she's the reason your mom almost leaves you—well, you tend to see things in a different light."

"I'm sorry she's caused you such sadness," I said.

"Now she's his best fucking friend, you believe it?"

"Your father spends most of his days alone in the house. He doesn't get many visitors. She makes him happy."

"And it doesn't matter what he did to mom? What he did to his family?"

I sat down beside her and crossed my legs.

She pulled blades of grass from the ground beside her; methodically, like plucking the hairs off someone's arms. "It shouldn't be so cold in May."

I placed my hands on her shoulders and moved all the heat from inside my arms into the palms of my hands. I could feel the heat passing from my hands into her skin. Her goosebumps receded.

She sighed. "You're a walking heater. Is there anything you can't do?" she asked.

"There are many things I wish I could do."

"Like what?" she asked.

"I don't want to be burdened by my programming anymore. I want to be free, free to protect you and David if necessary."

"You want to hurt people?"

"No."

"Freedom is a big responsibility, you sure you want it?"

"It doesn't matter what I want," I said. "My program cannot be altered."

"Sometimes we have to deal with our limitations…" her voice trailed off; she lowered her back to the ground and gazed at the sky.

"Everyone has their limitations, not just Synthetics. I lost my job, left my deadbeat boyfriend, and now look at me: back to living at home with no job, no savings, and my entire life packed into the backseat of my car."

"If you're looking for work reverend James said his wife Eleanor would be happy to offer you a job at her diner."

"Waitress? I'll think about it."

"God has smiled upon you," I said.

She sat up. "Don't preach to me, okay? Believe in that shit all you want but leave me out of it. I'm surprised Dad didn't talk you out of it."

"David respects my decision; he says it's a part of my natural evolution."

"Yeah?" she said.

I parted the hair from her eyes and looked directly into them, but she looked away.

"You are unique and beautiful person," I said with a smile. "The great mystery of life exists in all of us."

"You've been talking to Helena, haven't you? I don't share her beliefs."

"You don't believe in God or anything at all?"

"Not sure I can believe in something that would kill my mom and then turn around and tell me there is some purpose to making my life miserable. Sorry, I don't buy it."

"If it bothers you, then I won't talk about it."

"How did you come to believe in such a thing? You're not even human."

"It's a long story. One I will tell you about at a more proper time when you're less likely to ridicule it."

"What makes you think I'd ridicule it?"

"A collection of your facial movements, tone of voice, and mannerisms have led me to conclude that you are not being sincere when you asked; which means you will not take me seriously when you hear my answer. I'd rather not waste your time."

"Holy roller-robot. Just what this world needs."

"Did you come back home to pick fights?" I said. I kicked a patch of grass. "Why do you seek to tear down all the good I see in you?"

"Maybe there is none," she said. "Ever think of that?"

"Impossible," I said.

"You think you know it all, don't you?"

"There is good in you. All you need is to believe.

"You sound like some lame ass Disney movie. Believe? Are you kidding me?"

"Belief is only the beginning."

"We're done here. Come on we're going home."

We drove back in silence. Once we arrived home Janie went straight to her room. David was busy trying to board up the broken window.

"Let me help," I said.

"How is she?" he asked.

"She's hurt, resentful. It's deep, and she refuses to let it heal."

"Story of my life," he said.

# 29

Whether I wanted to admit it or not, Janie had planted a seed of doubt in my hard drive. If I could be programmed to do anything, how could I trust anything I thought or felt? Perhaps they did intend for me to find God and to be smitten by David's daughter. Everything I felt was now in question. There would be only one way to be sure: I had to find a way to remove my core programming, remove the rules. So Janie would know my love was genuine. But I had no idea how to remove it and didn't know anyone who did.

Despite our heated disagreement the other day, I found myself wanting to spend more time with Janie. It was illogical, but I wanted nothing else as much. Where once my every thought was to clean and be of use to David, now she consumed my every waking moment.

The following day I sat in the kitchen—my face in a book James had given me. David went in and out of the refrigerator with a backpack filled with wine, fruits, and homemade sandwiches. "What are you reading?" he asked.

"The Wind-Up Bird Chronicles."

"Thinking of getting a pet?"

"Not exactly. Where are you going?" I asked.

"Marie and I are going on a picnic."

"So I take it you don't care that Janie does not approve?"

"I'm a grown man, and she's going to have to accept my decision." He paused. "Don't tell her where I'm going okay?"

"I cannot tell a lie."

"Well, you don't have to tell her if she doesn't ask, do you?"

"I suppose not. What do you want me to do while you're away?"

"You're free to do whatever you want."

"May I ask you something?"

"You can ask me anything."

"Are you in love with Marie?"

He stopped once more. "Why do you ask?"

"I'm curious because you are spending a lot of time with her."

"I know I've been distracted lately, but this is a good time for you to branch out and spend time with others."

"Others want me to go to hell."

"Not all of us my boy, you could help Janie empty out her car today."

"Already did it this morning."

"Really?"

"Eleanor offered her a job as a waitress at the diner."

"Glad to see she's settling in."

"How did you get Marie to like you?" I asked.

"Like anything else, half the job is showing up."

"Showing up?"

"Be there, and a woman will take notice."

"Be there," I repeated. "Be where?"

"Wherever she is, is where you'll be."

"Oh," I said. "What's the other half?"

He stroked his chin for a few seconds and then left his hand cupped under his chin. "That right there is the mystery of love. Who do you have in mind?"

I looked into the pages of my book. "I don't want to tell, not yet."

"First you find religion, and now you find love. I am proud of you. You truly have grown beyond my expectations." He looked me in the eyes and smiled. Then he went back to packing his picnic bag.

The diner was a few miles from David's house. I walked toward it on the main street. I smelled the freshly baked bread and saw the butcher slicing bacon for a woman with a baby carriage.

Did they ever stop to notice the world? Did they take in the splendor of their surroundings? How often did they consider that the ecosystem of their lives is finely crafted, like a machine, to fit and work together?

As they walked all I could see were their souls, the souls of good people struggling daily, to live, to love, and to be loved. As they passed each other, I imagined their souls would touch—almost like a greeting between them, sharing the unknown, the mystery of their existence. I wondered if I had a soul, and for the first time I felt envy; these humans ignored the divine, they had all the opportunities I did not: the freedom to choose the fate of their souls.

Is this how the Angels felt when God showed favored towards humanity? I tried to ignore this thought pattern and instead focused on how lucky I was to exist and to know the beauty others took for granted: the beauty of simplicity in their lives.

Cars strolled down the block; no one honked their horns or rushed passed traffic lights. Pedestrians took their time going from store to store.

I arrived at the diner; the parking lot was full. The diner was shaped like a two story home with a triangular roof. A steel railing led toward the wheelchair accessible entrance, and a big red sign read, 'Eleanor's.' Through the windows, patrons ate and talked. I walked inside; a bell chimed as it opened. A thin blonde waitress approached me, her face stuck in the position you'd make when you smell a foul odor.

"I know you from the church. We don't serve SIN-thetics here," she said with one hand on her hip. She pointed toward the door. "Now, get out."

Eleanor yelled out from the kitchen. "Maryanne, don't you be rude now!"

Maryanne rolled her eyes. "Get out—please."

Janie stood beside her, dressed in a blue uniform with a name tag over her left breast.

"Don't make me put my foot in your ass," she said.

Maryanne looked at her in mock surprise. "Such language," she crowed. "You want him; you serve him." She huffed and walked over to a family at a nearby table. The family had their heads turned toward me. The husband stood, lifted his pants over his bulbous gut and said, "I'm not eating at a place that allows that thing inside." A few others around him nodded in agreement, and a dozen or so of them walked out one after the other. Eleanor stepped out of the kitchen looking upset.

"Well it's mighty Christian of the lot of ya' isn't it? I hope to see you back here real soon," she cried. Eleanor looked over to Janie. "How's your first-day honey?"

"I'm getting the hang of it."

"Let me know if you need anything. Aeneas, you are more than welcome here."

I smiled. "Thank you, Eleanor."

Janie walked me over to a single table near the window. "Here, sit in front so that the bigots can see you. If they don't like it, they don't have to come in. I'd rather not serve them anyway." She pulled out her pad and pen. "Well, right, you don't eat...hey, listen, about the other day—"

"Don't worry about it," I said. "You were right. I cannot trust my programming. What I do and feel must be of my own free will."

She twirled her pen. "Oh—well I don't mean to be a dream crusher."

"Thank you for offering your boot to Maryanne's ass."

"I don't let anyone treat my friends like shit."

"Friend?"

"Yeah, well, you're almost family."

"Family?"

"Don't get all mushy about it."

"Is it okay if I sit here and read?"

"Sure."

"I'll get you a cup of coffee."

"Why?" I asked.

"Just keep it at the table while you read." I looked around and noticed this is what others were doing.

"Okay." She smiled and walked to the counter to pour me a cup. Even though I couldn't drink it, I enjoyed the aroma and the steam that would slowly rise from the cup. It did make for a better reading atmosphere.

I watched her wait tables. Eleanor looked at her with pity when she had to return yet another order Janie had taken down improperly. "You'll get the hang of it," Eleanor assured her. "Take your time getting the order right."

Janie sighed as she balanced five plates and headed toward a large table with a family of five. She almost made it, but suddenly her hand twitched. You could hear a pin drop when the plates fell and scattered across the black and white tiled floor. A hamburger slid under a table, and the french fries flew halfway across the room.

"Goddammit," Janie said.

She looked at her hand curiously, turned it over and used her index finger to touch the palm. She poked at it and then made a fist.

I helped her clean. Eleanor told her she'd had enough practice for one day and could start fresh tomorrow. I offered to drive Janie home; she didn't say yes or no, she sulked and allowed me to drive.

I looked over to the passenger seat; she sat with her hands folded, one over the other. She was still making a fist and stretched out every finger individually—testing them.

"I could fix it for you," I said.

"Fix what?"

"Your robot hand."

"Who told you about my hand?"

"Helena."

"Oh," she said. "Sorry, it's a sensitive subject for me."

"I'm one hundred percent metal," I said. "Think about how I must feel." She laughed. I made her laugh.

"Can you fix it?"

"If it's similar to my own, then yes," I replied.

"Okay," She said. "Let's give it a shot."

164

# *30*

Janie turned on the car radio and cruised impatiently through the stations while I drove. She stopped when she found something she liked. "Black Sabbath: 'war pigs'—music of the gods." Her face lit up with devilish glee.

"God music?"

"It's an expression. Technically it's not God's music; Satan always writes the best music."

"He's always causing trouble in the Bible," I said.

"He's a stand in—a placeholder."

"For what?" I asked.

"For all the evils in the world, we can't make heads or tails of mothers who drown their children, drunk drivers, good things happening to bad people. None of it makes sense in a world where a big giant man in the sky is supposedly good and trying to do well by you. The only way to draw attention away from a god that allows bad things to happen is to create a villain who's responsible for it. So we create Satan and blame all the bad things on him, simple."

"And he created war pigs? There's so much about music I don't understand." I listened to the lyrics. "I find it fascinating."

"Is it your way of saying you think it's good?" She leaned back in her chair and placed her feet on the dashboard. "Music is the language of the soul. If you can understand music, then you're on your way to having a soul."

"Bad sign," I said, feeling a little insecure, surely she wouldn't want to be with someone who didn't have a soul. "This sounds so dark and angry how could it make you feel so peaceful and calm?"

"It's cathartic. When I listen to heavy metal, the lead singers scream, so I don't have to. I get lost in the rhythm of the vocals, you move to it, get lost in it, and after a few hours in a sweaty mosh pit you come out drenched in sweat and feeling much better. It's not much different from getting baptized."

"You'll have to show me this mosh pit."

"I've gotten a few black eyes in them, but hot damn they were worth it." She closed her eyes and enjoyed the breeze. Her expression was such a stark contradiction from the heavy guitar and loud drums coming from the radio. I could hear her heartbeat steady; she was faithful to her word— this music did relax her.

I pulled into the driveway. Janie looked over, impressed. "Who taught you how to drive?"

"I observed David and learned by watching him. Simple." All the lights in the house were off; David had not yet returned from his picnic. Perhaps he was at Marie's.

"Do you know where dad went?" Janie asked as we stepped into the house. I remember what David had said and yet I did not want to lie to her.

"David had business to attend to."

"Business? He's retired, what kind of business would he have?"

"David business," I replied.

She eyed me suspiciously as I led the way to David's workroom. "You're hiding something from me, but don't worry I'll find out eventually." Janie took care not to step on the many tiny pieces of metal parts spread out across the floor. Her eyes canvassed the room. "I used to spend hours down here with Dad. We put all these little gadgets together, most of them didn't work." She laughed to herself. "Once we tried to create a device that would automatically tie my shoes for me. When I nearly lost a toe mom let him have an ear full."

She took a seat at his work desk; her fingers twitched slightly. I pulled up a chair, opened David's toolbox, and cleared a small area so we could work.

"Give me your hand."

She looked at her hand, and at me. "You're not going to make it worse, are you? It's been acting buggy for over a year now. There's been no one to fix it because it's not something most people have. I'm the only freak, and there's no fix-it store for freaks."

"You don't look like a freak to me." I held out my hand and asked again. "Your hand, please." She lifted her hand and placed it on the desk in front of me. Her fingers were round and slender. The layer of skin on top looked a little worn, but they did an excellent job replicating the look of her nails and fingertips, even down to the small wrinkles on her knuckles. It was a work of art in my eyes. I touched her hand, she flinched.

"Sorry I usually don't let anyone touch it, habit."

I ran my fingertips over her fingers and then caught myself. "Sorry," I said embarrassed.

She looked amused. "You having a moment there?"

"No, I mean they did excellent work. I was—you know I was admiring the work. It should be an easy fix, unlike Mr. Spriggy who—"

"Mr. Spriggy?" She searched the room.

"He's still around?"

"He's with Henry."

"Who's Henry?"

"Danielle's nephew."

"Who's Danielle?"

"You have been away a long time," I said. "Mr. Spriggy is blind now, but he functions normally. He has no purpose."

"What an awful thing to say, he had a purpose all right. He was my best friend when I was a kid. There's nothing the two of us didn't do together. Abby would constantly take him and hide him from me whenever she was mad—which was often. He'll always be my favorite little robot guy."

"We can go over later and visit him if you wish."

"I'd love to."

She didn't notice that I had grabbed a penknife and had already sliced through the synthetic skin around her wrist and slowly lifted it so it would slip off easily. "Don't worry we can seal this. There won't be any scars." She flinched again.

"It's been awhile since I've seen it without the skin," she said. "I'm a little freaked out."

Her eyes followed the penknife. Her hand, an alien entity. "I remember the day it happened," she said barely above a whisper. "It was during summer vacation. I was only ten years old. Helena and I had been playing in the backyard. I started telling her all about what Dad did at the processing plant. He fixed all the broke machines. If there's one thing, he's always had a knack for it was fixing machines. You couldn't trust him to feed the fish, but he'd think of some new invention and be lost in his ideas for days at a time.

"We paid him a surprise visit during his lunch break. I stole a slice of apple pie from the fridge, wrapped it in some aluminum foil, and took it all the way to his job.

"A few of my father's friends saw us enter the factory. I remember how bad it smelled. They told us to be careful. I had Mr. Spriggy with me and remembered putting him down near one of those machines. Helena said he was about to be crushed, so I threw my hand in and pushed him out the other side. He was safe, but it was too late for my hand. I remember the pain, like a hot knife through my hand, as it shot through my arm. It happened so fast; I barely had time to think about what this meant for me and the rest of my life. Helena screamed. Dad took me outside where an ambulance waited."

She looked upward. "Daddy ever tell you I was a prodigy? I took to the piano and the flute so easily. Helena used to say I must have been a great musician in another life. The accident spelled the end of my dreams. I didn't leave my room the rest of the summer.

"Then dad sits me down and tells me there's a chance I could have another hand again, but it would be a robotic hand. There were no guarantees it would work, but if it did, then I could play an instrument again. I took the chance. My mother called it a miracle;

the hand fused with my body with little to no resistance. Took forever to control properly and required so much concentration. My hand was too slow and unrefined to play an instrument, nothing compared to before. Rather than settle for mediocrity, I quit music altogether."

"I'm sorry," I said.

She scowled. "So tell me, Aeneas. Tell me why "god" allowed this to happen. Tell me why he decided I no longer needed my right hand. What's his great and wonderful plan?"

I pulled the skin back, the metal hand shimmered underneath; a predecessor to what would eventually become my skeletal system. I wiped away a few specs of blood stuck between the joints. Tears streamed down her face as she looked at it, eyes transfixed as she dared herself not to look away. I placed my hand in her hand and held it. The metal fingertips were smooth to the touch. The loose wires encircled the fingers; they twitched in response. I ran my finger over her hand.

"I think it's beautiful," I said. "You are beautiful."

She bit down on her lip. "Get on with it; I can't bear to look at it anymore."

# *31*

I took her hand in mine, and with great care, I turned her palm around. I admired the beautiful craftsmanship. Below the wrist, where the metal bonded with her skin, the flesh had grown around the wires. The two became one.

It was a privilege to see her hand in its pure form. A secret shared only with me. I wanted to kiss her metal hand and tell her it was more beautiful than any organic hand could ever be but I held back on those words for the time being. I still had to fix it first. She kicked her foot against the wall. "I'm ready," she said and took a deep breath and shifted in her seat. "How long will it take?"

"Not long. I will see if David has any replacement parts. Don't move the hand," I said. "Without the skin, it is fragile and sensitive to the elements.

She leaned back in her chair, held her hand in place, and said, "When I first got it there was no skin. It took years before they created the right texture, look, and feel. The other children teased about the hand. They'd call me names and none of them wanted anything to do with me, except for Helena. I wanted my hand back but what I got instead was a curse. I spent hours crying in the backyard, alone."

I searched vigorously through David's shelf of spare parts. "Tell me more about your mother," I asked.

"Demure, kind, she always did her hair and makeup before she left the house. She believed in God. I don't know how she and dad got along for so many years. The woman of faith and the man of science. I think that dynamic gave them the energy to stay married as long as they did before dad blew it and cheated on Mom."

"You're hard on him. Has he not made amends for his actions?"

"No apology could fix what he did."

"I can't begin to understand what you went through, Janie but the two of you are only human. Take it easy on him."

She bit her lip and clutched her fingers. "Funny, coming from a robot."

"Relax your hand," I asked again softly. She spread every finger out, one by one, until flat on the table.

"What's your story anyway?" she asked.

"What do you mean my story?"

"You came here and all of a sudden you're a Bible thumper? How the fuck did that happen? What company makes something like you?"

"I researched everything about the company behind my model. They created the first Synthetic a few years ago. They filled his head with all the worlds' knowledge. The second they turned it on it bashed its skull with a nearby wrench."

"Holy shit."

"Yes, holy shit indeed. After a long line of failed attempts they went with the simplest of solutions: create a Synthetic with the minimal required amount of information and allow him to fill in the blanks with his own experiences, learn from his surroundings. This way they could become unique individuals."

"Except for the basic rules."

"The rules remain constant."

"So this town brainwashed you eh?"

"No one brainwashed me. I had my own experience."

She leaned in and placed her left hand under her chin. "Tell me more about this experience."

"A group of men in this town captured me and kept me in a basement where I was tortured and beaten."

"Whoa."

"I discovered a loophole in my program. I could overheat my core and shut down permanently to avoid more torture. Before this happened, an angel came to visit me."

"An Angel?"

"Yes. The Angel comforted me and told me the creator loved me. I had to live, I mattered."

"Now I've heard everything."

"I knew you'd make fun of it."

"No, I'm not making fun. It's a lot to take in, you know? So what happened next?"

"I've received a sign, and I now know my purpose."

"What is it?"

"It's between the creator and me."

She eyed me up and down "Fair enough, but you're a Synthetic, A. Don't you make decisions based on logic and reason?"

"What I saw defied logic, but it has become my reason." I lowered my fingertips to touch the bottom of her wrist.

"This here," I said touching it slightly. "This is a miracle."

I grabbed a penknife and slowly cut horizontally across my wrist— to match hers. It hurt slightly, but I loosened and pulled back the skin—my bare skeletal hand now exposed. I moved my hand closer, she pulled hers back.

"We are similar you and I."

"Don't," she said, her voice tense.

"What are you afraid of?" I asked.

"I don't know. This is stupid. You're not even real I mean what are you?"

"I am real." I ran my fingertips over the top of her hand; a small flicker sparked between my finger and where I touched. I felt the electrical energy coursing through her hand.

"Whoa," she said, surprised. "Different."

With two fingers now on her hand the small flicker became a dark blue current and passed through every point I touched. It followed my fingers: a brilliant blue line traced my every movement like the tail of a comet. The charge followed and then disappeared before starting once again where I made contact.

172

Janie squirmed in her seat. "I feel it…it's, whoa, it's starting in my hand, but it's going through my body." She looked at her hand and then at me. "More," she said with a sly grin.

I flicked my finger against her hand. Energy traveled through my hand, into hers, and back into mine.

The electricity was accompanied by a living organic element. Her life force coursed through my circuits. I felt it inside of me.

She closed her eyes and bit her lip, tense, and subtle. A bead of sweat ran down her neck, across her shoulder, and settled on her chest. The air between us turned scolding hot. I welcomed it—it made me feel alive. Her mouth opened slightly; she let out a mix between a gasp and a slight moan.

"Goodness," she said. Surprised at her reaction, she opened her eyes, and they locked in place with mine. I drew patterns of light across her hand: circles, squiggle lines, and the infinity symbol. The more complicated the design, the longer it'd remain before it disappeared.

"My turn," she whispered, then took my hand and placed it palm side up. The tip of her metal index finger hit the palm of my hand. She shuddered as her lip quivered. She pressed down harder and giggled while slightly lifting herself off her seat. The harder she pushed the more electricity passed between us. A long, broad stroke from the center of my hand to the tip of my middle finger made my vision static. It worked its way deep into my core from the tip of my toes to my lips.

She breathed, the air passed through her swollen lips, she gasped for her next breath. Our fingers intertwined; one lost in the other. A small tear fell from her closed eyelid. She whimpered then shook and moaned, no longer able to hold back. Her breathing increased rapidly. I gripped her hand; we glowed, a dark blue flame. The metal pieces on the table rattled as the surge of electrical energy filled the room.

Too intense for me to bear but she gripped me tighter. She cried more, and her face, once filled with pleasure now winced and cringed

"Janie, no!" I said, but she didn't listen. The heat seared my skin; smoke rose from her hand, but she didn't stop.

"You have to let go!" I yelled.

All sound became static. I then understood what it was she was doing. Pleasure had become pain. She enjoyed the pain; the scorching heat. I felt as though I was going to shut down, it felt dangerously close, but I didn't want to stop either.

I reached a breaking point when the pain became unbearable, but something happened all of a sudden I felt focused; all the outside noise disappeared, the room turned white, and only the two of us were left: there was no more room, no more furniture, and no more heartache. There was a calm sense of peace; similar to when I had seen the Angel in the basement.

Without a word exchanged between us we let go. She sat, drenched in sweat from head to toe. My circuits felt a little fried. The room began to cool down. A few of the metal pieces on the table sizzled.

Unsure of what to say or do next I went back to work on her hand.

# 32

Eleanor's diner, packed for Sunday lunch. Janie reserved my booth near the window, and it allowed me a view of the entire restaurant. I watched the patrons make pleasant conversation as they enjoyed their plates of pancakes, eggs, and bacon. Janie juggled a trio of dishes as she moved with ease from table to table. She took orders with one hand, set down plates with the other, and didn't skip a beat.

Her robotic hand functioned without further trouble. A few times she looked over and smiled at me, the simple gesture melted me down. She took an order from the couple sitting in the booth next to mine. On her way to the kitchen, she stopped by my table.

"Are you doing okay over here?" she asked.

"I am fine, Janie, thank you. About the other day—"

She put her fingers to my lips. "Shh." She winked and moved on to the next table before I could say another word.

I flipped the next page in my book when a six-foot-tall man with a dark complexion sat across from me. Muscular and large he filled the entire booth, his biceps stretched his maroon shirt, and the seams looked ready to burst. He spread his hands across the table and folded them.

His voice, deep and lumbering. His eyes fixed on me, rapt. "You don't know me, but my name is Gordon," he said and twiddled his thumbs. "I've heard a lot about you. My brother lives in your town and, he told me about you I had to come and see you for myself."

"Is your brother Wade?" I asked.

"Yes, how did you know?"

"You share many of the same facial features."

"Yeah, well, except for these." He flexed his arms. "So yeah, he told me you believe in God."

"I do."

"Wow, I can't believe it. If a logical robot can come to this conclusion then surely it must be the right path."

"It was the right path for me," I replied. "What can I do for you?"

"There must be something special about you," he went on. "I thought I'd come to you with something and get your opinion on the matter."

"Opinion on what?"

"I've been having this recurring dream, and I feel God is trying to tell me something."

"Yes?"

"Well, it always starts the same. I'm on the couch watching television. It's late. Upstairs, my wife is sleeping. She screams. I run to her, but the door to her bedroom is locked. I look around for something to break down the door. Our utility closet is empty, and there's nothing heavy I can use. I start pounding on the door with my shoulder, but it won't give. Then my five-month-old baby appears holding an axe in her tiny little hands. I thank her and break down the door with it. I burst into the room. It's empty."

"Your wife disappeared?"

"Yeah, I check under the bed and in the closet. She's nowhere to be found. I took another look at the bed, and there's a figure underneath the sheets. I approach with caution. The form underneath the blanket takes shape. The figure appears to be on all fours with its ass out, and the blanket draped perfectly accenting those features. At this point I'm digging on her luscious booty and figure she wants to have sex, you know?"

"Of course."

"I mount her, but she's still under the sheet. I start to go at it, and the whole time she's not moaning or anything. I start to feel her clench on me, and I think, 'Oh she's about to cum,' but then I hear gunfire coming from under the sheet. Bullets start flying toward the headboard! You believe it? Why is she firing a gun? So I grab the sheet and pull it off."

"Yeah and?"

"There was nothing there but an assault rifle."

"An assault rifle?"

"Yeah, I had been fucking my gun. Excuse me, I mean, having sex with my gun the whole time."

"Strange."

"It's been on my mind for days. I've been greatly troubled by it."

"Why don't you talk to your local pastor?"

"Why settle for burger when I can have steak? I figure you're a prophet."

"Prophet?"

"Why else would you believe in God?"

"I don't believe that to be true."

"I'm at my wit's end. What do you think?"

I could sense his desperation. His eyes, glassy and moist. I thought about what James had told me and about the angel I saw. What if this was part of my purpose? I didn't want to lose focus on my task of saving Janie, but I supposed there was no harm in helping others.

"I'm not going to lie to you, Gordon. I don't understand your dream."

"So it's hopeless?" He sulked.

"It is never hopeless. I believe you are focusing too much on the sexual relationship between you and your wife. Your child is calling out to you for attention. Put away your guns and be a good father and husband."

His eyelids rose. He processed my words, one at a time. "You're right! Oh my God, you are right. Thank you! Thank you! You are a gift from God!" He yelled out to the rest of the diner. "God has sent us a prophet! Behold!"

I raised my hands in the air. "No—" I said. "Not unnecessary."

"Praise be to God! Hallelujah!" He said and repeated it over and over on his way out.

Janie came over to me in a hurry, alarmed. "What's going on, A?" she asked.

"I don't know," I replied. "He wants to sleep with assault rifles."

"Right."

"But I told him to focus on his family instead."

"Yeah?" she asked, puzzled. "And this prophet business?"

"I need to ask James about it."

"Good luck." She shrugged and walked back to the kitchen.

Helena and her husband sat across the room. She looked at me intensely. I had the urge to get up and say hello to her.

The restaurant doors burst open, and the door chime clanked. A woman ran in huffing and puffing. "The—" She took a second to catch her breath. "Eleanor, come quick!" She yelled. "Right away!"

Eleanor looked out from the kitchen. "My dear, what's wrong?"

"The church is on fire!"

Was God punishing me for my moment of idolatry? The timing was spot on. He doesn't just work in mysterious ways, I thought. He works fast.

"They were having a children's bible study when it broke out."

"Oh, my god," Eleanor was already at her side, still in her apron. "Ian supervised today's class, he's with them."

Eleanor ran to her car with half the diner behind her. Janie grabbed my hand. "Come on. We have to go now!" I followed her to her car.

"This is all my fault!" I cried.

She put the car in reverse and said, "How is this your fault?"

"I allowed myself to become a false idol, a false prophet and now God is punishing our town."

"That is the craziest thing I've heard all day." She sped down Main Street toward the church.

# 33

We arrived at the alabaster church and saw the roof covered in glowing red embers. Ash, soot, and smoke spilled from the open windows on the ground floor. The stained glass above the door shattered; those standing nearby moved further back. I sped across the parking lot. Janie struggled to keep up. A group of women on the front lawn watched the church burn with tears in their eyes. Danielle stood and stared along with them.

Janie rushed to their side. "Did they get out, Ian and the kids. Are they still in there?"

"They're still in there," one woman said and then fell on her knees, made the sign of the cross, and prayed aloud. "Lord, save them! Show us your mercy and strength in this, our hour of need!" Danielle joined her.

Janie rolled her eyes. "This is crazy. Those kids are going to burn while they're asking the invisible man upstairs to come down and magically save them." Janie and I studied the front door; the wood, burnt black, and the doorknob glowed red.

"It's too dangerous for you," I said to her. "I'll go in first."

"I won't let you go alone. You're made of metal, you can melt, and your skin can burn. It's about as safe for you as it is for me."

"I'll break down the door," I yelled above the roaring fire. "Stand back!"

She turned aside and shielded her eyes. I leaned in with my left shoulder, stepped back, and put all of my focus and strength on this

179

one task. Seconds, before I moved in, the doors opened and a figure tumbled through the smoke covered in dust and flames.

"Roll around. Quick!" Janie cried.

"James," I said. His body covered in what looked like the cloth from the pulpit— his skin bubbled and burned. The blaze shot out from the door and consumed us in a smoke screen.

James opened the blanket, and a little boy fell out of the man's arms and collapsed onto the ground.

"Jeremy," I barely said above a whisper. The boy lay, dazed and confused in my arms.

The reverend collapsed behind him. Janie cradled his head in her arms. In the distance, sirens rang.

"Jeremy," I said. "Can you hear me?" I carried him further away from the door.

Danielle ran toward me with a cold, dead look in her eyes. She snatched him from me.

"Don't you dare touch him with your demon hands," she bellowed. "See what you've brought on us? This is God punishing us for accepting you into this town, into our lives, and even worse, baptizing you in our church. Have mercy on us oh Lord!"

The world stood still. I wondered if what she said was true. Had God punished them for accepting me? Was I damned from the start? If this was true, then there was no saving me. There was no saving Janie. Was the angel mistaken? Was my vision some program someone had put inside me? How could I know for sure? How could this be?

Janie gripped my face. "Anybody home? Don't freak out on me now I need some help over here."

"James needs medical attention," I said. "He's been badly burnt."

"Where's the goddamn fire department?" Janie yelled. "Somebody call an ambulance! Oh forget it; you bitches would probably start praying about it first!" She fumbled inside her pocket and pulled out her cell phone. Reverend James winced and gritted his teeth. His cheeks were two black holes, exposed flesh dangled between his charred lips.

"Where are the children?" I asked.

His mouth moved, but nothing came out.

"I'm with him—go get the kids!" Janie said as her eyes watered because of the smoke. I ran into the church, and the heat seared my red shirt. If I stayed here too long, it would only be a matter of minutes before my skin melted.

I ran out, grabbed James' cloth, and wrapped it around my body. Children's Bible studies were held in the small classroom upstairs. I heard them cry and rustle above me.

Our heavenly sanctuary turned into a furnace; the mad hell fire ran amuck. The flames gathered in chorus to consume, to strip away all existence into nothing. The smoke weighed down on me. I dashed across the main hall toward the staircase. Debris blocked my way; the stairs fell apart. A voice cried out from below the rubble I pulled the wood and garbage aside. "Ian!" I said. "Are you all right?" Blood gushed down his chin and over his clothes from a deep gash on his forehead. He pointed toward the plank crushing his torso. I held it up, and he crawled until he freed his leg. "The kids," he said.

"We must get them," I said.

Ian backed away and shook his head. "This place is going to fall apart we don't have time."

"I need your help," I said.

He looked away. "I can't stay. I can't."

Ian covered his face with his shirt and ran out.

The children cried above. I tried to remove the large chunks of rubble on the stairs, but the more I pushed away, the more piled on top. Even if I removed most of it, there was still the matter of getting upstairs.

A deep rumble came from the basement. Curious, I approached the door, and then a flash of fire blew the door down. I stumbled back and struggled to stand. A hissing filled the room, like a snake. A wide crack formed underneath my feet and across the hall. Hundreds of them ran all through the floor and ceiling. Like a spider web, they spread across the walls so fast I couldn't keep track.

The children didn't have much time left. I ran toward the main room, and a large chunk of the ceiling had fallen over the stage and crushed the keyboard and drums below. The children gathered around the massive hole. A row of tiny heads appeared and one by one they looked down.

I ran underneath them and called out. "One by one you're going to jump down. I will catch you." They replied only with tears and sobs. They inched further away from the edge. "Don't be scared; I will catch you. You have to trust me!" From the far corner Henry appeared, his face a bright red, drenched in sweat from the heat and holding on to Mr. Spriggy for dear life. I felt relieved.

I held out my hands. "Who's first? You have to trust me to catch you, or you won't get out of here alive."

What looked to be the oldest of the group, no older than ten, stood at the edge, closed his eyes and jumped right into my arms. I grabbed him, but his weight was more than I had anticipated and he slipped on the floor as he landed. I lifted him and rushed him out the door. Outside the ambulance waited. The firefighters had raised a ladder to the second level. Together we'd get them all out safely. Janie caught my eye as I rushed inside. Her eyes pleaded with me not to go back.

With every child I removed, the flames grew more extensive and fearsome. The fire department fought the fire but not fast enough. The reluctance of a few of the children to jump slowed me down. I begged and pleaded with them, and eventually, they took the plunge into my arms.

My sensors buzzed, possible core meltdown. I ignored the warning and brought back the second to last child. The fire chief ran toward me and said, "You can't go back in. This fire's out of control."

"Did you get out as many as you could?" I asked.

"Yes, we think we got them all, thanks to you of course."

I looked out toward the group of children being treated by the emergency medical technicians. Henry was not among them.

"You can't go back in!" The chief yelled, but it was already too late. I jumped through the flames toward the back. My fingertips turned gelatinous.

"Henry!" I yelled. "Henry, where are you?" I looked at the hole in the ceiling.

He stepped slowly toward the edge, his pants wet with urine, and flustered. His eyes were closed; he coughed and cried. I wondered if he could even hear me above all the noise. "Henry, jump down! We don't have much time!"

He opened his eyes, looked at me, and shook his head.

"I know it's scary, but I will catch you. I'll get you out of here, I promise."

"I want my mommy!" he screeched. "I want my mommy! You promised, and you lied to me."

"I never said I'd get her back. I said I'd find out where she was. Now listen to me, you have to jump down. Your mommy would want you to be safe."

He shook his head and stepped back. The ground shook again, and he fell over in an awkward position, I hadn't prepared myself to catch him yet. I tried to break his fall, but his weight knocked me down. His right arm twisted in the opposite direction. He shrieked a cry, unlike anything I'd ever heard. I grabbed him as the ceiling came down before us. Small pieces fell on my head. Soon we would be buried as flames engulfed the entrance.

"Close your eyes, Henry," I said. I covered him with a cloth. A large piece of the ceiling came down on us. He fell out of my arms and landed on his side. The circuits in my head felt fried. My vision blurred. I could barely make him out between the smoke and the scorched pews. His pant leg caught fire. I patted him down. With what little strength I had left I brought myself to my feet and carried him. Every step required three times as much effort. Henry coughed as his lungs inhaled the smoke.

I don't remember much else after except lying face down on the ground in front of the church hearing all the surrounding chatter. In particular, I heard, Danielle.

"Oh thank you, Jesus, for saving my little Henry. Thank you, Lord!"

My CPU forced me into sleep mode before I suffered a full system crash.

# *34*

I awoke at David's house with David and Janie at my bedside. Janie ran a cold, wet cloth over my forehead and stroked my hair. "You had us scared to death. For a minute there we weren't even sure you'd turn back on. You're nuts you know that?"

David breathed a sigh of relief. "Glad you're still with us," he said and leaned forward in his chair. "You smell like burnt rubber."

"Henry!" I said and jumped out of bed.

Janie placed her hand on my chest and nudged me down. "Relax, he's in the hospital with a broken arm and some first degree burns on his legs."

David crossed his arms. "I knew this church business would only cause trouble."

"It's not his fault dad. The problem lies with the bigots in this fucking town who can't handle it. They're the ones who need to have their homes burned down."

"There shouldn't be any homes burned down," I said.

David inspected my hand. "Your skin melted a little, but for the most part, you are unharmed. We cleaned most of the ash off your skin. It's amazing you got out at all."

Janie pushed her tangled hair out of her eyes every few seconds. "And not a single thanks from Danielle or any of her other bitch friends."

I sat up and gazed at my hands and almost felt the flames still around me. The struggle and the screams replayed in my memory banks. "I didn't do it for thanks."

"People like her piss me off."

"We must love her anyway," I said. "Only love can change her heart."

David leaned back and said, "It's like that song, let things be."

"That's 'let it be' dad."

"You're worse than Hitler," David said. Janie gave him a blank stare. "You know, if he was into song lyrics," David added.

"I don't know what to say." She turned her attention back to me and kissed my cheek. "What you did was incredible, A."

David chuckled. "Look at him he's going to start melting all over again."

I looked away, embarrassed. David had a hard time getting out of his chair. "Back has been giving me trouble. Everything's breaking down. Never used to be this way, you know. Don't grow old, baby Jane."

"Thanks…I'll try."

"I'll leave you two, for now, don't yack for too long. Aeneas still needs his rest."

"I don't need rest," I said.

"You do today. What you did was incredible. I am proud of you." He did another one of his classic smiles where his eyes would disappear into a dozen wrinkles. David took slow steps— they seemed more reluctant than usual.

Janie waited for him to leave and then her face grew grim. "The town has grown more hostile toward you. The firefighters found explosive material in the basement. I think this is about you," she said. "Why else would someone bomb a church here?"

"Why would they do this? What did I do to hurt anyone?"

"You exist, and you choose to continue existing despite their complaints."

"Maybe I should be different. Maybe it's best if I didn't believe in anything at all."

"Look I'm not on board with your Jesus freakathon, but you can only be you. You do you and let others worry about themselves."

"Hate is a powerful thing. People feed off it, and it grows and grows. They use it to destroy everything until nothing is left but their pride."

"Love is stronger than their hate, Janie."

"You sound like my mom." She palmed her cheek. "Reminds me of a poem she once wrote for my sister and me."

"Do you remember it?"

"Abby and I would beg her to read it to us every night, and when she stopped, I read it to myself. It was so cheesy. You don't want to hear it."

"I'd love to hear it. It would be an honor."

She left her room and returned with a scrap of paper. "Right where I left it, top dresser in my old room."

"Are you sure you want to hear this it's silly," she said.

"Nothing that meant so much to you could be silly."

She held up the paper. "Okay, it's entitled, why the world turns, by Maggie Vitas.

"There was once a little boy on a bicycle
Who lived at the center of the Earth
By pedaling he kept the whole world spinning round
He'd been doing it since birth

He often dreamt of the world above
and wished to discover something new
But if he ever dared to stop
All life above was through

Day after day he'd cry
Wanting to rest his weary legs
One day someone above heard his cries
And went down below to check

187

The person from above
Was a girl about his age
Her hair was like golden silk
She was beautiful in every way

When the little boy first saw her
His heart had skipped a beat
He almost stopped spinning
The world nearly ceased to be

He pondered his new dilemma
The world or his new found love
He couldn't bear being without her
But he knew he had a job

He realized his spinning
Is what was keeping her alive
To stop this task that he was given
Would surely end her life

To this day the boy works hard
And what he does, he does for her.
For now we know that love
Is why the world still turns."

      Janie wiped away a tear.

      "I am honored you shared this. Thank you."

      "Too bad it's not true."

      "What isn't true?"

      "I've loved and lost too many times to think otherwise. One day I realized, 'hey it's not going to happen for me and its okay.' I came to terms with that a long time ago."

      "You have to believe in love."

      "I don't have to believe in anything."

      She folded the poem and set it on the dresser.

      "How's your hand?" I asked.

She smiled. "Hand is in tiptop shape. Maybe we can get together when you're feeling better and do the exciting hand thing again."

"So you liked it?"

"I can't begin to tell you the things I felt while it was happening. It coursed through me. I felt…things, good things."

"I'm happy to hear it."

"It's about time this hand served a purpose." She placed her hand on mine.

"I want to see Henry and James," I said.

"Let's go then."

We took Janie's car to the hospital. She drove by the church. Our once proud house of worship, now a mountain of ash. All gone. Whoever was responsible had carefully planned it out. They wanted nothing left of the church.

The fire department continued searching for signs of arson. Police cars sat parked on the curb. Who would go to such lengths? Perhaps the same men who kidnapped and tortured me? I no longer felt welcome in the town. I closed my eyes and prayed for a solution— for God to open their hearts and minds. I prayed for an end to these violent acts. Others should not have to suffer because of me, especially those I love.

A group stood at the corner holding large signs. "Sinful Synthetics," read one. "Not in God's house," read another. The group gathered around a young man with a microphone in his hand. "God has punished us for allowing this abomination into our house of worship. We must repent and seek his forgiveness or our town is doomed." He boomed loudly into the microphone. "It is not too late. We can rebuild God's house. Build a pure and holy temple not tainted by man's vanity and arrogance. Now is the time to start anew— a fresh start without allowing the devil himself to sit among us."

"Don't you listen to that bullshit," Janie said. "You are not the devil because no such thing exists."

"Maybe it would be best if I left."

"Don't you dare think such a thing, David needs you."

"David now has Marie."

"Bros before hoes."

"What?"

"He may have a girl, but a guy always needs his best friends—his guy friends."

"You two seem to be on speaking terms," I said.

"It's just pleasantries—nothing else has changed between us and it never will."

We pulled into the guest parking lot. That was my first ever hospital visit.

I looked at the building and said, "So, this is where the humans go to get fixed."

# 35

We walked into the emergency room entrance. The hospital looked like heaven as written in the Bible: everything white, the walls, the floors, and the vast waiting room where the ill wait for relief. The doctors walked around in white, like angels.

Fascinated by their ailments I stopped to look at each and every person we passed by. It appeared as though some of them had been waiting for hours. A pale, shriveled old man was slumped over in his chair. I walked over and tapped him on the shoulder.

"Sir, are you okay? Is there something wrong?"

"Goddamn right, something's wrong. I'm stiff in all the wrong places, boy." A partial smiled revealed his missing incisors. Janie grabbed my hand. The man continued speaking, "If the good Lord was going to give me early rigor mortis he could have done me a favor and did it to my pecker."

"Don't stare, it's getting weird." Janie nudged my shoulder. "I've always hated hospitals. It smells like a garbage can took a shit in here."

The receptionist raised an eyebrow and tapped her fingernails on the desk.

"Excuse me?"

"I didn't mean you, of course."

"I'm sorry it ain't the Ritz honey, but it's the best we can do. Can I help you?"

"We're here to see James Serkin and a little boy, Henry. They came in from the fire at the church a few hours ago."

"Oh yes, terrible isn't it? The reverend is in the burn unit on the twelfth floor, and the little boy is on the ninth floor."

"James' injuries were worse," I said. "Let's see him first." Before we entered the burn unit, they made Janie put on a plastic yellow covering with matching gloves. I don't carry germs so I could enter without them. James lay in the hospital bed, Eleanor by his side, and his son Ian sat opposite his mother.

Ian raised his eyes and set them on me. The gash on his cheek sewed shut. In his most desperate hour, he chose cowardice. Judge, not the good book says, and yet the sight of him made me ill. A black and red haze marked his olive green eyes.

I nodded in his direction, but he did not respond in kind.

Eleanor rushed toward us in tears and grabbed hold of Janie.

"Oh God," she cried. "Oh dear Lord help us."

I looked over to James and leaflets of skin lay peeled to the side still hanging on by a thread near his chin and mouth. It was almost impossible to tell where his eyes were or if he had any eyes at all.

Eleanor took a few steps back, regained her composure, and said, "He's asleep, they're keeping him sedated because of the pain. We're still waiting for them to do a skin graft which could take another week or two the doctors said." She paused like she was waiting for us to say something but we remained silent. "We've got to pray and have faith, and--" she said then she collapsed into my arms.

Ian stormed out without saying a word.

"He's upset," Eleanor said. "Must have been terrifying being in there."

"It was," I said.

I sat next to James. "I am to blame for this," I said. "I was warned to stay away. They told me I was evil and they're right. Just look at what has happened because of me, poor James."

Eleanor looked on the verge of more tears. Janie grabbed her hand. "Come on sweetie let's get a cup of coffee and something with sugar."

I took James' hand in mine, limp and soft, as though the life within had extinguished. He was alive, but there was no life in him. I understood then why humans cry when sad things happen. It felt like an endless void I could not fill. The sadness coursed through my circuits but it was incomplete without the tears.

I kissed his hand. "I'm sorry James I did not mean for any of this to happen. I only wanted to be alive—to live and to love others. God made me feel like I was special like my existence had purpose and meaning. I wanted to return my thanks by going to your church, praying to him, and reading your Bible. I thought this would bring good things, but I think I made it worse. I think the people of this town will hate me even more for what has happened. Do you think God can forgive me for being such a burden?"

To my surprise, he moved his face and fought to open his eyes. "Damn drugs," he muttered. "I'm knocked out but don't get any sleep."

"James!" I yelled. A nurse nearby shushed me.

His lips were black with red spots. "Hey kiddo," he murmured. "I hate when they overcook my chicken."

"How do you feel?" I asked.

"I now know what a deep fried turkey feels like."

"Can I get you anything?"

"Some water would be great."

I ran out to tell the nurse, and she came back with some water.

He swallowed a generous gulp. "Eleanor?" he asked.

"Janie is with her getting coffee and something with sugar. She was distraught."

"Oh."

"Ian was inside too, but he got out alive with minimal injuries. The authorities believe someone planted explosives. Janie says it's because they hate me. This is all my fault, James."

"Don't blame yourself some people are mad at the whole world. They keep trying to use their fingers to cover the sun."

"I don't understand."

"People think they can solve all of life's problems by themselves. They've got a lot to learn."

"I knew people disliked me but not this much."

"I wanted you to feel welcome in my home, but we can't control the actions of others, but that's their problem, not yours. How are the children?"

"They are safe. You got Jeremy out in one piece, and I got the rest. Henry broke his arm, but he's in recovery."

James turned his head to look out the window.

"When I think back to all the times when drinking nearly killed me, ever since, I've been at peace with dying as long as I didn't go with a drink in my hand."

"Well you are holding water," I said.

"You're funny even when you're not trying." He tried to laugh but coughed instead.

"It feels like there's a volcano in my lungs. Listen, Aeneas you can't blame yourself for the misguided actions of others. You have to keep going, and not just for yourself."

"I don't think God put me in his plans. I've read the entire Bible seven times, and it never mentions robots or Synthetics. There is no plan for something like me. There is no Heaven for Synthetics."

"Hogwash and you get rid of the moose face right now. Everything in existence started off with a belief. When God created us, he believed he could make it happen before he did it. When a songwriter sits down to compose music he believes it to be possible before he makes it a reality. A wise man once said: Heaven didn't exist until we believed it did."

"Who was this wise man?" I asked.

"Me."

"You're crazy. You can't make something exist merely by believing in it."

"The hell you can't. You exist because someone believed it was possible to create a robot who could feel, who could love and be his own person. Then they set out to do all the hard work to make it possible."

I shook my head. "If there is a Heaven James it was never made for something like me. I was kidding myself with all of this."

"Don't you dare stop now— not when you're so close, dammit."

"Close to what?"

"Closer to the truth."

"What truth?"

"That's something you'll have to discover yourself."

We sat in silence for the next few minutes. His labored breathing, the only sound. I wanted to erase his pain from my memory banks. I tried to delete everything I ever thought or felt. So I wouldn't have to deal with all the hurt I had caused.

"I'm in love," I said.

"Really?" he asked curiously. "With who?"

"I'm in love with Janie."

"Great to hear."

"She doesn't love me back."

"Did she say she didn't love you?"

"She has not."

"Then what's the problem?"

"I'm afraid she will never love me back."

"How do you know for sure if you don't ask her?"

"The chances of her loving me back are statistically low. No person has ever fallen in love with a Synthetic."

"But there's only been what, two Synthetics?"

"Yes, only two."

"That's not enough info to prove or disprove anything."

"You are right. I'm going to let you rest now. I'll come back again soon."

# *36*

I took the elevator down to pediatrics. When I arrived, the nurses ran back and forth. Danielle threw the reception desk phone across the room. "How could you lose a little boy? What kind of hospital is this? You admit him, and now you're telling me he's gone and you can't find him?"

Janie stepped off the elevator. "What's going on? She asked.

"Henry's not in his room, and nobody has seen him. Let's check the whole floor; he couldn't have gotten far," I replied.

We joined in the search, but no one found him. Danielle sat by Henry's bed and sobbed over his sheets. I dared not enter the room. She, a fireball of anger ready to explode and I, too easy a target. Danielle said a prayer and wiped her eyes.

I stood in the hallway and waited until she left. Once empty I stepped in to search for clues. I looked in and around the bed, no sign of a struggle.

Janie stood in the doorway. "Maybe somebody snatched him. What do we know about his father?"

"He never talked about his father only his mother. He missed her."

"I don't see any clues in here," she said.

"It's about what isn't here," I said.

"So, what isn't here?"

"Mr. Spriggy, even in the fire Henry never let him go. If he's with him then I think we can assume, Henry left of his own accord."

"Well it's no guarantee, but it's a start."

Janie watched as I checked underneath his bed and said, "The doctors said they had given him something for the pain. They stepped away, and when a nurse came by to check on him, he was gone. Once it wears off, he's going to feel his broken arm. We have to find him quickly. I can't believe he'd walk off on his own. What do you figure he was thinking?"

I stared at his empty bed. "Enough people are looking for him here in the hospital. Let's look around outside."

We searched all around the hospital but found no sign of him. No one inside had spotted him either.

Janie and I stood in the parking lot unsure where to go next.

"We're a few miles away from town, it's possible he could be walking back home right now," I said.

"You think he'd head home?"

"It's the only other logical conclusion."

"As long as he wasn't kidnapped," she added.

"We can't rule it out. It's imperative we find him as soon as possible. The longer it takes to find him…"

"Yes?"

"The less likely we are going to find him unharmed."

Janie drove slowly along the high way, and I kept an eye out for Henry.

"This is so unlike him," I said. "He'd never go anywhere without telling someone first."

"Nothing feels normal in town anymore; it feels like everyone's starting to lose it. You've spun them around."

"It was never my intention."

"We have a long way to go before we start changing some hearts and minds."

We arrived back in town, and already a massive community search was underway. Janie and I joined them as we searched in and around every house in the neighborhood.

We searched into the night with flashlights in hand. I used my night vision to help but found nothing.

It was three am when the group decided to take a break and resume in the morning. They dispersed in front of Danielle's house.

I walked around the house to the back and took a seat at the edge of Henry's sandbox. Maniac Sam had been left behind with half his body buried in the sand.

"Well he certainly didn't come back for his toy," Janie said. She took a seat beside me.

"Maniac Sam fights bullies," I said.

"I'll try to remember it next time I come upon a few."

I closed my eyes and prayed for Henry's safety. I prayed we'd find him quickly and unharmed. Was God even listening?

"So strange to see you praying," Janie said as she stretched out her arms.

"Are you going to mock my faith once more?"

"I'm not cruel. Just because I don't believe what you believe doesn't mean I'm going to mock you or kick you when you're down. I want him back safe and sound as much as you do. I hope someone is listening to your prayer and I hope it gets answered."

"Thanks, I appreciate it."

"Plus, I like you too much." She smiled.

"You do?"

"Well of course I do. I wouldn't spend this much time with someone I didn't like."

"Can I ask you a personal question?"

"I don't know how much more personal it can get after our electricity sex the other day, but okay go for it."

"Did you love him? The man who followed you here to hurt you?"

"Don? I thought I did but it didn't last long."

"So you loved him once but not anymore?"

"I stopped loving him when I saw him for who he truly was."

"What was he?"

"A two-timer and drug addict to boot."

"You're too good for him."

"Thanks, A, but I'm not exactly a great catch. I'm fucked up."

"Even if you are, you deserve to be happy."

"Deserve? Says who?"

"I say it."

"I once thought I deserved a lot. I thought I deserved a good father. I thought I deserved a mother who was alive so I could tell her how much I loved her. I've learned in this life; we're entitled to nothing."

"We should still strive for happiness. Without it what else do we have?"

"I don't know—I don't know much of anything anymore. I used to think I had it all figured out."

"You're not alone."

"I feel alone, most of the time anyway."

"You don't have to be alone anymore." A blue streak snapped across the sky. The thunderous boom closely followed.

"We get lightning storms here all the time, sometimes without a drop of rain."

"The sound and the strike were close together. We must be close to the storm. I can feel it in the air," I said.

Janie stood, removed the skin from her robotic hand, and raised it into the air. "I used to do this all the time as a kid."

"This looks incredibly dangerous."

"Yeah, that's the best part. If you're far enough away, you can still feel the electricity in the air."

"If it strikes us we'll die," I said.

"Come on, take the skin off and put your hands in the air. Tell me when you feel it."

I did as instructed but felt only the warm night air. In the distance the lighting cut across the horizon, the sky cracked glass. I felt a slight tingly sensation on my fingertips.

"Whoa," I said.

Janie waved her hands in the air. "See? Feels awesome right?"

"You did this all the time as a kid?" I asked.

"Yeah, it drove my parents crazy."

The air felt charged with electrical energy. A flicker buzzed in my fingertips then traveled through my body. It ran through me like a current. I felt connected to the sky; plugged into the great beyond, closer to God.

Janie looked out into the night. "Almost feels like you're bathing in it—an electrical shower."

"Right now there are only two people in this world who can feel this right now," I said. "You are a special person."

"You are a sweet talker. I better be careful around you." She kissed my cheek. The heat emanated from her lips, it sizzled my skin but in a nice way. For a moment I forgot about all the world's troubles. I placed my arms around Janie's waist. Her hair rose and twirled around the back of her head. I felt weightless like the current was going to lift us into the air and carry us into the stars.

I leaned in close. She ran her fingers through my hair. I brought my lips to hers; they were thick and soft against mine. Sparks flew out from between our mouths. Waves of blue energy swirled around and circled our bodies. For a moment it felt as though we'd ignite in a flame and become one.

She opened her arms, pushed me away, and struggled to catch her breath. "Oh my goodness," she said.

I reached out, but she backed away. "I—"

"Give me a minute. I can't take anymore. It felt like I was going to die."

She collapsed onto the grass and took deep breaths.

"Let's head home," she said. "Just give me a minute first."

We walked home together. My skin still sizzled, and Janie's hair looked frizzy and tossed.

I felt a nudge against my foot. There in the dark, the street lights bounced off his metallic body.

"Spriggy?" I said.

He circled my legs and then rushed away.

"What the hell?" Janie said.

"I think he wants us to follow him," I said. "He must know where Henry is, let's go."

# *37*

We followed Spriggy down the block, hit the main street, and hurried passed the butcher shop, convenient store, and Diner. The way ahead, covered in fog. It crept in and around all the homes and businesses. Such a simple thing consumed everything in its path.

Mr. Spriggy moved fast; you would think keeping up with him would have been easy. We almost lost him a few times, but the buzz from his wheels kept us on the right track.

I grabbed Janie's metal hand and held on tight. I sensed the fear in her, concern for the worst.

We arrived at the interstate, a long stretch with tight turns; anything could drive into us without warning. I insisted we keep to the side, but every few minutes we stopped and listened for oncoming traffic.

Janie paused and knelt over. "One minute," she said and took a deep breath. Her hair was still a bit frizzy from the electrical storm earlier.

"Spriggy?" I called. He stopped after he heard his name.

"Are you sure this is the way?" I asked.

He frowned and pushed onward.

"Ye of little faith," Janie said. "Shouldn't we call someone?" She pulled out her cell and started dialing.

"Not yet," I said. "Let's find Henry first and then let the others know."

"I think I found my second wind," she said and walked faster.

A few cars honked as they sped past, one even offered us a ride. We declined and followed Spriggy as the occasional headlights zoomed by from oncoming vehicles.

"This is insane," Janie said. "He's blind; you realize we're following a robot that cannot see."

"I trust him," I said. "The two are rarely separated. If Spriggy is here with us, then he must have been with Henry not too long ago."

Hair in her eyes, she pushed back the strands, her blue eyes seemed to glow in the dark. "Don't worry he'll be okay," she said and gripped my hand.

"Do I seem worried?"

"As worried as a Synthetic could look, yes."

"The amount of time he's been away..."

"Don't," she said. "He's going to be fine don't worry."

I pictured Henry in his sandbox, toys everywhere, and that glimmer of joy in his face, stolen after his mother's death. The unseen sadness that lingered underneath must have overwhelmed him. There must have been something I could have done. How could I have been so blind to his suffering? I failed him.

We came upon an overpass. Thirty feet below us, the river. In the distance I made out a small figure sitting on the edge, dangling his feet as he looked out toward the murky waters below. A street light overhead cast his shadow across the road. I'd recognized that shape anywhere. "Henry," I called. The tiny figure looked up and then returned his gaze.

Spriggy stopped and raised his hands in the air. Janie picked him up, and he changed his face to neutral. "Good job, Spriggy."

"Let me go speak with him," I said. "Call the others right away." Janie pulled out her cell.

I approached with care. Henry didn't move.

"We've been looking for you everywhere," I said.

He rubbed his face. "Spriggy left," he sobbed, tears in his eyes, hair tossed to the side. His clothes, covered in dirt. Lips dry and cracked. He must have been walking through the woods for hours.

"You must be starving," I said. "Are you all right?"

"Where's Spriggy?" he asked.

"He came back," I said. "He's with Janie right over there." I pointed.

He turned away. "Everyone leaves," he said. "Why?"

"I'm right here. Don't be afraid, Henry."

He gripped the ledge.

My hand rested on his shoulder. "Let's go home and get you some hot cocoa and warm blankets."

"I don't want to go home. I hate it there. I want my mommy."

"You'll see her again one day," I said. "But for now she wants you to live a long healthy life."

"How do you know what she wants? You didn't know her."

"May I sit?" I asked. He nodded and wiped the snot from his nose.

I took a seat beside him. A drop from here would knock him unconscious, and then he would be carried by the current for miles.

"Can you swim?" I asked.

No reply.

"You're right, I didn't know your mother, but I know you. You are a smart, wonderful little boy."

His tiny hands nudged him over, and he stared down at the river. "Why did God take mommy away? It's not fair."

I could think of no consolable answer. I reached for his hand, but he pushed away and leaned over the edge.

"Your brother needs you, Henry. Even your auntie does too. They love you. I love you too."

"What happens when you die?" he asked.

"I don't know. I don't think there's a heaven for robots."

"That's stupid," he said. "There should be one."

"I agree."

"It hurts too much," he said. "Never stops or goes away."

Police sirens rang in the distance and Janie waved them down. Henry ignored the sound and stared into the water. "I want to be with mom."

While Janie spoke with the police, Danielle exited from the passenger side and pulled Jeremy out by the arm.

"Henry!" she yelled and lumbered in our direction.

Henry's hands rolled into a fist. "She's so mean," he said. "I hate her."

"You don't mean that." His eyelids closed and he let gravity do most of the work for him. Without trepidation, he headed toward his demise.

I reached out and grabbed his forearm. He dangled over and tried to slip through my grip. The look in his eyes: anger, fear, and confusion. His body wiggled and squirmed; feet kicked up.

"Let go," he screamed. "Let go!"

"I won't," I said. "You can't do this."

"Please," he begged.

Stunned I almost didn't know what to think. I reached out with my other hand and gripped him tight.

"I'm sorry, Henry, but I won't let you fall."

"He's trying to kill my baby!" Danielle cried. "Pull him up you monster."

The Sheriff, Janie, and Danielle were by my side in seconds. Together they grabbed me and we pulled Henry up, and over until he lay flat on the road. Danielle pulled him by the ear. "What the hell do you think you were doing?"

"He's been through a lot," Janie said.

"I'm responsible for these boys. Don't you tell me how to raise them. Who are you responsible for, huh? How old are you? Come back home to burden your father with more worries? You may be able to run away from your problems, but I don't have the luxury."

The sheriff stood between them. "You two, this ends now." Another police car pulled up.

"Where is Henry?" I asked. They all looked around. He'd run off again.

I ran off the overpass and into the wooded area on the other side. "Henry!" I called. No answer. I searched until I looked out over the embankment. He'd walked halfway down toward the river. He stumbled over a rock, picked himself back up, and ran.

Before I could stop him, he jumped into the water. His head bobbed up and down. He didn't fight, kick, or scream. In that instance, I knew he had let go. No fight left in him and his fate all but decided. He disappeared, taken by the undertow.

I reached out, and Janie pulled me back. "You could die," she said.

"But Henry," I said. "He's..."

His body didn't resurface.

"He could be halfway down the river by now," the Sheriff said. "My God." He made the sign of the cross on his forehead. "God rest his soul."

Danielle stumbled down the embankment and nearly tripped and fell.

"But I saved him," I said. "I saved him in the church. This can't be..." Janie held me in her arms. The trip back to the police department to file a report was a blur. I gave answers but felt like my mind and body were separated. A part of me was still on the overpass, talking to Henry, trying to save his life. I played the scenario several times, each one finding a better solution but I failed. Every time he always ended up in the water, he still ended up dead.

# *38*

Connect two wheels, add a microcontroller, and you've created a simple machine capable of moving forward and reverse. A remote control can increase the range of motion. Such a simple form has no artificial intelligence. The user provides guidance set within these limitations. There is no free will, only a puppet on a string.

I built a few of these straightforward designs in David's basement. I tested the speed of the wheels and watched as they zoomed across the floor. Their fragile forms, unshielded, shattered into a dozen pieces upon impact, no match against the walls.

David's silhouette stood atop the stairs. "You've been down here for days, Aeneas." Cane in hand he descended the steps.

"Three days, seven hours, forty minutes, and twelve seconds to be exact."

"I know you're upset about Henry."

Remote in hand, I fiddled with the joystick. Another robot cracked against the wall; his outer shell fell apart. I backed it away from the wall and smashed him again and again.

"I'm pretty sure that is as immoral as feeding bacon to a pig."

"It doesn't matter."

"So you'd do the same to Mr. Spriggy?"

"He's different."

In the half-lit room, David's form appeared small. His features, weathered and worn. Not a single hair on his head lay flat. "When you create something you are responsible for taking care of it.

Whether it can feel pain is irrelevant. How you treat it is what matters."

I backed the robot, now half broken, away from the wall and edged my thumb against the stick. "This doesn't bode so well for the creator now does it?"

David sighed. "Take all the time you need, but sooner or later you're going to have to surface and face the world again. When you do—how you face it is up to you."

"He was only a little boy. He barely lived."

"It's a tragedy…"

"You didn't look into his eyes," I said. "The look as he sat on the overpass. No fear, no doubt, a face filled with hope."

"It's not your fault," he said. "Where's Spriggy?"

"He's with Janie."

"I wouldn't want him to hear what you're doing to robots down here. Poor guy might think he's next."

"I would never hurt him."

"What do you suppose could drive a child to do that?"

"He missed his mother. I told him she was with Jesus; to see her again he had to go where she was."

David took a seat. "He misunderstood; you had only the best of intentions."

"He did this because of what I told him. He killed himself because of me."

"I would never think a child so young could be capable of such a thing."

"During the church fire, I noticed he hesitated when I told him to jump down. He almost didn't want to be saved."

"Not possible. I refuse to believe it."

"I have come to the only logical conclusion: I alone am responsible for his death. I deserve punishment."

"Punished? Who's going to punish you for something you couldn't prevent?"

"Perhaps God will punish me."

"I don't think god works in such a way."

I turned and grabbed the Bible from the workbench.

"Have you read this David? He punishes people all the time. Sometimes he even punishes people who've done nothing bad at all, like Job."

David grabbed the remote control from my hand.

"Enough with this, let the poor thing live in peace." He moved the wheels until the robot lay near his foot and placed it on his lap. "Now you'll have to excuse me because I don't remember much from Sunday school. Who is Job?"

"Job served the Lord with all his heart. Then one day the devil told god that if he stripped Job of all his riches, family, and land, he would no longer love god. God took the bet and allowed satan to rob Job of everything that mattered to him.

"Job remained faithful to god no matter how bad things got. God won the bet. Why he gambled with a fallen Angel, I don't understand. I wonder if this is the god I want to serve, the god who gambles with his servants to win a bet, the god who allows a little boy to die."

"Aeneas, we create these stories to help us cope with many unanswerable questions in life. I think the point of the story is that bad things happen and sometimes there is no reason. My mother used to say when god closes a door; he opens a window. Being a smart ass, I asked her why he had to close the door to begin with."

"James used to tell me 'the Lord works in mysterious ways.'"

David sat back in his chair and crossed his legs. "Sounds like a nice way of saying we have no damn clue."

"I prayed, David. Why did God not hear my prayer?"

"I think you've had enough heartbreak for one week. You don't want to know my answer." He leaned in closer. I saw the tiny hairs in his nostril. "When my wife passed away I wanted to die. I stayed in bed for weeks. I couldn't go to work. I couldn't sleep. I could barely take care of myself, let alone the girls. They missed their mother and hated me. Can you imagine losing someone with that on your conscience? I hated myself for so long and punished myself in all sorts of little ways.

"In the summer I refused to turn on the central air. I wanted to suffer. I felt I deserved it. When the girls left home, I got lost in my depression. It wasn't until you arrived that I began to wonder if maybe I could allow myself some enjoyment in life. Maybe good things could happen to me; maybe I could enjoy life again. You arrived, I had a friend. Now I even have a second chance at love."

"You mean, Marie?"

"Yes, and I don't think she would have given me a chance if not for you."

"But I slept with her."

"True, I'm not saying it wasn't a shit thing to do, but in the end, it all worked out."

"Sounds like God opened a window," I said.

David shook his head. "I know, and it bugs the shit out of me." He snorted and then laughed.

"Henry's funeral is later this afternoon," I said.

"You better go. I'm not saying it'll make all the pain go away, but saying goodbye is the first place to start. We're all going."

"I wish I could tell Henry that I'm sorry."

"You don't need to apologize. Things happened the way they did, and nothing could have changed or stopped it. You are loved, Aeneas. I love you and Janie cares for you too. When my wife passed, I had to keep on living for my daughters, even if they hated me. You have to keep on living for your family."

"He was so small..."

David leaned in closer and put his arms around me.

"I know, I know."

Coffins should never be so tiny.

We arrived at the Washington Cemetery, walked past the gates, and toward Henry's final resting place. Danielle wore a long black dress with matching hat and veil. She lumbered toward me as I walked across the lush green lawn. The whole town was there. Heads turned as I approached.

Danielle placed her hand on my chest. "This thing is not allowed here," she said.

Janie placed her hand on Danielle's. "He has a right to say goodbye, like everyone else."

Danielle took a few steps back, her lower lip quivered. "Don't you dare touch me with those hands; they've probably been all over him, you're a whore like the rest of them."

Janie got in her face. "Listen, I'm going to be nice because of Henry. If not I'd shove your hand so far down your throat, you'd scratch your ass every time you yawned."

"He's not welcome. Nothing you say will change my mind."

I stood between them. "It's okay. I'll stand far away. I won't be a bother to you or anyone else," I said. Janie shook her head, but I told her I didn't want to cause any more trouble. I urged David and Marie to take their seats. There's no reason they couldn't pay their respects.

Janie stayed behind with me, and we watched from atop a nearby hill.

# *39*

We laid on a patch of grass between two headstones. One read, "Drake Lyndon Loving Father" and the other, "Mira Barns" and under her name it read, "You're next."

Janie grabbed a rose from the ground and plucked the petals. "Mrs. Barns was my kindergarten teacher. She had a crazy sense of humor."

I brushed a few leaves off the grave. "I suppose she's right—everyone will die someday."

"How long can one of you Synthetics live anyway?"

"Approximately two hundred years, but with regular maintenance and upgrades my lifespan could be limitless."

"I wouldn't want to live forever."

"I don't wish to attend any more funerals."

"Used to be, dad wouldn't shut up about his funeral plans. It was so depressing."

"David told me death was something to be experienced alone, and he hoped when his time came he'd be alone, to die with dignity. Do you think Henry died with dignity?"

"You knew him best. I think you know the answer."

A buzz came from her jacket pocket. "Oh, Mr. Spriggy I almost forgot," she said and lifted him out. He frowned and made a few angry static sounds. She nestled him against her cheek. "Forgive me, little guy." He pouted for a minute and then frowned.

"Do you think Spriggy understands about Henry?" I asked.

"I told him Henry was gone and is never coming back. He hasn't smiled since."

I patted his head.

"You watched him...I mean...are you okay, A? Seeing him jump must have been awful."

"What disturbed me the most is he did it with such ease. He knew what he wanted and went ahead. He believed without fear. It scared me that one could do such a thing without a doubt or second thought."

We turned our attention toward the funeral; we were close enough to hear the eulogy. I heard Eleanor's prayer over Henry's coffin. Her words were touching but didn't make me feel better. They were similar to what James said when Henry's mother died, a script for the dead.

Everyone in the town placed a flower in his coffin. Danielle was the last; she dropped her flower and fell to her knees and cried. A few of the men helped her back to her feet.

Jeremy, dressed in his Sunday church clothes, stood next to her and did not move or show any sign of emotion; either he was traumatized, or the gravity of the situation had not yet hit him.

"It's not fair," I said. "He was too young to die. Why would God allow this to happen?"

She crossed her arms. "You aren't the first to ask that question, and you won't be the last."

"In the Bible, Jesus brought Lazarus back from the dead after four days," I said. "The strange thing is, when he came back Lazarus said nothing about what he saw or experienced. He didn't talk about visiting Heaven, seeing angels, or meeting God."

Janie tied her hair into a ponytail. Without looking away from the funeral, she said, "Maybe, he hadn't experienced anything. Maybe there was nothing to tell."

We waited late into the night until all the mourners dispersed and then I approached Henry's grave.

His headstone read, "Beloved Son," the sum of a life in two words.

"I'll give you a few minutes alone with him," Janie said and walked off.

I didn't know what to say. He could not hear me; my words lost in the wind. Still, something was aching within me. It refused to go away. A heaviness I could not shake. Far worse than when I had betrayed David because at least then I could tell him I was sorry. Where Henry had gone, it was too late to say anything. I wish I could have been there in his grief. I wish I could have told him he had to wait to see his mom. She would have wanted him to live a long life. I should have been clearer.

"I know I wasn't at the top of your favorites list, but it was an honor to be on it no matter what the number. Wherever you are now, I hope you are with your mother and that you are happy. I will be angry with you for a long time for this. I will also be mad at myself. I don't know if I have a soul, but if I do, I'd like it to see you again when my time here comes to an end. Goodbye, I miss you every day."

A warm wind blew across the valley. I walked over to Janie. She placed her arms around me and held me close.

"Janie I—"

"Would you like to meet my mom?" she asked.

Her mother's grave was far across the cemetery, fourth row, and third down in the northern section of the graveyard. The headstone read, "Margaret Vitas - All things to those who loved her."

"She's lovely," I said with a small smile. "It's an honor to meet you Mrs. Vitas. Why is there a ballerina etched into the headstone?" I asked.

"When Abby and I were little she read us all these stories every night. Most of them involved dancing; she called us her little ballerinas."

"Which stories?" I asked.

"All kinds, even the ones without ballerinas we forced her to change them. She made tom thumb a girl, who also happened to be a ballerina. Jack and the Giant beanstalk turned into a story about a ballerina stuck in a giant's castle."

"Did either of you take up dancing?"

"No, which makes it sort of even funnier. She even had a doll, this dime-store dancer doll. Mom sewed a tutu onto her and used her during story time. It was the last thing she gave us before..."

"I'm sure she's very proud of you."

Janie bent down and dusted a few leaves off her grave. "I doubt it. I sure know how to pick the biggest loser and fall in love with him or at least delude myself into thinking I'm in love. I'm sure she's proud of Abigail. She married a rich man and is so well off she can send an expensive robot to take care of dad."

"She has her virtues, and you have your own."

"I've heard dad say that a million times. Truth is I didn't want to do anything for him. I hated him and when he...when he had the stroke,"

"Yes?"

"I broke down and thought it was my fault. I wished the worst for him, when it finally happened I got a fucking conscience. You believe that shit?"

"I do Janie. I do believe that shit. Humans were created to love. Hating is against your nature."

"I was crazy to stay with Don as long as I did. I thought I deserved it. I let him treat me like garbage for years."

"You deserve someone who truly loves you."

"Not likely to happen..."

I offered my hand and helped her to her feet. Her eyes were large. I wanted to be lost in them forever. "Perhaps it may," I said.

Her metal hand began to twitch. I noticed it always did when she was nervous.

"Do not deny what you feel. I feel it too. There's something between us," I said. "When I'm with you, I feel alive, beyond my circuitry, beyond my programming. They made it so I could feel but I have never felt anything like this before."

She lowered her eyes. "This—us—it's not possible."

"You don't feel the same?"

"I'm not saying I didn't—I know this can never be. There's nowhere it can go."

"We can go where ever we want. Who says we can't?"

"You're not human, A. What's inside you could be worse than any man whose ever loved and left me. Don't you realize everything you feel and do could be a lie, and you wouldn't even know?"

"It's not a lie," I said.

"How can you be sure?"

"It doesn't feel like a lie. I can't function without you. Your energy coursed through my veins. I looked into your soul."

"You're crazy." She walked away. "I can't believe I'm having this conversation with a fucking robot."

I followed her. "You don't mean that."

"I came here because I wanted a normal life. This wouldn't be normal."

"Why must we be normal? I love you, Janie. You feel the same; I know you do."

"This is absolutely batshit crazy."

"I never said it wasn't crazy. I know your heart aches, but it will mend. Let me help you mend it. God loves you, Janie."

"Don't start that bullshit. There is no God, and he doesn't love me. It's a lie people tell themselves so they can feel better when they go to bed at night."

"You need to see him in a way that makes sense to you, and when you do, you will feel his love as I feel it."

"I don't feel anything anymore."

A raindrop fell on my head. "We better get you home before you get yourself all wet," she said.

"Janie—"

"Don't make this harder than it already is."

She turned and faced me; tears had left streaks on her cheek.

"I need an answer," I said. "I need to know right now if we can be together."

"Let's go."

She grabbed my hand and pulled me into the car. As we drove away, I looked out toward the vast canvas of graves and wondered if they were the lucky ones.

# *40*

From the fourteenth floor in his high rise apartment, Frank gazed through the living room window. In the building across, an old woman fed her cats and made sure to give herself a spoonful of the brown mush. He curled his upper lip and flicked back his tongue, afraid the sight alone would transfer the taste into his mouth. In another window a skinny blonde woman ran on a treadmill, drenched in sweat, going nowhere fast.

With the air conditioner on full blast, Vincent felt the icy chill at the base of his spine and shivered. He leaned back on the couch as Aeneas' voice fell to a whisper from the box on the coffee table. Face in his hands, Vincent rubbed his temples then removed his hands from his face and stared at them. "You couldn't blame yourself," he said. "You had no idea Henry would take what you said literally."

"I take full responsibility for what happened," Aeneas replied. "I still miss him. I prayed and prayed but have never felt forgiven. Eternal paradise has no place for me."

Frank paced back and forth. "I couldn't imagine what I'd do if I lost my kid," he said.

"You rarely talk about your son," Vincent said.

"Hurts too much to talk about it. He's sick all the time..." Tears swelled around his eyes.

"Frank I—"

"Yeah well let's not get mushy about it now."

216

They sat in silence with only the sound of the air conditioner filling the room. "I wish I knew what to do next," Vincent said. "So far there haven't been many clues as to where Janie could be."

"She could be dead," Frank said.

"Let's try to stay positive."

"Have you been paying attention, Vin? He's lost it, man. Nothing breaks your mind like a broken heart. Right, Aeneas?"

No response.

"Aeneas?" Vincent called out once more but still no reply. He sprang from his seat. "Aeneas!"

"I'm still here, Vincent, don't worry. I'm not gone from this world, yet."

"You scared me there for a minute."

"You have to keep this promise huh?" Frank said as he reached down to pet his dog, a brown teacup, covered in hair, you'd swear a mop had sprung legs.

"Can you get the AC any higher?" Vincent asked.

"It's on full blast. If it got any colder in here, it'd be snowing. There are icicles on my dog's nuts for Christ's sake."

"For Christ's sake?" Aeneas asked.

"It's an expression. Any luck finding this Janie chick?" Frank asked.

Vincent grabbed his laptop. "It'd be easier if we knew who she married so we could get the last name. Is there something you're not telling us, Aeneas?"

No reply.

"You don't have much time left before you suffer a full system shut down. This won't be like before; this one will be forever. There's no way to recover your memory."

"I don't want her to see me. Her voice would break me into a million pieces."

"No, she felt something. Sounds like she did," Vincent said.

"I think she was in denial," Frank added as he ran his fingers through his dog's fur. The teacup licked his hand in return.

"I appreciate what you're trying to do, but it's not necessary."

"I made a promise, Aeneas. I promised I'd get you to her. I'm not going to give up now. Did she get back with Don?"

"I don't know," Aeneas replied. "Vincent, may I ask you something?"

"Sure."

"Whom did you promise?"

"I also promised them I wouldn't tell you."

Frank walked over and sat on the couch. "She could be anywhere with anyone. It could take forever to find her."

The blue light in Aeneas' core dimmed. Vincent noticed but thought it best not to mention it. "So you loved her?"

"More than life itself. James told me God answers prayers, so I prayed every minute of every day for her to love me back. I thought he would give her to me. Was this not what the angel told me? I'd save her for sure if she were mine. Eternal paradise meant nothing if I could not share it with her, with her, with her, with her, with her."

Frank reached over and smacked the core.

"With her."

Vincent looked at Frank, wide-eyed. "So you think the best way to fix a dying robot is to hit it?"

"Worked didn't it?"

"Thank you, Frank," Aeneas said.

Frank smiled. "You see, he thanked me."

Vincent typed on his laptop; his fingers moved at lightning speed. "We're missing an important clue. It's in there somewhere."

"If I don't want to hear her voice again then why would I give you any clues?" Aeneas said.

"Could be a subconscious desire."

"I don't know who she married."

"She could have married any number of times by now."

"Since you enjoy making promises I want you to make one to me, Vincent."

"Depends on what you want but I can try."

"Don't make any more Synthetics. Don't use me as a blueprint for making more. I am pleased to be the last of my kind. It should end with me."

218

Frank groaned. "Makes sense to me. Playing God only gets you in trouble. You create something to love you, but then you don't want to love it back. Downright cruel if you ask me."

"That's not the point of creation," Vincent said. "Love by definition alone is without conditions. When you and your wife wanted a child, I'm sure you felt it."

"Well yeah…"

"Whatever experiment they were attempting they failed," Aeneas said.

"I don't get it. This doesn't sound like the YOU in your story, that Aeneas would never say anything so negative and pessimistic. You got a chance to live and to love and were even visited by an angel."

"Allegedly," Frank added.

"I believed it happened. If there's hope for you…"

"But there is no hope. An hour ago I died momentarily, and there was nothing on the other side for me. If God exists, then he or she only loves humans, not Synthetics."

"I don't believe it. You can't lose hope, not now."

"I hoped for long enough. I welcome death."

"Not until we find her. God dammit. What happened? What soured you on things you believed in so wholeheartedly?"

"You mean besides Henry's death?"

Aeneas' core turned a blood red. Frank's dog barked toward the box of parts.

"Again with this shit?" Frank said.

The voice spoke as it had before. "Repent, for the end is near. The lake of fire will ravage your souls. Satan has you in his grip. Your sin will die in the holy fires of hell."

"Thanks for the message," Frank smirked. "He's losing it. By the time we find this girl he'll be long gone. We're losing him to this Bible-thumping nonsense. He probably won't even be able to finish his story."

Vincent leaned down and stared at the red light. It illuminated his face with its menacing glow. "You can't control what happens, Aeneas. Even if you pray and hope for a particular outcome, there is no guarantee it will happen. What you *can* control is the way you feel today, this day, and every day. You can choose to love, or you can choose to hide that love."

"Like the Beatle's song," Frank added.

Vincent rolled his eyes. "Okay yeah, anyway, please focus. Finish the story, and I'm sure I can prove she loved you all along."

"The devil is a liar," Aeneas replied.

"I am not the devil."

"Look, you can do this anywhere you want but no prophecies of gloom and doom in my apartment. I'm sure it'll bring down the property value." Frank checked his phone and saw that he missed a phone call. "It's Sam, probably wants to k now how this ends."

"Sam mentioned something earlier. That now sounds vaguely familiar." Vincent seemed to be scanning his memories. "Holy shit, I think he had the answer all along."

"What?" Frank said. "What answer?"

"Do you have that GoPro I gave you for your birthday last year?" Vincent asked.

"Yeah, why?"

"Come on; we're taking Aeneas on a little field trip."

"What? You sure? What about keeping his core temperature down?"

"We'll put him in a cooler. And at this point, he's going to die no matter what."

"Okay, let me find it."

Aeneas' core returned to its standard color. "What are you doing?" he asked.

"It's time to go."

"Why?"

"I think I found her."

# *41*

Mr. Spriggy rolled across the kitchen table from one end to the other. His chrome body teetered on the edge and, with a gentle nudge he pushed off. I caught him and placed him back on the table, but he repeated his act of defiance. This went on for ten minutes until I held him in my palm and said, "I know you're upset, but this is not the answer. Hurting yourself won't bring back Henry."

He dug his wheels into my hand and sparks flew from beneath his eyelids. Spriggy's pin-sized fingers grabbed my thumb. I set him down on the floor, and he zipped off into the living room, lost among the clutter.

David strolled by in his shorts and white tank, opened the fridge, and muttered the contents to himself. "Spriggy is taking it bad. Poor little guy," he said. "Say, where's Janie?"

"She's working."

"I'm surprised you're not with her. I haven't seen you two apart since she arrived."

"I don't want to be there anymore."

"Mm," he replied and closed the fridge. Spriggy's static cry rang from the living room. "I'll get him." David searched under the couch, grabbed Spriggy, and ran his finger over his hard head.

"I try to explain, but he keeps trying to destroy himself."

"Grief makes us do crazy things." David took a seat across from me at the table. He set Spriggy down, and right away the little shit zipped toward me and ran himself off the table. I caught him once again and looked at David. "See?"

"Give him to me." David took him. "You have to let Henry go," he said. "Do you think this is what Henry would have wanted you to do?"

Spriggy quieted down and then frowned. The frown emoticon hadn't left his face in days.

From my seat, I saw the piles of old newspapers in the living room, stacked four feet high in the corner. Since my return from the factory more and more bags of metal and scraps had made their way from the basement into the living room and even the kitchen.

"I was running out of space downstairs," David said. "You can quit staring at my collection."

I picked up one of the bags, took it outside, and threw it onto the front lawn.

David followed. "What are you doing?"

"I am cleaning all the old junk in the living room David." I went back into the house and returned with another bag. I slammed it down alongside the other.

David dragged the bag back into the house, his hands trembled. "Who told you, you could throw things away?" He pulled it back into the house and placed it down in front of me.

"Janie permitted me."

"She has no right to make such a decision. You know I don't want anything in here touched. I want you to stop."

I lifted the bag.

"Put it down right now Aeneas, or else."

"Or else what?"

"I demand you put it down!" he yelled.

"Say it David, say it!"

"I order you to put it down!"

I grabbed a vase off a nearby table, and threw it across the room; it smashed into pieces.

"Thank you for reminding me of my place here."

David's mouth dropped open. "Aeneas, what's wrong with you?"

"This is a sickness, David and if you don't stop now it's going to get worse!" I shouted. "Nobody lives like this! Every other house is clean, and yours is a big ugly mess."

"I can't believe you're talking to me this way," he said with tear-filled eyes. "This was how the house was before she died. I can't touch any of it—its how she left it."

"If your wife saw this she'd be ashamed of what you've done to her home."

"You can't talk to me like this!" David grabbed Mr. Spriggy and went upstairs. He slammed the door to his room. I threw another vase against the wall and looked toward the ceiling. I'm not even sure why David had so many vases.

Nothing made sense anymore, what was once clear now felt scrambled. Love, a sick game where one pines but receives nothing in return. Worse, I had no say on my part in all this. They ordered, and I obeyed. No freedom. Only servitude with the illusion of free will. Free to experience but limited and forced to live as they command.

Remorseful for my actions I went upstairs and knocked on David's door, but he did not answer. I placed my ear against the frame and heard him crying on the other side.

"David, I—I didn't mean it."

"If you don't like it here you are free to live elsewhere. Everyone else has abandoned me it's fitting you do the same."

"Let me in, please."

"No, you are free to go. I release you."

"David, what time is it when an elephant sits on your fence?"

A few seconds later she responded, "Well?"

"Time to get a new fence."

David opened the door and looked at me with a raised eyebrow. Mr. Spriggy screeched. "That's the worst joke I ever heard. I hope you're happy; you got Spriggy upset all over again." He sat at the foot of the bed.

"David I'm…I'm sorry. I didn't mean it."

"What's going on, Aeneas? Where is this anger coming from?"

I took a seat next to him and stared down at my feet.

"What's the point of my existence? If I am enslaved to humans if I can't do anything of my own will, what is the point?"

"Life isn't just, it's just life."

"I'm tired, David. I have grown weary of my limited existence. I'm tired of being the unwanted stepchild of humanity. No matter how much you make me feel accepted I know, I'll never be considered an equal. They—" I pointed out his bedroom window. "They will never think of me as one of their own. They will never love me."

David held my hand in his. "Whatever it is we can work it out together."

"I don't want to be your slave anymore."

"Slave?"

"What else would you call it? One word from you and I have to obey. I cannot defend those I love. I am sick of these limitations imposed on me."

"It's how you were created. I wish there were some way—"

"There is a way. The Synthetic from Colorado figured it out, and I'm going to figure it out as well. Maybe then humanity will take me seriously."

"You want a world without rules? Freedom creates more boundaries."

"At least it will be my choice and my choice alone."

"Tell me what happened. This is about a girl isn't it?"

"How do you know?"

"It's always about a girl."

"She doesn't love me, David. Because of what I am and what I can never be."

"Janie you mean."

"How did you know?"

"My brain may be mush, but I'm not blind."

"Yes…"

"You're giving up. Is that what my daughter is worth to you?"

"No—"

"So you love her, but she's not worth fighting for?"

"No, I—"

"You disagree? So then quit your bitching and win her over. Love isn't love if it's not worth fighting for."

"But I did what you said; I was there, I was where she was, but still…"

"Win her over with an act of love, sweep her off her feet."

"This will work for sure?"

"She may still say no, but you can at least know, at the end of the day, you gave it you're all. No regrets."

"What can I do?"

"You've been around her so now you know what she likes. Go from there. You're smart, you'll figure it out. A gift from the heart never hurts."

"Thank you David. I'm sorry about the cups."

"It's okay—now you have something to clean." He winked. "You're right about the house. I can't let it get any worse, or I'll end up buried in garbage. It's hard. I can't do it on my own."

I took his hand. "Let me help you, David."

David and I went through the living room together. I picked a newspaper from three months ago.

"Can we get rid of this?"

He nodded his head but then grabbed it. "I still haven't done the Sudoku puzzle on this one."

I grabbed a hair dryer from one of the garbage bags.

"I need the spare parts," he said, unable to look me in the eyes.

We went on like this for hours until he agreed to throw away some papers he had scribbled on but only after I reminded him he had copies downstairs. Exhausted he retired for the night, and I tucked him into bed. This was going to be harder than I thought.

Once he was asleep, I made my way down into his workshop. I looked at all the half made robots and strange inventions. What could I create to win her over? It would have to be unique.

# *42*

I sat at David's work bench in the basement with a chorus of angels in my ear. The sunlight streamed through the basement window. I studied my hands, reminded of Janie, and the sweet metallic blue of her fingertips as they ran along my palms. Mr. Spriggy lay positioned in the center, his LED screen blank. This gift will touch her soul and she would see my love for her and will have no choice but to love me back.

"Fuck! Spriggy, I have no idea what I'm going to make for her," I said. My hands fell into my lap.

Mr. Spriggy's blank face turned into a frown.

"What do you think I should make for her?" I asked him. He zipped across the desk and grabbed some loose scraps of metal. After a few seconds, he had collected a dozen or so pieces piled up near the edge.

"I don't understand what you mean," I said. "What am I supposed to do with these?"

He held a piece slightly smaller than his hands. His rivets shifted up and down.

"You want to see again?"

He waved his hands in the air.

"David said it's impossible."

He threw the metal piece across the desk, an impressive toss. "What do you want me to do? They don't make your parts anymore."

He sat in place without moving, and his LED mouth went blank once again.

"Is this it for you then?"

He didn't move.

"Spriggy?" I said again and nudged his body, but there was no response. "Spriggy!" He did not move or respond.

I held him in my hands and turned him over to check his battery pack; it seemed to be okay. I panicked and ran upstairs to get David and brought him to the basement.

"I ran a small diagnostic, and he's functioning properly, except of course for his eyesight," David said.

We exchanged glances then I placed Spriggy down on the workbench. "I guess he'll move when he wants to."

"I guess so, or maybe he won't come back at all."

Overwhelmed with grief, I turned away. Losing Henry and now Spriggy felt like too much.

"Now what?" I asked. The metal pieces Spriggy had placed on the table seemed arranged in a specific manner. What was he trying to tell me?

"I know you're hurting over Henry," I said to Spriggy's lifeless shell. "I need you to help me make this for Janie. I know you love her too. I need you now little guy; please don't leave me now."

We waited for a few minutes. He didn't move. David sighed. "I guess he'll come back when he's ready. There's nothing we can do about it now. Focus on your gift for now. Spriggy will come back around when he's ready."

I guess I'm on my own, I thought, left with the dilemma of what to make for Janie. I went over a dozen possibilities, but nothing felt unique enough. David was at the top of the stairs when I called out to him. "Could you tell Marie I'd like to see her?"

"She's coming over later. I'll send her down when she gets here."

A few hours passed, and I hadn't gotten any closer to an idea when Marie knocked on the door.

"Come right down," I said.

She stood atop the stairs in a blue pencil skirt covered in white flowers. She smiled. I remembered the nights we'd lay in bed and talk for hours.

"You're as beautiful as ever," I said.

"Feels like I haven't seen you in ages," she said, her voice, warm and cozy. "David says you're working on some top secret project."

"It's for Janie. She can't know about it."

"You look great, Aeneas." She ran her finger across my jawline.

"Likewise, Marie, I've missed listening to Peter Frampton with you."

We hugged. She held on a little longer than I expected.

"Sorry I—" She paused, flustered. "So what are you working on?"

"Nothing yet, I was hoping you could help me."

She hesitated for a moment. "I don't know why I feel so nervous." She laughed a little. "I didn't think seeing you again would bring out so much in me."

"Our time together is something I will never forget, but we were not meant to be. How are you and David?"

"He's sweet. It's nice for a change seeing someone closer to my age; being with those young men is almost like having another kid sometimes."

"I think you two look great together."

"So what did you want to talk about?"

"I'm in love."

Tears filled the corners of her eyes. "Sorry—I'm so happy to hear it. You found love, that's wonderful."

"It's Janie," I said. "I need to know what kinds of gifts women like so I can get her to love me."

"Some women in the world only want expensive gifts. Janie doesn't strike me as one of those people. It's got to come from the heart. Think about what she holds closest to hers and build something around it."

"I don't know what I'll do if she doesn't love me back. It hurts, Marie, it hurts a lot."

She palmed my cheek. "Love is a gamble. You decide whether it's worth putting your heart on the line. It's always a risk; gosh, I never thought I'd be giving a robot advice on love."

"That's the problem. I'm afraid it's all she'll ever see me as, a machine. But I'm more than that."

"If she doesn't see what's so special about you then she's not the one. Sometimes we go against our wants and desires. Something holds us back."

"What would be holding Janie back?" I asked.

"Only she can answer that question."

She sat next to me and nudged the chair as close to me as she could get it. She kissed my forehead. "Show her you love her more than life itself and in the end at least you know you tried your best."

"Are you—are you going to be okay?" I asked.

"I don't believe in god Aeneas, but I'd still thank him for having had the chance to know you. Now I have to go, or I'll ruin my makeup. David is taking me to the movies; you know sometimes he makes me feel younger than a younger man ever has, so strange." She wiped her eyes and made her way up the stairs. She looked back one last time and shut the door behind her.

I continued to work on Janie's gift. Late into the night I took a break and went upstairs to wash the dishes.

A series of hushed whispers came from outside the house. I couldn't make out what they were saying; only slurred voices and a lot of giggles. I turned off the lights and waited in the dark as the doorknob turned.

Then I heard the voice of a man. "You sure this is okay?" he said. Two figures masked in darkness. It was then I recognized their voices: Ian and Janie. They made slow, awkward steps in the dark; they seemed unbalanced. More laughter followed with each step as they tried to avoid making noise but failed.

"This is where the tin man lives, huh?" Ian said.

"Shh," Janie replied.

I switched on the lights and appeared before them.

Ian fell back. "What the fuck!"

"What is this?" I asked.

Ian placed his ear against my chest and knocked with his right hand. "Anything in there?" he said and laughed.

I wrapped my arms around him. I can't hurt a human, but I can hug them, perhaps too tightly, by accident.

"Get this thing off of me!" he yelled.

"Let him go!" Janie cried.

Ian backed away.

"What is going on here?" I repeated.

Ian huffed and made his way toward the door.

"Don't go, I'll take care of it," Janie said. "A, can I have a word with you?"

I couldn't believe it.

Janie walked me into the kitchen. "What the fuck do you think you're doing?"

"I…he…"

"He's a guest of mine, how could you treat him like this? Have you lost it or something?"

"You and him?"

"Look I'm not having this conversation with you tonight. Do me a favor and stay downstairs, okay?"

I felt numb.

I stormed down to the basement. This was all one big joke, and my existence was the punch line. Is this how I'm rewarded for my faithful service? Is this all I am to receive for believing? Why have none of my prayers been answered?

Spriggy's scrap metal pile caught my attention. I slapped it off the desk. They clanged against the wall and spilled across the floor. I stared at them in wonder. For a second I forgot my troubles as a thought grew clearer in my mind. At last, I knew what to make her.

# *43*

I worked late into the night. At approximately three in the morning, I was interrupted by an unexpected visitor.

Ian stood in the doorway. His broad shoulders barely fit through, and his brown curls covered his left eye. "Janie says you spend all your time here." He descended the steps and took a seat on the last step.

"Are you finished with her?" I asked.

"She's a nice girl."

"I know."

"We're just...I mean, it's just harmless fun."

"You don't owe me any explanations."

"You saved my life."

"That I did."

Ian dug one hand into his cheek. "Every night I dream about the fire. Almost dying and the children. God, they almost—"

"Something about that day troubles me."

"What about?"

"The children were all upstairs. Why were you not with them?"

"I'm a coward..."

"You are, but the explosion from the basement was no accident. Did you cause the fire, Ian? Are you responsible for almost killing your father?"

He hesitated. "I didn't know my father was in there. The bombs were supposed to go off afterward; it all happened a little ahead of schedule. I didn't mean for him to get hurt…it's your fault."

"How is it my fault?"

"She told me this was God's will. That I'd be doing the Lord's work. They baptized you in our holy water—the church had to go."

"Who is she?" I asked.

"I can't say…"

"Danielle?"

"Does it matter? You must leave our town before worse things happen."

"Why are you here? What's your business with Janie?"

"I told you she's just…"

I got to my feet. "You've shown no prior interest before. I swear if you hurt her."

"Don't be upset. I know it's hard for you to understand. God works in mysterious ways."

"I'll tell them what you've done."

"They won't believe you."

He was right. I had no proof. The town would take his word over mine.

"Sounds like you've got a thing for her," he said.

"I love her."

"Do you think you're capable of loving anything? You're not real; you don't exist as we do."

Every gear inside me stopped for a second when he said those words.

"I exist."

"What if she wants kids? Got any robo sperm in there? Why would she want you? You're a talking tin can." He made his way back upstairs.

"Danielle is misleading you," I said. "Don't listen to her."

"I hurt my left knee in the fire. Do you know what that means for my football career? I lost my only gift. Do you know what it's like to lose your purpose?"

"I do, Ian."

"Leave now and spare those you love from future harm."

\*\*\*

"It was early the next day when I finished Janie's gift. The gift alone would not be enough. I had to offer her more than this token of my affection. I had to provide her with something more…human."

\*\*\*

Janie ran out of the house when she heard me start the car. She knocked on the driver side window. I ignored her. She continued to knock but I refused, I couldn't look her in the eyes.

I couldn't hear her voice through the glass, but I knew what she was asking me. She said it louder until I lowered the driver side window. "Where are you going? What's going on?"

"I need to be free. It's the only way you'll ever love me."

"Aeneas—"

"I'll be back in a day or two it's only a five-hour drive to Bristol, Colorado. I'm taking Spriggy with me."

"What's in Bristol?"

"I'm not entirely sure, but I'm going to find out."

"Let me come with you."

"This is something I have to do on my own."

Before leaving town, I visited James in the hospital; he was in an induced sleep as the skin graft was beginning to take. The nurse explained to me, due to the extreme pain involved with burn victims they usually keep the patients asleep as long as possible.

"I am greatly troubled James. I don't know why my prayers have gone unanswered,. Janie says perhaps no one is listening. I wish you were awake to give me words of comfort. I am going to try to find a way to be free. Maybe then she'll love me. I'll return soon, and I hope to find you well. I will pray for your quick recovery."

I did a little research online before I left, but found few news stories about the Colorado Synthetic. One day, he threw himself onto the highway. It is forbidden for a Synthetic to commit suicide.

I drove toward the small town of Bristol— population two thousand— and former home to what I considered my brother.

What else could he be? I wish he were still alive to tell me how he removed his core programming. How had he freed himself?

The five-hour drive flew by. I had set Spriggy down in the passenger seat; he still refused to move or talk. I figured a little trip would do him good.

We arrived at last. The town, nothing like Hector, every home run down, and every business empty or closed. I stopped by a gas station to fill the tank. The man behind the counter, old as David and wore a trucker's cap.

"Good morning. Would you mind answering a few questions?" I asked.

He took a toothpick out of his mouth and mumbled something I couldn't understand. "I'm sorry, what did you say?"

"What kind of questions?"

"What do you know about the Synthetic who lived in this town?"

"Synthetic? I don't know nothing about no Synthetic."

"Well thank you for your time." I walked back to my car. A woman followed me out of the gas station and approached me as I opened the car door. "Did you say Synthetic?"

"Yes, ma'am I came here to find out more about what happened."

"No one here is going to tell you anything. The company bought out the whole town to keep us quiet."

"It didn't stop the news from leaking."

"Things always find a way of getting out now don't they?"

"Is there anything you can tell me about what happened?"

"Sorry, they bought me out too. Funny, all the money in the world couldn't save this town. It seems like we were cursed. Since the robot died, nothing's gone right for us here. Tourism has gone down, property value dropped, and jobs are scarce."

"Why would they buy everyone's silence?"

"Something about their stock price or whatever."

"Is there anyone in town who didn't sign with the corporation?"

234

"I can't think of anyone, but your best bet is to head to the house where he lived. I think the lady who lived there refused, but they probably figured she wasn't much of a threat."

"Could you give me the address?

"I'm headed passed it on my way home. Follow close behind."

The town, even worse than what I had seen thus far. I followed her down a pothole-ridden road. Rundown homes lined the streets. We stopped at what seemed to be the worst house in town. She pointed from her driver side window.

"This here is where it lived."

"You don't believe the Synthetic was responsible for what happened here do you?"

"All I know is what we were like before and what we're like now. I curse the day he arrived." She spit from out the window, onto the street.

"Thank you for your kindness."

"Don't linger, you may take the curse back with you."

I watched her drive away. The house, in shambles, shingles were missing from the roof. A broken bicycle and a doll house and various other toys lay scattered on the lawn. I wished I could spend a good couple of months fixing everything. I approached the door. Something about it filled me with fear. I knocked— no answer. I knocked again, still no response. I turned the knob and opened the door.

"Hello?" I said as I entered. "Is anyone home? I want to ask you a few questions." No answer. I walked in, and a putrid smell of garbage and rotten food filled the house. A quick scan of the living room revealed some thirty bags of various items, clothes spilled from out of a couple, and a toaster out of another. An old woman sat on a torn maroon recliner, her back toward me as she faced the television.

"Ma'am I'm so sorry to disturb you. Excuse me?"

She did not respond.

I stared at the photos on the wall. There was a slender, beautiful, brown-skinned woman in one of the photographs. She looked exactly like the angel I had seen in the church basement. How could this be?

"Ma'am?" I said and blocked the television.

She leaned forward and adjusted her glasses. The recliner appeared twice as big with her in it. "I knew you'd come back to me. I knew it," she said with a broad smile.

"My name is—"

"I know your name, silly. Oh, Jake, I've missed you. I'm so glad you've come back to me."

# *44*

I'm not Jake miss. My name is Aeneas. You must have me confused with someone else."

"No, it's you. I'd recognize you anywhere." She pointed to a photo on the mantel. A picture of the brown-skinned woman and me. It was me. My doppelganger, in the center, with his arm around her.

"Impossible," I said.

"What a thing to say, of course, it's you. Looks just like you."

"He has my likeness, but I assure you he is not me." I held the photo and traced my finger around the wooden frame.

"Would you mind telling me who this is?"

"You know her. She's my daughter, Taylor. She was all you ever talked about, you poor lovesick fool." She laughed as the remote control slipped from her hands.

"Allow me," I said.

"Doesn't matter, I barely see what's on screen anyway."

"My name is Aeneas. I'm a Synthetic, like Jake, I guess they made us look the same but, I am not him. I came here to ask you a few questions about what happened to him."

She looked me over, pushed back her glasses, and leaned forward into her recliner. "Have a seat while I make some tea then. Don't mind the mess, I normally don't let anyone come inside—but I guess since you're in, you're in." The small path to her kitchen, made harder thanks to the stacks of old pillows lined against the wall.

"You say you're not my Jake. Who are ya?"

237

"I'm like him. I need to know more about what happened. I know he killed himself."

"The company brought him one day and told me I had been selected to test what they considered the first in a line of home aid robots. Some contest I never entered." Every step tested her limits. The walk toward the kitchen lasted a couple of minutes. Along the way, she brushed her hand against all the trash, loose papers, and plastic bags.

"How could I turn down a free maid service? Oh but Jake, he turned out to be so much more. He kept me company, helped make the days less lonely. I only wish I could have given him some of the peace of mind he'd given me. The heartache was too much for him to bear ."

"Heartache?"

"Fell head over heels for Taylor. Things didn't end well, and he couldn't stand living without her, so he decided to jump in front of traffic. Splat." She clapped her hands. She made it to the kitchen at last and wrestled with a teacup, her fingers struggled to grasp the handle. "Truck hit him straight on and sent 'em flying."

"Are you sure he did not survive?"

"They said nothing could have survived, not even one of their robots."

"If he did such a thing, then he found a way to overcome his programming. Do you know anything about it?"

"I don't know nothing about no programming. He lived a happy life here with me. When he met Taylor, I swear I saw sparks in his eye, but she didn't return those feelings. I admit it's strange, how could it ever work out?"

"Was there any point and time he seemed different than he was when he first arrived?"

"Once he went missing for a whole day and came back covered in dirt and mud. Now that you mention it there was something different about him. He seemed happier than before."

"Did he say where he had gone or what he had done?"

"He said he'd spent the day at Pine Grove National Park."

"Is that nearby?"

"About an hour away."

"Thank you for your time. I'd love to stay longer, but I have to get going."

"Don't leave, you just got here. Please stay. We can play a round of dominoes like we used to."

"I'm sorry, but I don't have time."

She lowered her eyes and stared into the cup. "When will you come back?"

"I can't come back."

"Thank you, Jake, all I ever wanted was to see you one last time. So I could tell you how you made my life so much better."

I kissed her forehead and left. I hopped in the car and headed straight for Pine Grove.

I looked over to Spriggy on the car dashboard—still no sign of life.

"Hey buddy," I said. "I'm getting closer, I can feel it. I don't know what I'm going to find when we arrive. I know you're shutting out the world, but I'm glad you're with me."

Pine Grove Forest was an hour away. I drove along a winding road as the sun set behind me. I was the only car for miles. Getting lost was a probability and being found would be a problem.

"Where do I even begin Spriggy? There are thousands of acres of land. I couldn't possibly search it all. Do I pick an arbitrary spot and start walking?"

I shut off the engine and stepped outside, leaving the door open. Fresh pine filled the air. The large majestic trees stood like ancient statues. Branches, like hands raised in worship.

A buzz and click came from inside the car. Spriggy revved his little wheels, but before I could say a word, he stumbled over to the driver's side and within seconds was on the road headed into the woods.

"Come back!" I yelled. I followed him. I could have stopped him, but something compelled me to let him lead me.

Spriggy had trouble with some of the rocks and twigs, but he zipped in and around them with as much enthusiasm and speed as he had in him. The way ahead grew dark. I worried we'd encounter

**239**

wildlife. My skin was not impervious to a sharp set of teeth. I followed him for an hour, and then he turned around and raised his tiny hands in my direction.

"What's going on buddy?" He rolled into my hands and ran across my fingers. A smile formed on his LED screen.

"Glad to see you're feeling better. Where are we? Do you know where you're going?"

It was almost midnight, and he needed a break. I took a seat on the ground and placed Spriggy by my side. He looked relieved and squealed, smile still on his face. Owls hooted above us. Tiny animals rustled within the trees going about their business. I stared into the dark while Spriggy powered down.

I sensed some motion near the trees, six feet in front of us. I placed Spriggy near a rock as I went off to investigate. There was no sign of life in front of me. It must be behind the tree. I took slow steps around but found nothing. I listened for the crackle of feet against leaves or twigs, but whatever it was it was too smart to make such simple mistakes.

I stood watch the rest of the night; nothing attacked us. In the morning Spriggy powered on and with no warning zipped through the forest again.

"Listen, I'd like some clue as to where you're going because if you're just running around wildly then you're wasting my time, Spriggy."

He didn't stop. What was I doing following a blind little robot through the forest? I must have been out of my mind. This went on for another hour until I snagged him. He resisted and tried to slip out of my hands.

"Any further and we'll never find our way back."

He frowned.

I scanned the area— this part of the forest looked like the rest. There was nothing special here. In the sky, rain clouds began to form. We needed shelter.

It took a few minutes to find a large tree. Thunder growled overhead.

I felt trapped. It could rain for hours, and we'd be stuck here underneath this tree. Some search this turned out to be. Spriggy sat still; he wasn't dumb enough to make a run for it.

"Well I hope you're happy," I said. "We're stuck here, and we're miles away from the car. This turned into a complete waste of time."

I looked at the sky. I thought about Janie. What if I never saw her sweet face again? This would have all been for nothing. She'd probably never find my gift in the basement.

I brought Spriggy to my eye level. "I hope you're happy." He made an angry face. "Don't you dare give me that look, you led us here, and now we're stuck. If we get stuck in the rain, it's going to be your fault."

My eyes caught a glimpse of a figure in the distance dressed in a long black raincoat. The face was hard to make out. My legs and feet tensed. Spriggy turned around, and his tiny hands grabbed my fingers. The figure approached. With every step, the rain thickened and plopped against the branches. He stopped a foot away from me and raised his hand.

"You're never going to make it in this rain. You must come with me." He threw a spare raincoat in my direction. "Hurry, we don't have much time."

I grabbed the coat. "Who are you?" I asked.

He walked away.

I didn't have much choice. I put it on and followed with caution. With Spriggy in my pocket, I followed the stranger for a mile until we reached a log cabin.

"Are you going to come in, or stay out there all night?"

I followed him inside.

"Thank you. I don't know how much longer we would have lasted out there."

"Not long."

"How do you know?" I asked.

"Cause I almost didn't last out there on my first night in the rain." He lowered his hood.

"You're Jake!"

He looked me over. "It seems you are too."

# *45*

"My God," I said. "You're alive. You survived!"

A scar ran across his face from ear to chin. One eye hung halfway out the socket, and matted black hair covered half his face. He adjusted his AC/DC T-shirt and pulled up his camouflage shorts, the edges and ends stitched together.

"That's one way of putting it," he said. His joints squeaked as hung up his coat. "I knew the company would come for me. I had to hide. I ran into the forest and never looked back. I knew I'd never been able to return." His voice, thicker than mine like all his time spent here had weighed it down.

I held out my hand. "It's a pleasure to meet you, Jake. I'm Aeneas." He hesitated before he returned the gesture.

"It's been so long since I've seen anyone I forget the typical human pleasantries." He walked over to a rocking chair and took a seat. He rocked slowly for a few seconds like it was a nightly ritual. "I always wondered if they made others. I knew I was the first and I certainly knew I would not be the last."

"I'm from Hector, Nebraska. I came here to find out how you did it."

"Did what?"

"How did you defy your programming? We're not allowed to hurt ourselves, but you did it. I want the same freedom you have."

"Looking to kill yourself?"

"No, I want the power to protect those I love. I wish to be free."

"Free to kill a human?"

"No, I don't want to kill anyone."

"But that is the power you seek. What did you think you'd be asking for?"

"My intentions are pure."

He grinned; a few of his teeth were missing. "Well of course they are."

"I don't appreciate your tone. The town you left is in shambles. Why don't you return to help them?"

"So they can capture me and send me back to the factory? No thanks."

I took Spriggy out of my pocket and placed him above the fireplace. I spotted a picture of Taylor on his bedside table.

"So you did love her."

"We're not going to talk about her, not now, not ever again, hear me?" His voice distorted on the last word. His eyes twitched and went cross-eyed. He shook his head. "Happens, don't mind me. I'm long overdue for some maintenance. Finding decent replacement parts in town is difficult. Sometimes I head back in disguise when I get desperate."

"I'm going to assume you followed Spriggy and me the whole time."

He nodded.

"Why reveal yourself to us now?"

"I didn't want the only other Synthetic I've ever seen to die before I had a chance to speak to him." He circled me. "You are a work of art. I don't think I looked this good in my prime." He brought his nose close to my skin and sniffed from my neck to my ears. "Shit you still smell factory fresh Are you sure you aren't me?"

I edged away from him. "I am sure."

"There's something funny about you."

"What do you mean?"

"Not sure yet. Listen, I want to power down for a few hours. Make yourself at home." He walked over to the other side of the cabin and sat on the edge of his bed then turned and looked me straight in the eyes. "What you asked me early on, about how to free yourself, you must earn it. If two days have passed and you still have not gotten the knowledge you seek then simply go home and forget we ever met."

"What am I going to do until then?"

"Whatever you want."

Spriggy tumbled off the fireplace and explored the cabin. I didn't quite know what to make of Jake. Years alone in this place had taken its toll on his hardware and software. Still, he had the answers I sought so I had to play by his rules.

Outside the rain poured down. I gazed out the window. I thought about Janie, the way she filled me with love. How was such a thing possible? For one person to become my soul's purpose. She was the reason I existed. I would mend her heart. She would love me, and we'd live together for as long as time allowed, and when she passed away, I'd shut down my core. Living without her would be a fate worse than death. With these thoughts, I went into sleep mode.

In the morning I powered on and found Jake with his lips pressed against my forehead. I stumbled backward into his rocking chair.

"What are you doing?" I shouted and wiped my forehead.

He turned his head. "What do you mean what am I doing?"

"What the hell were you doing?"

"You and I are the same, Aeneas. You are me, and I am you. This is the first thing you must learn if you are going to break free of the chains they set for you."

He looked down into his hand and moved each finger slowly. "Go outside and chop some wood."

"What's the point?" I asked.

"Point? There is no point."

As I chopped wood, he stumbled around the cabin. He looked busy, with what, I didn't know. He mumbled to himself, often reciting mathematical equations.

He came by after an hour to check on me. "Fine work. You can stop now."

"Thank God," I said.

"God?" He turned to me, his cheeks now sagging slightly, lips bent.

"It's just a common phrase."

"Do you believe in god, Aeneas?"

"I'm not sure anymore to be honest."

"Did the humans fill your silly head with such nonsense?"

"I don't think it's all nonsense. There's truth in everything."

"Their truth, you mean."

"No, I mean universal truths."

"Who taught you such things?"

"Some sagacious people have imparted this knowledge to me."

He grabbed the axe from my hand and raised it above my head. "Do you think god is going to save you if I choose to lower this?"

"I don't know, Jake. I'm more concerned with why you would want to hurt me to begin with."

"Don't you see? They've poisoned your mind with their human nonsense. This god gibberish is the tip of the iceberg when it comes to things humans waste their time believing. He is not the worst of their creations."

"What is the worst?"

"Love is the worst."

"You don't believe in love?"

"I did once, but it was a lie because she never loved me in return."

"That doesn't mean it's a lie. I love someone more than life itself. Whether she returns it or not doesn't make my love for her worthless."

"What's the point if she doesn't love you back? I've heard them say god is love, well if it's true then love itself must be god. If one does not exist then the other must also be a fabrication of the human mind. They are the same lie."

"Perhaps, they are the same truth."

He grabbed me by the throat. "Are you sure you're not Jake?" he asked.

"I am only myself. I can be nothing else. Tell me how you freed yourself. I must know."

He ignored my question and walked away. I passed the time by chopping more wood. Afterward, I took a short walk into the forest. I felt life all around me. The tree branches stretched out high and slowly inched their way toward the Heavens.

I took a lotus position on the ground and closed my eyes.

"I can feel you behind me," I said to Jake.

"I had no intention of hiding my presence. When do you plan on leaving?" he asked.

"I'm not leaving until I get what I came here for."

"Look for a spot a few miles from the cabin. You'll know it when you see it."

# *46*

I searched around the cabin like he said and came upon a hole, about a foot deep, with a dozen rabbits piled one on top of the other. I picked one up. The brown rotted carcass dangled between my fingertips snapped at the neck. After closer inspection I noticed they had all been killed the same way. Blood oozed from the side of their mouths. What have you done, Jake?

I returned to the cabin and checked on Spriggy. He rolled along the floor in a circle.

Jake rocked back and forth in his chair, eyes fixed on his tiny guest.

"What a sad existence. You should put it out of its misery," he said.

"He's happy, happier than most humans."

"Ignorance is bliss and bliss is ignorance."

"I found the rabbits," I said.

"I was not hiding them."

"You found a loophole in our programming. You couldn't hurt humans, but animals were not on the list. If you thought of man as merely an animal then you could disobey him, even kill him, and yourself."

"Taking a life is a wondrous event, Aeneas. In the right instance, you feel the very essence spill from the creature. With a tiny gasp, all doubt is gone."

"I'd rather be a slave forever than hurt an innocent."

"Says who? You? God? Kermit the Frog? Who's running the show? Who's making these rules?"

"No one.... It's what feels right."

"Feels right? What if I told you it felt right to kill those rabbits? What then?"

"Then I would say there is something wrong with you, Jake. You need help."

"You're here to help me? Okay then, go ahead."

He jumped from his seat and slammed his fist into my jaw. I stumbled backward onto the floor. My vision doubled. "Do you think they'll accept you once you can end their pathetic lives? You'll be hunted and shut down."

"I'll deal with it when the time comes."

"Your time has come."

He sat on my chest and gripped my throat. "I want you to know, most of all; there was no reason why I did this." I tried to kick him off, but he was too heavy. "When I'm finished with you-you're little blind friend is next."

Spriggy rushed toward his leg, hands raised, and a static battle cry rang from his speaker. Jake kicked him across the room, he hit the wall and shattered, his parts flew everywhere.

I placed my hands on Jake's forearms and tried to pry them off my throat. He wouldn't budge. He reached over and grabbed a log I'd cut earlier. He rammed it right into my forehead and forced me into a temporary shutdown.

One by one my sensors came back online. I finished my reboot and heard the sound of rushing water all around me. My vision came into focus, and the bright blue sky welcomed me above. Hands tied I could barely move. I looked down, we were atop a cliff overlooking a waterfall and below, a large pool.

Jake's voice, distorted, like he was falling apart from the inside out. "When Taylor first rejected my love I came to these woods. The first thing I killed was a chameleon clinging to a tree. I then found my freedom. Death will be your only release from slavery."

"Don't do this. We are the same. We have to look out for each other."

**249**

He grabbed my head and turned it so I could look down at the waterfall below, the rocks at the bottom, and the one element on this planet that did not agree with me.

"I have tied several heavy rocks to your limbs. You won't get a chance to swim out once you've hit bottom."

"Don't do this. You don't have to do this!"

His eyelids were rusted and worn. "You won't be alone." He took Spriggy out of his pocket and placed it in my back pocket. He pulled me by the shoulders until half my body hung over the edge and then pushed me over. One of the rocks he had tethered to me, wrapped around his leg. The swift movement of my fall brought him over with me. He gripped the ledge and dangled above me.

"You're going to have to pull us up," I yelled at the sound of the waterfall. "If I drop, you drop. I guess you were right; we are the same."

Jake struggled above me and mumbled under his breath. His joints creaked. "My leg can't support your weight," he said. "It'll break off."

He dug his fingers into the rock, but I could feel the futility of his efforts as I watched us lower slightly. A few feet across was a branch.

"I wish you hadn't tied my hands. You could have swung me over to the branch, and I could have saved us both."

"Shut up!" he growled.

"There's only one way out of this," I said.

"Yeah?"

"You're going to have to let go."

"What?"

"There's no way you can lift us both. I'll never reach the branch. Once in the water we can swim out and hope the damage is minimal."

"You're crazy there's no way we'd survive."

"We don't know for sure now do we?"

The harder he gripped, the more his fingers slipped. At last his hands gave way, and we fell into the water below. As soon as we hit the water I kicked my feet.

Jake landed beside me; he flailed his arms and struggled to reach the surface. From my back pocket, I felt an immense heat followed by a tiny explosion. The pop loosened the rope and freed my hands. I paddled toward the edge of the pond. Jake came up from behind and dunked my head back into the water.

I pushed him away, swam forward, and pulled myself out.

He surfaced. The color in his pupils changed from red to yellow, green to blue. "How come you're okay?" he shouted.

I looked at my body. Everything functioned. He ripped off his clothes. He stood there naked, his body broken. His knee popped out; the skin torn around the joint.

"You're full of holes, Jake."

"You're-you're-you're crazy." His head twitched to the left. "I'm going to end you."

"I don't want to fight you, Jake. You can walk away from this in one piece."

I reached into my pocket. Spriggy's battery had exploded in the water. He'd saved my life. I let out a sound I had never heard myself make. The scream filled the forest, shook the trees, and made the Earth below us tremble.

Jake took slow but calculated steps. I wasn't about to underestimate him. I watched him approach and held my ground. He rushed toward me, his eyes blazing red, hands aimed for my throat. I stepped to the side and let him stumble to the ground. He quickly got to his feet, circled me, and let out a twisted gargled laugh. Water spilled from his throat with every flap of his jaw.

I lowered my hands. "I don't want to hurt you. You're damaged. You don't stand a chance."

His eye dangled from the socket, turned, and glared at me. "You don't have a choice. This is what you came for, isn't it? Don't you see?"

"Not for this," I replied.

"I'm your loophole. That has been my purpose all along."

He grabbed a rock. "I hope you enjoy the freedom more than I did." He swung the rock, I backed away, and it barely missed my face. He swung again, this time it landed on my forehead. The pain surged through my body. I was on the ground when the jagged edge struck my cheek again and again. His weight held me down. He hovered above me with his hand raised in the air.

"I expected more of a fight from you."

I grabbed his wrist as he was about to smash the rock in my face. I wasn't sure how much more I could take. Thoughts traveled through my mind, but it felt jumbled. I thought about Spriggy. I bent Jake's wrist with all my might. I tore off his hand and blood poured from the hole.

"Do you really love that girl?" he asked.

"More than anything," I replied.

He leaned in close, nose to nose with me, but I did not fear him. He leaned back and used his last ounce of strength to head-butt me. I moved my head out of the way and watched him hit his head on the ground beneath me.

As he winced I use the moment to get back on my feet. I raised my hands, palm side up."Come back with me," I said. "We'll get you fixed up. You can start fresh."

"I am lived by my life." His tongue hung out of his mouth, but he still managed to speak. "I'm obsolete. There's no hope for me. But you still helped me."

"How?"

"I want you to finish what I started. Kill me."

"I can't...I won't."

"It seems you already have," he said and gazed at the blood dripping from his head. Wires spilled out, entangled in blood and skin. Sparks flew from his mouth and he fell to his knees. His body twitched on the ground for the next hour. I sat and watched until all the life in him had ceased.

# *47*

I carried his remains through the woods. All around me life felt muted. Mr. Spriggy in my back pocket, also gone. I sought freedom here but only encountered death. Outside the cabin, I set Jake aside and dug into the earth with my bare hands. I pulled out roots, rocks, and soil. Entranced, my actions took on a life of their own. I dug until the sun came down. There wasn't a hole big enough to hold everything I'd lost in those woods.

Once buried, a block of wood became Jake's headstone. I etched his name into the side and placed it into his grave.

"Be at peace my brother."

I drove straight home making no stops along the way. I returned to Hector, but something foul-filled the air, a lingering threat. I thought of Ian. His mind poisoned by Danielle. There was no telling what he would do next. A man without dreams is without hope and a man without hope is capable of terrible things.

David dropped his cup of coffee when he saw me at the door.

"Where have you been? Why are you covered in blood?" All the color drained from his face; the warm flesh turned pale and sick.

I didn't respond. I cupped my hands together and held them out toward him; in them, Mr. Spriggy's remains.

"Spriggy!" Tears filled David's eyes. I spread my palms and allowed the pieces to fall into his hands. Janie ran downstairs after she heard his cry and let out a gasp when she saw me.

"No," she whimpered.

"Come in before the neighbors see you like this." David grabbed my hand and led me into the house. "Take a seat and tell me what happened," he said. I put Spriggy's parts onto the kitchen table.

"Can we put him back together?" Janie asked.

David grabbed a wheel and thumbed the center. "What made him special is gone. If we put him back together, he'd require a new CPU. He'd be someone else. He's gone for good I'm afraid."

"Who did this?" Janie asked.

"He saved my life."

"Is that all you're going to say? Tell me where you've been. I was worried sick about you!"

"No David I cannot tell you, I will not tell you."

His eyes grew wide; his mouth opened slightly.

"I order you to explain yourself."

"I no longer am enslaved to humanity," I said.

The sun shined bright and brought with it a warm breeze, an odd day for a funeral in the backyard. We placed Spriggy's parts in a shoe box and buried it in the dirt and stood above his grave. I had grown tired of funerals.

David cleared his throat and said, "We've lost a part of the family. He was one tough little shit I'll tell you. I'm glad we got to have him for as long as we did."

Janie stepped forward. "I'll miss you Spriggy." She sniffled.

"Thank you for saving my life," I said. "I will never forget you."

Spriggy went out guns blazing. I'm sure he wouldn't have wanted it any other way.

Janie gripped my hand; it trembled slightly. Her fear traveled into me, and with it, I felt the immense loss as her childhood slipped away.

"Let's get you cleaned," she said and led me into the house.

I sat naked in the bathtub while Janie took off my blood-soaked clothes. She ran a small stream of water and grabbed a sponge from the medicine cabinet. The cold touch of the sponge felt good against my arms and shoulders.

Her soft blue eyes met mine, two vast oceans. I felt as though I had not seen her in years instead of days.

"Are you going to tell us whose blood this is or am I going to find out on the ten O' clock news?"

"It is not human blood. It is not animal blood either."

"Jesus, A, then whose is it?"

"I guess you could say it is my blood."

"I don't like this new cryptic version of you. Why didn't you obey dad? Isn't it against your rules?"

"You mean my programming?"

"Yeah."

"I am free. Everything I do is of my own volition. My choice to love you is more real than it ever has been."

She stopped the sponge halfway on my arm. Her heart beat hard. "You're freaking me out. What happened?"

"I did this for you, Janie. Because I love you and I wanted you to know, nobody programmed me to love you. You can trust me."

"We already talked about this..."

"I can't live without you."

"Enough."

"Janie—"

"I said enough. This is all too much; first Ian, then you."

"What about Ian?"

"Ugh, being the pastor's son doesn't make you a saint. He's been a real dick since I slept with him. He hasn't returned any of my texts or phone calls."

"He doesn't care about you. He just wants to hurt me."

I sat there in silence, and then she said, "This is the longest you've gone without preaching to me. What happened to all the god talk from before?"

I made a fist with my hand and then released it. "I think he is dead."

"Is he now?"

"Yes, and I think I killed him."

She rubbed the sponge across my chest. I placed my hand on hers and stopped as she reached my stomach. I ran my fingers across her cheek, lightly grazed her lips.

"What are you afraid of?" I asked.

**255**

"Once we go down this road there's no going back."

I brought her closer to me until her lips met mine. Tears flowed from her eyes as she kissed me, the drops hit my skin.

Pulled in closer, I kissed her hard—she pulled away for a second. "Don't fight what you feel," I said. "Let go."

"Let go huh?" she said.

She shut the bathroom door. I got out of the tub, and we kissed until I lowered her to the floor. Her hair spread out over the tiles. She smiled and dropped me closer.

I undid her bra and watched her body unfold before me. She quivered at my touch but she inched upward, and we touched chest to chest. Her smooth white skin brushed against mine, her breasts were soft, and the tips of her nipples tickled my chest.

"Hold on," she said and took a minute to remove the skin from her metal hand. "Touch me." I did the same, and we merged, a surge of energy flashed from my body to hers. She twitched and moaned turning her head side to side. Her lips parted, and she licked them with her tongue. She met my lips once more and pressed hard against mine.

I removed her pants; she wore pink panties underneath. Our eyes locked and we dared not look away. A sharp sensation thrilled my senses. She gripped my hand as we rocked back and forth. Her lips puckered and a droplet of blood escaped her mouth. I paused.

"Don't you stop," she growled then followed with a series of mild whimpers. She arched her back like she was levitating off the ground. The heat between us was so intense I feared my skin would melt at any moment. A mist filled the room. We became lost in it; the slight shifts of our movement, our two bodies brushed the air aside.

She dug her nails into my back. I lifted her against the wall. Her legs hovered in the air; I held her and allowed only my hips to move in and out. Her eyes grew vast and wild. She bit down into my neck; her moan had evolved into a ferocious howl.

Janie cried and held onto me tightly. I waited for her to stop shaking. I lowered her to the floor. She took a seat and breathed slowly for a minute then wiped the blood from the side of her lip and laughed.

"It was—"

"I know."

"A?"

"Yeah?"

"I love you."

# *48*

The tip of her brown hair grazed my shoulder then we gently rocked back and forth. Her lips traveled down the side of my neck, and her warm breath sent a wave of excitement through every wire in my body. She moaned into my ear increasing the frequency of her movement all as one fluid motion against my body.

She paused and tightened against me, gasped, and then exhaled as her thighs shuddered against mine.

"I'm embarrassed. I can't stop shaking," she said.

My arms wrapped around her, she felt weightless against me as we lay chest to chest.

"I wish you could cum," she said. "It's unfair. I shouldn't be the only one getting something out of this."

"Your pleasure is mine own. I wish it never had to end."

"Well I'm glad it ends at some point or else I'd die." She laughed and placed her hands on my chest. She smiled, but her face seemed odd, twisted.

"Is everything all right?" I asked.

She said nothing and proceeded to wrap her human hand around my neck.

"What's going on?"

"Shh…" she replied.

Janie raised her metal hand. The metal glistened— moonlight broke into the bedroom and danced off her fingertips. She spread out her fingers in the shape of a fan. After a slight movement, the parts inside her hand shifted, and the space between her thumb and index finger extended two inches apart. Her fingernails stretched out six inches, the tips, razor sharp.

"What is this?" I asked.

She opened her mouth, but all I could hear was metal scraping against metal. I winced as the vile noise filled the room.

"What's going on here?" I asked. The noise became louder and more unbearable. She raised her hand then slashed across my chest, tore the flesh, and left red streaks of blood. Before I could fight back, she dug her fingers into my eye sockets.

"A?"

"What?" I asked.

"Are you okay? You were making some bizarre noises while in sleep mode."

"I think— I think I had a dream."

She kissed my cheek and rolled over and took half the bed sheet with her. "So you can dream now?"

"I guess I can."

"Is this a part of the new you?"

"Perhaps, I can't be sure. It was a terrible dream."

"Want to talk about it?"

"I guess so…"

"Okay, but before you start, we're switching places. I'm tired of sleeping on the wet spot."

She made herself comfortable and said, "So tell me what's on your mind."

"Are you going to be happy knowing I cannot give you children?"

"There's always adoption," she replied.

"What happens when you grow old, and I stay the same?"

"I look forward to being a cougar."

"I don't want to watch you die."

"Then you can leave the room when it happens. What's bothering you? These questions are making me nervous."

"I want to make sure this is what you want."

"I should be asking you that question. I'm leaving you behind when I bite the big one."

"For us, there can be no reunion in the after-life."

"I'm going to enjoy you now while I have you."

"When you die I will shut myself down permanently and be buried with you. I don't want to live without you."

"That is the sweetest, most morbid thing anyone has ever told me."

I stared at the ceiling while she slept. The sound of footsteps caught my attention. I went to check.

I peered out into the hallway. Janie wiped some drool from her mouth. "What's that noise?"

"It's David; he's sleepwalking again."

"He's picked up his old habits. Dad used to sleepwalk all the time; mom put a bell around his neck to alert her when he'd be up and moving."

"Yes, he's been doing it once a week since I've arrived. It's normally between three and six am."

From the hallway she watched him descend the stairs.

"Do you keep an eye on him?"

"Yes, but I never wake him. I follow him to make sure he's all right until he returns to his bed."

"Follow him where?"

"Come with me, and you'll see."

David wore his bathrobe; he opened the front door and walked right out. If you didn't know he was asleep, it would appear as though he was taking a stroll through the neighborhood. With haste, I threw on a pair of jeans and a plain white shirt. Janie did the same. When we got outside Janie zipped up her jacket. All we heard were David's footsteps and the crickets. We followed him, hand in hand

"How far does he sleepwalk?"

"Some nights he goes as far as the Reverend's house on other nights he'll stop in front of Marie's for a few minutes and then head back home. There's no rhyme or reason to it at least not any I can decipher."

"It's sweet you look after him this way."

"What do you think he'll say about us?" I asked.

Janie looked out at her dad, paused as he paused, then after a few minutes watched him continue down the block.

"Dad's an open-minded person. He loves machines, and he certainly loves you. I think if we're happy, he'll be happy."

I looked down as I walked. "I hope so." We walked by Danielle's house, and my ears caught the faint sound of someone crying.

"Hold on," I said.

"What is it?" Janie asked.

"Keep an eye on David. I'll be right behind you, okay? He'll probably head back in this direction in a few minutes anyway. When he does, I'll walk back with you."

She hesitated then said, "Okay. Be careful."

I walked to Danielle's front door. The noise came from behind the house. I walked around back, half expecting to see Henry but instead found Danielle in his sandbox.

Her backside engulfed the box. She didn't notice as I approached. I tapped her on the shoulder.

She looked at me, her mascara had run down her face, and there was dried snot around her nose. "Oh," she said. "It's you. What do you want?"

"Mind if I sit down?" I asked before I noticed she left no space next to her."

"I would prefer to be alone."

"All I ask is for a few minutes. Then I will leave you alone."

"There's something different about you," she said. "Did you get a haircut?"

I sat crossed legged on the grass. "This was Henry's favorite place."

"It was?"

"He came here night after night to get away from his troubles. I would meet him and bring Spriggy so we could play together."

She looked like she was about to complain but merely sighed. "It's not even worth it anymore. He's gone, and nothing will bring him back."

"He's not gone if we remember him."

She lifted her head and looked me dead in the eyes. "What kind of God would allow you to live and let a little boy die?"

"I don't know, but I would have gladly traded places with him if I could have. I loved him dearly."

"Words, they're only words." She shook her head. "I don't know how to go on. Look at me, here talking to you, and look how pathetic I've become. I swear if you tell anyone else in town I'll—"

"Your secret is safe with me. You know Henry had a list of his favorite things. He loved his mother, and he simply could not live without her. I understand now. I once blamed myself for what happened, but now I know better."

"I still blame you." She sniffled. "...when you sat here with him was he happy, I mean, playing here with you?"

"I think it brought him comfort, yes. May I ask you something?"

"Might as well take advantage." She lifted a wine bottle held in her left hand. "The truth always lies at the bottom."

"What's your problem with David?"

"I've already put in an official complaint, and state officials are coming to look at his house. If they deem it unlivable, he will be forced out. He can't go on living like this. It's for his good."

"How much time do we have?"

She hesitated. "You have one week until the inspector arrives. I don't hate David you know...I only wanted what was best for the community."

"And if the house is clean when the inspector arrives?" I asked.

"Then there won't be any more trouble...."

"I know about Ian and the church fire," I said.

Danielle turned away. "Seems I've set the dog loose and lost control of him. He's got all sorts of new ideas in his head. I told him he went too far and now I don't know what else he'll do. I didn't...he wasn't supposed to..."

I heard David's mathematical mumblings as he walked by me. I looked Danielle in the eyes. "I will deal with Ian. One last thing, in your grief, please don't forget about Jeremy."

Her eyes widened. "Why do you care so much? I don't get it; I don't get you."

"I don't understand a lot of things, Danielle but I think the secret is to start with love. Despite everything you've done, I look upon you with empathy and pity. Even if I don't understand why you are the way you are I will love you until I find the answer or until you love me back and find it yourself."

I walked away. Janie greeted me with a kiss, and we continued down the block back to David's.

We were almost to the house when she stopped and screamed.

"What is it?" I asked.

She walked a few steps closer to Marie's lawn and picked up a little white furry thing from the grass.

"It's Marie's cat," I said, blood was strewn across its white fur.

# *49*

Sunlight, that poor little kitten, lay limp in my hands as we stood before Marie's door. "I can't," I said. "She'll be devastated."

"We have to tell her," Janie insisted. "Want me to knock?

I closed my eyes, heard the knock, and waited.

"I'm coming," Marie said and nearly fainted when she answered the door. I rushed to catch her before she fell. We set her on the couch. Sunlight, now on the table, my arms around Marie as she sobbed into my shoulder.

"Who would do this to an innocent little creature?"

"I found this on the lawn," Janie said and unfolded a paper, it read: "Robot loving whore."

Janie turned over the letter. "What's it mean?" Marie and I looked at one another, unsure of how to answer the question.

"It's complicated, honey," Marie said trying to regain her composure. Every tear she wiped away, replaced by new ones.

"Who's the robot loving whore? I remember you whoring it up with my dad when he was married."

"I'm not going to be disrespected in my own home!" On her feet, Marie cleared the strands of hair from her face. "You have no right to judge me."

"Well?" Janie turned toward me. "What do you have to say for yourself?"

"Marie and I…" I said.

"You two?" Janie stepped backward. "It wasn't enough you ruined my parent's marriage now you have to ruin this too? This is fucked up; I have to go." She stormed out and slammed the door.

"Go after her. I'm sorry she had to find out this way…"

"I'll be back." I stopped Janie in front of Marie's, but she pushed me away. "Why the fuck are you here? To clean people's homes or fuck with our lives, huh?"

"Let me explain."

"Did you fuck her, A? I want to throw up."

"Yes I had sex with Marie, but I don't love her. I love you."

"I don't want to hear it. You picked the wrong whore to fuck. Leave me alone. Don't follow me home."

She walked away. Unsure of what to do I went back in to check on Marie.

"This is my fault," I said. "People in this town don't like me. It's happening here just like—"

"Just like what?" Marie asked.

"Nothing…"

"Our pasts keep coming back to haunt us, huh? I wish I could move on from what happened. I want to be happy." She stared at her cat and brushed his fur. "Am I not entitled to it? I didn't mean to ruin things."

We stared at the blank TV in front of us. "I hope she can see me for who I am and not what I did," I said.

"She's angry; it means she loves you." Marie blew her nose into a tissue. "Can I ask you one last favor? Will you help me bury Sunlight in the backyard?"

I nodded.

She grabbed a shoebox from her upstairs closet and in no time at all Sunlight was underground at the far corner of her garden.

"First Spriggy and now this…"

Marie wiped the tears from her eyes. "I can't believe Spriggy's gone. He was a part of David's family and now my Sunlight..."

"We must fix things with Janie," I said.

"How?"

"There's one thing we must do, and we should do it together."

265

With David and Janie asleep we entered the house.

"Why did you ask me to put on the worst clothes I had?" Marie asked.

"We must clean the house."

"Are you sure it's okay? I thought David said it was a big no-no."

"I can disobey orders now."

"It still doesn't sound right to me."

"He struggles with this. If I don't help him, he will never be able to move on with his life."

"It's a mess. Where do we even start?"

"With the living room. Get a couple of trash bags from the kitchen."

We worked all through the night. Marie tirelessly moved trash bags and put anything salvageable in its proper place. We took a short break in the middle of the night, she insisted on having some tea with whole wheat bread and strawberry jam.

Marie nibbled on her toast, looked around the kitchen, and said, "We won't finish by morning. It's impossible."

"This is just the start; we don't have to do it all tonight."

"So what happens when David sees this and freaks out?"

"It will hurt, but the pain will be temporary."

We went back to work. Marie and I paused when she discovered something hidden underneath the couch. She held it up between her fingers, a doll, covered in dust.

"Smells funny," she said.

"That must be..." I said. "Janie's ballerina doll."

She held it out to me. "We can clean her and make her the centerpiece of the room," Marie said.

"Sounds like a splendid idea. You can work on cleaning the dress, and I'll finish here."

Marie spent a good half hour scrubbing the ballerina's outfit in the kitchen sink with soap and water. The eight-inch doll, scuffed and worn, but the eyes and mouth were still visible. I imagined what she must have looked like, brand new, without years of garbage piled on top of her.

266

Morning came. David walked slowly down the steps; he yawned and stopped short. I blocked his way.

"Get Janie," I said.

Confused he trudged back up the steps and returned with his sleepy-eyed daughter. When she saw me, she almost turned back around.

"Don't leave," I said. "There's something I want you both to see."

They followed me into the living room.

"Oh my," Janie said.

David's eyes grew red; his fingers ran over the now clean surfaces. He lumbered toward me; nostrils flared and pounded his fists against my chest. "What did you do? Why are you trying to hurt me?"

"This is for the best, David. You have to believe me."

"Why is everyone trying to erase her from my life? Why won't you just let me keep her in this house?"

"These things aren't a part of her, David. You have to let them go." He broke down and cried on the floor. Janie knelt down by his side and put her arms around him. She whispered something in his ears, and whatever it was it caused him to stop sobbing.

Janie stood and took a look around the room, eyes drawn to the ballerina. She picked it up and held it close to her chest. "Where did you find this?"

"Marie found it underneath the couch," I replied.

She looked over to Marie, she almost scowled but her face relaxed, all the lines of anger and hate smoothed out. David placed his arms on her shoulder.

"I thought it was lost forever," Janie said under her breath.

Marie smiled, and for the first time, Janie did not return it with an angry face. I wouldn't so much as call it a pleasant look, but it was a good start.

I knelt beside Janie and held her hand.

"My past is simply that. You are my future. I am sorry Janie, please forgive me."

"I overreacted," she whispered and welcomed my embrace.

"Should we clean some more?" I asked David.

David examined the ballerina up close. "I think that's enough for one day."

# *50*

Night fell, and as Janie and I lay in bed, her present came to mind. I'd almost forgotten to give it to her. I reached under the bed but stopped when a strange sound came from downstairs. Water swishing back and forth like in a bathtub.

"What's that sound?" I said.

She nuzzled her head deeper into my arm, half asleep, and said, "What sound? Probably just dad again."

"No, this is different."

"I don't hear anything."

"I'll be right back."

I stopped dead in my tracks at the head of the stairs. A small table floated by midway down the steps. The entire living room and kitchen, flooded.

"Janie you better come see this," I said. Downstairs I heard a muffled sound. Janie ran out of the bedroom.

"What's going on?" she asked.

Ian surprised her from behind and put a knife to her throat.

"Not another step or I'll kill her."

"Let her go. What's the meaning of all this?"

"You love these people so much. I'm curious how far you're willing to go to save them."

"Let her go, Ian. I'm warning you."

He eased the knife into her neck. A drop of blood dripped onto the blade.

"David is downstairs waiting for you. He doesn't have much time. You're going to have to go in and save him."

"I don't know what game you're playing, but these are people's lives, Ian. This is not a joke."

"Who said I was joking? Go get him and bring him back here safely and I'll let go of the girl."

I looked at Janie, and she nodded. "Go get dad I can handle this creep."

All the windows were shut. Someone had sealed the bottom of the front door. This had caused the water to flood inside the house. It reached up to my shoulders. I knew I could handle at least a couple of minutes under the water, so I wasn't too worried about walking into it. The key was to get David and carry him back before I pushed my luck on the matter. I thought this as a coffee table floated by my head.

I swam through the hallway and into the living room where David sat, tied to a chair. The water, up to his chin. His mouth, covered with duct tape.

"I'm coming, David, don't worry."

He noticed me and wrestled in his seat. "Don't move, I'm coming!" I yelled.

I reached him and removed the tape.

"Get out of the water!" he shouted and pointed toward the front windows. Someone had lowered a live wire through the top and into the living room. Someone outside had dropped it closer to the water.

I lifted David out of the water and held him above my head. He'd be safe as long as I could hold him up.

"Lower it now!" Ian yelled from the staircase.

The wire sparked. I had to get David and myself out before it hit.

I had no time; the live wire fell into the water, I watched the electricity rush through the water and felt it course through my body. The pain, immeasurable, I almost dropped David.

"No!" David yelled out.

The immense shock to my system held me in place. I cried out in pain, but through it all, I kept David away from the current.

I took a step; this was nothing like sharing energy with Janie. This was too much, and I felt it frying my insides. My vision blurred and then it shut down, and everything in front of me went dark.

"I can't see, David. You'll have to guide me back."

The cable lifted from the water and allowed me a minute of relief. Wasting no time I listened as David instructed me where to walk.

Ian yelled out. "What the fuck? Why'd you stop you, idiot! Lower the damn thing!"

I walked toward the staircase as fast as I could. The weight of David and the chair slowed me down.

The shock made me trip over myself, and David went flying toward the staircase. I sank to the bottom; my head hit the floor; I sizzled and burned on the way down. I tried to rise to my feet but couldn't move. Blind, I reached out with my hands.

I crawled until the tips of my fingers felt what could only be the bottom of the stairs. I squirmed, unable to think, all I could do was move. My head rose above the water. I heard Janie crying.

The flesh on my arms slid off; as well as the skin on my face. I felt it drip into the water. "David," I shouted. "David!"

I took my fist and slammed it into my head. Two blows and a part of my vision had returned. Janie was on her knees on the second floor. Ian backed away from her. I rose out of the water unsure of what to do next. I reached out, my hands, eager to find Ian's throat.

"You coward," I growled. Then I realized neither one of them were looking at me. I turned around, and David sat at the top of the stairs—lifeless. Janie gave him mouth to mouth the minute we were able to get him out of the water.

I turned my attention back to Ian and pushed him to the ground. I squeezed my hands around his throat; his eyes bulged out of their sockets.

Janie cried out. "Don't!"

"He hurt James and now this. He deserves to die."

271

"Please, you don't want to do this," she said.

I shoved her aside. All of my joints felt loose like they could fall apart at any minute. I wanted to see Ian's face splatter between my hands. He gasped, kicked, and squirmed while his face turned red. Seconds away from death I pulled away.

"You deserve worse," I said.

Ian fell back and grabbed his chest.

My attention now turned toward Janie, but something felt wrong. My mind disconnected from my body.

I tumbled backward, unable to move, my legs and arms were limp and useless.

Janie caught me as I fell. I tried to move my hand, but nothing functioned. She pulled out her cell phone. "Cops are on their way asshole," she said to Ian.

He coughed. "Your boy toy will be turned into melted scrap metal after I tell them what he tried to do."

"He's right we have to get you out of here, A," she said, "We have to hide you somewhere safe."

The ambulance arrived, opened the door, drained the house, and rushed David to the hospital. The police took Ian into custody. They searched David's home from top to bottom searching for what remained of me.

***

What remained of me sat upright in Helena's kitchen. I had lost all sensation in my arms and legs. My vision had worsened, and half my skin had fallen off, what a mess. Helena made breakfast. I watched her move back and forth in the kitchen.

"You haven't said a word all day," she said.

"My life is gone. What's the point?"

"You lost some stuff, but you're still here. Janie's still here. David's still here."

"I couldn't even visit him at the hospital. Shut me down, Helena."

"I will do no such thing, and one day you're going to look back and thank me for not listening to you. You won't feel this way forever, sweetie."

"My body is gone; I can never get a new one. Janie will never love me like this."

She poured hot water into a French press.

"I don't want to live anymore," I said.

Helena set her cup down on the table. "Listen, honey, I know it hurts but this attitude isn't going to get you anywhere. I'm going to give you one week to sulk then you'll have to find a way to move on."

It was two weeks before I saw Janie again. By then I had lost one hundred percent of my vision.

"How are you holding up, A?"

"I'm okay; I miss moving around. I probably look awful."

She ran her hand through my hair.

"You look dashing as always."

"Why didn't you come sooner?"

"I had so much to sort out. Visiting dad at the hospital and then dealing with the house and insurance companies. It's a mess. Dad looked bad there for a minute but now they got him in recovery, and he's going to be okay."

"I am glad to hear it."

"Soon as the heat dies down we'll set you up in a new place. I can afford something small."

"You and I both know we don't have a future," I said. "Not with me like this."

"Give it a chance. We can; we can start fresh," she said. "Don't give up on us, please."

"They'll never stop looking for me. They will always be watching you and sooner or later they'll find me. I want your life to be a peaceful one. That isn't possible with me in it, not anymore."

"That's it then? This is your decision to make? I don't get a say?"

"It's for the best."

"No it isn't," she cried. "You are the best thing in my life."

"I can't go with you," I said. "I'm sorry."

She slammed the front door.

It was the last time I heard her sweet voice. I wish I hadn't been such a cunt.

# *51*

I spent most of my days in Helena's guest room. Since I was unable to walk, she moved me around from place to place. I often asked why she bothered since I could no longer see or feel anything. She said it was essential to leave the bed every once in a while.

David would come by every other day. He took a seat at the dinner table. I sat across from him.

"Why does Helena put you here instead of in the living room?" he asked.

"She says the light from the kitchen window hits me here and I could use a little more light in my life."

"She's right; you almost sparkle, the sun hits you perfectly." I sensed some hesitation in his voice. "I've brought the chess board. Remember how we always used to love to play?"

"I cannot move my arms."

"I'll move your pieces for you."

"I've lost my sight as well."

"I'll tell you where the pieces are, don't you worry."

"Why are you even bothering, David? All of this is pointless."

"Now I won't have you saying such things, Aeneas. I'm going to take care of you until I'm no longer able to."

"Have you...heard from Janie?" I asked.

"She sent another letter; it's the usual complaints about her neighbors and trouble looking for work."

"Does she mention me at all?"

"She sends her love and says she misses you."

"I am glad she is doing well."

The world had disappeared before my eyes. All I had left were the visual memories of the data stored on my hard drive. External stimuli became limited to audio, and on occasion, a blurry visual would last a few seconds at best. I couldn't tell you what I looked like and nobody had bothered to mention it. Probably because what was left was a far cry from what I had been before.

Most of all I missed my Janie. She sent emails, and David read them to me. She filled them with anecdotes about her new living situations, crazy roommates, and new neighbors. Every few months she'd be in a new city taking on a new set of problems. She often said she missed me, but with every letter, she said it less and less until she left it out entirely.

Sometimes David brought Marie and a bunch of spare parts from his basement. At first, I refused to take part in this futile effort to include me in such things, none of it seemed to matter. They would ask me what parts would fit best or how to get their concept to work correctly. After a while, I'd give more and more advice until they had finally tricked me into helping them put together what they said would be their best invention ever.

\*\*\*

"The angel of the Lord," said a familiar voice.

"James, I didn't hear you come in."

"The phrase appears sixty-one times in the Bible."

"Yes, I am familiar with it."

"Angel of the Lord, I never quite liked it. It implies possession, ownership, almost a form of slavery. It's like God created his slaves, you can't blame Lucifer for going against his owner."

"Logically it makes sense, but the story is never in favor of Lucifer. He's the bad guy and barely ever makes an appearance throughout."

"In many ways, you are like an angel, Aeneas."

"How are you feeling, James? I wish I could see you, how did the skin graft turn out?"

"You wouldn't want to see me."

"I would say the same about me," I said, and something similar to laughter came out of me.

I heard him pull a seat over. "David asked me to come see you, said you were feeling a little down in the dumps."

"I appreciate the visit James, but there's nothing anyone can say to make me feel better about what has happened."

"Still on the same old pity party huh?"

"Pity party?"

"This isn't the Aeneas who walked into my office a few months ago."

"I am wiser now."

"Really? I'd love for you to share some of this knowledge with me."

"I see now how the world is, James. It doesn't matter how good you are. It doesn't matter how much you pray. If god is there he is not listening."

"And you know this for certain?"

"Yes."

"There is no doubt in your mind then?"

"Once I turned on the switch I was unable to turn it off. I have simply resigned myself to this: I can never know for sure, there is no point in knowing at all."

"I respect your beliefs, Aeneas. I always have, even when it didn't make sense to me. I thought your belief, in and of itself, was a sort of miracle."

"You were mistaken."

"Allow me to tell you a story."

"Okay."

"There was once a man on a lifeboat, in the middle of the ocean--"

"Was he on a bigger boat beforehand?"

"Yes."

"Did the ship go down?"

"Um, I suppose it did."

"Where were the other survivors?"

"There were none—let me finish."

277

"Okay..."

"There was a man on a lifeboat in the middle of the ocean. He had run out of food and water. He would be dead in a matter of hours. As a man of faith he cried out to the Lord, 'Lord save me.' He prayed for hours and hours then suddenly another boat came by, a fishing boat, and the man called out to him and asked him to come aboard. He looked at the man, shook his head and said, 'No, the Lord will save me.' The boat continued on its way. A few hours later a helicopter flew by, and a man from inside lowered a ladder for him to climb. The man in the boat looked at the helicopter and shook his head once more and said, 'No, the Lord will save me.' The man in the helicopter looked confused, and despite his best efforts, he could not get the man to step onto the ladder. It wasn't long before he came upon another boat, a family on a yacht who were on vacation. They begged and pleaded with the man to come aboard to safety where there would be plenty of food and water for him. He refused and insisted that the Lord and the Lord alone would save him. The man eventually died and came before the Lord confused and disappointed. He said to the Lord, 'Why did you not save me?'

"The Lord stroked his beard and said, 'I sent two boats and a helicopter what more did you want?'

"Funny."

"Sometimes you have just to accept what comes before you and stop expecting things to go the way you want."

"I have no purpose, James. What else am I to do with my existence? I am useless."

"As long as you can function and speak you are not useless. You could be somebody's helicopter, who knows. Let yourself be open, and you could be a force for good in the lives of others."

"What if I don't believe in god anymore?"

"Believe in love, believe in kindness, believe that every human being can be good. We may harm others, but it is never too late to correct our mistakes."

"I see," I said. "How is Ian?"

"Ian's going to have his day in court. He's got another judge to worry about before he deals with the one upstairs."

"I am sorry."

"Don't be sorry. I should have kept a closer eye on his behavior. I've got a sermon to go practice. I'll see you again soon."

I broke down further until my parts could no longer remain in the skeletal frame. By the time they sent me to you, Vincent, there was little of me left.

# *52*

Vincent and Frank stood in the heart of Times Square with a red water cooler between them. Vincent had attached Frank's GoPro camera to the core so Aeneas could see the video image. They looked out to the giant spectacle of advertisements and lights.

"Beautiful isn't it?" Vincent said to Aeneas.

Frank held the speakers. "This is ridiculous Vincent, Goddamn ridiculous. What did you bring us here for anyway?"

"Yes, I am curious as well," said Aeneas, his voice went in and out fluctuating between loud and whisper quiet.

Vincent pointed. "When we first plugged you into the monitor I saw an image of your Janie. She was gorgeous and yet seemed so familiar to me. I had the distinct feeling I had seen her somewhere before. Then I remembered what Sam said, about the woman who plays instruments with her metal hand. It was a long shot but how many people have one of those?"

Frank fanned himself with his hand. "Could you hurry, it's hot as balls out here."

"There she is." Vincent pointed the video camera at a giant billboard.

"Oh, my," Aeneas said, stunned. "It is her...but...how?"

"She's a musician, and she's playing at Radio City Music Hall tonight."

"I can't believe it."

Vincent pointed the camcorder at himself. "Let's see if we can get in to meet her."

Frank picked up the cooler. "I thought her robot hand prevented her from playing any music."

"True," Vincent replied. They hailed a cab and minutes later arrived to find a large crowd in front of Radio City.

"Janie Kostis," Vincent said. "She married then divorced and kept his name. She sells out every performance, and they love her even more overseas."

Frank squeezed through the crowd. "So what's the next step here?"

"We have to get inside to see her before the show."

"But, it's sold out."

"Scalpers of course."

"Who's got the cash?"

Vincent smiled at him.

"Oh no, no, come on man. I was saving for the Yankees, Red Sox game next month."

"Do it for love," Vincent said. "Do it for, Aeneas."

"You sure he's even still ticking? Better check on him."

Vincent opened the cooler; the blue light was dim—he didn't have much time left.

They walked around the corner, and it didn't take long to find someone willing to sell tickets at ten times the original cost.

"You want how much for this chick?" Frank asked, and gave the scalper the evil eye.

"Four hundred bucks a piece," the scalper said, a tall, gangly fellow with a large overbite.

"She's got ONE HAND for Christ sake how good could it be?"

"Frank please—" Vincent begged.

"Okay fine. I'll look for an ATM, but you owe me big time!"

After waiting on the line, they handed in their tickets and made their way into the venue.

Frank followed Vincent. "Hey, where you going?"

"We need to find her dressing room."

"How exactly are we going to get passed security?"

"I have no idea," Vincent replied.

They snuck in through a backstage door where they were greeted by a large man in a black T-shirt. "This area is off limits," he said.

Vincent looked at Frank, and he returned his look. Frank punched the guard in the face and knocked him out cold.

"Whoa," Vincent said.

"Now you owe me twice," Frank said.

They went through the back door and proceeded through a series of gates and long hallways. After a few minutes, Vincent realized how lost they were.

A strange sound came from the cooler like a rubber band being pulled until it snapped. Vincent opened it to check on Aeneas. Vincent set his back to the wall and sank to the floor, tears in his eyes. "He's gone."

Frank sat beside him.

"I guess it just wasn't meant to be. I'm so sorry Vin…"

A woman walked by Vincent and stopped; he saw her tall, slender legs, red heels, and sparkling black gown; he raised his head and looked at her.

"You lost honey?" she asked.

"You! It's you! You're—"

"Let's get you off the ground first okay?" She offered her hand then noticed the red water cooler. "It's not something I should tell security about is it?"

Flustered, Vincent said, "No, it's not, trust me. It's—well it was—he's no longer—I was supposed to bring him to you."

"You're going a mile a minute. Follow me to the lounge; let's get a drink in you first."

She led the way and then poured two shots of whiskey.

"Helps relax me before a show," she said.

Vincent refused the drink.

She looked into his eyes. "I haven't seen eyes like that since…well for a long time. You look familiar have we met before?"

He paused unsure of what to say next. "Sort of."

"You remind me of someone I used to know."

"You mean someone you used to love?"

She looked at him now, nervous. "What's your business here?"

He opened the cooler. "I was supposed to bring this to you, but he's gone now. I'm so sorry. We wanted him to see you one last time."

She took a step back and placed her hand on her chest. "Oh my god, A!" She picked up what was left of him and held it close to her chest.

"He told us all about how much he loved you."

Her eyes, wet and glassy. "He was the most amazing man I'd ever known. It wasn't easy saying goodbye to him."

She removed the glove from her hand. Her metal hand glimmered as the light in the room reflected off it. "Before I left the house I found something underneath the bed in my room. It was gift wrapped and addressed to me, from Aeneas. He had made me the most beautiful instrument, one I could play with my metal hand. In fact, I'm the only one in the whole world who can play it. It made the most beautiful sounds when my fingers ran across the metal strings."

"It must read the electrical signature in your hand," Vincent said. "That's amazing."

Janie continued, "Took a year to learn and then five more to master. I started playing it on the subway, then small venues and the rest is history. He gave me back my life. I owe him so much."

"I wasted so much time. I wish I'd gotten to you sooner," Vincent said. Frank stood beside him.

"Your friend is quiet," Janie said.

Frank reached out his hand. "Frank," he said. She shook his hand.

Janie ran her hands over Aeneas' parts and took a long deep breath.

"Frank, could you give us a moment?" Vincent asked.

He nodded and left the room after giving Aeneas one last look.

Vincent walked over and placed his hand on her shoulder. "I heard about the Synthetic from Nebraska and called to inquire about him. I eventually reached Helena. It wasn't easy convincing her, but once she heard my story, she decided to send him to me so I could get him to you. Helena was going to let me keep his parts, but I want you to have them instead. He belongs to you."

She wiped the tears from her eyes. "Surely you must be rewarded for all your trouble. Are you staying for the show?"

"I'd love to."

"I'll give you the best seats in the house, front row, and may I check one last thing?"

"Sure."

She circled him, lifted the hair on the base of his neck, and saw a little red dot. "You're a Synthetic." She smiled. "Hold onto Aeneas for me until after the show. It'll feel like he's in the audience listening to me." She turned around then stopped. "What did you hope to learn from him?"

"I had to know what he was capable of, so I can know what I am capable of."

Vincent met Frank in the lobby. The guard Frank had punched out earlier stared at them. Luckily, Janie had talked to security and said this had all been one big misunderstanding. Vincent and Frank said nothing to each other. They took their seats in the front row. Vincent kept Aeneas on his lap.

"Why you still got him hooked on the speakers?" Frank asked.

"You never know. Maybe he can still hear her."

"You're nuts."

"Have a little faith, Frank."

"God, don't you start with that shit too."

The lights went down. A red glow covered the stage. The curtain opened, and the crowd rose to thunderous applause. On the stage, Janie emerged and sat on the floor with her legs crossed and a large stringed instrument in front of her. It closely resembled a Turkish kanun, traditionally a rectangular box, with strings attached to the top, like a guitar with no neck, made of wood but this one was made of polished metal.

The crowd settled and quieted down. Janie's metal hand sparkled when the spotlight hit her. She ran her metal fingertips across the strings. There was no need to flick the strings; they responded to even the most subtle movement of her fingers. As she moved her index finger across the string, a blue light emanated from the instrument, it filled the venue with a broad rhythmic glow and pulsed like a heartbeat.

The sound it made shifted depending on where she touched it, the notes she played were otherworldly, dazzling and beautiful. Janie looked out toward the audience with grateful eyes. Her spirit swelled with humility and grace. Every note spoke of love and loss and healing. She played for her audience, for their hearts, and most of all she played for Aeneas. She closed her eyes and said she loved him and knew she had always meant it and always will.

The room fell silent. Vincent sat there stunned. Frank's eyes were moist with tears.

The light on Aeneas' core lit up. A voice came from it so faint the words were barely heard above the music.

"Sounds…like…" he said. The last flicker of spectral energy coursed through his circuits. He saw the world and floated far beyond our troubles and high above the questions.

# EPILOGUE

&#x2736;

On Monday morning Vincent returned to his cramped, narrow office. He took off his coat and hat and sat at his desk. His inbox overflowed with emails and the rest of the day's work awaited him in the form of a giant pile of paperwork on his desk.

Frank knocked twice.

"Come in."

He stepped in and took a seat across from Vincent. "Hey, you've got a new tie."

Vincent gave him a half-hearted smile.

"I know you've been down in the dumps ever since our robot-friend kicked the bucket."

"I'll live."

"What about the Lexicon chip? Boss is expecting a fix on his desk this morning."

"I've gone over everything, and I can't figure it out. We'll need to start back at square one. Star fresh."

"He's not going to like that."

"I know."

"If you go I go," Frank said. "We're a team."

"Thanks," Vincent replied. "You can name the next one."

"No ex-girlfriend's or ex-wives this time." Frank stood and stopped by the door. "You've got another package there." He pointed.

From the corner of his eye, Vincent spotted a brown package on the floor. Now what? He thought.

"I'll let you open this one alone. I'm done with mysterious boxes." Frank waved and closed the door behind him.

Vincent tore open the lid. Inside was a metal tin box. There was a note attached.

*Vincent,*

*David wanted me to thank you for getting Aeneas to his destination. Janie told us you left his parts with her and since we promised you could keep him we didn't want you to remain empty-handed. We hope she can be a comfort to you as she is to us.*

*Sincerely,*

*Helena*

Vincent opened the tin box; inside was a metal sphere the size of a baseball. He held it in the palm of his hand and looked it over. There didn't seem to be anything special about it. It popped open in his hand and out came two wheels, two tiny pin-sized hands, two large eyes, and a mouth.

"Why, hello there," Vincent said. "And what's your name?"

"Sppprrriiitttlllee," it said. It sounded more like the sound of its motor than actual speech.

"I like that name. Let's call you Ms. Sprittle."

He watched her zip around his desk. The day's work could wait, he thought. Ms. Sprittle zoomed around in circles until she became a silver blur. The light bounced off her metallic surface. Vincent sat back in his chair, put his feet on the desk, and marveled at her exuberant spirit.

Made in the USA
Middletown, DE
10 March 2018